# mina borsalino
# flips out

## Sara Marx

# Bella
## BOOKS

2012

Bella Books, Inc.
P.O. Box 10543
Tallahassee, FL 32302

Printed in the United States of America on acid-free paper
First published 2012

Editor: Nene Adams
Cover Designer: Kiaro Creative

ISBN 13: 978-1-59493-312-7

## Dedication

To all the usual suspects, especially Petey, because he wanted me to dedicate a book to him. Thank you all for your love and for keeping me sane. Well, relatively sane.

## About the Author

Sara lives with her family in Southwest Florida where she writes, sips coffee, and chases dogs and kids.

# CHAPTER ONE

The general population does not respond well to Mina Borsalino.

I'd been saying it about myself for years, and for just as many years, my wife Fiona had been correcting me. She'd laugh it off—she laughs off a lot of things—and gracefully wade to higher ground with me firmly in tow, disregarding the hiked eyebrows all around us in response to something I'd said. I don't mean to offend anyone. It's just a side effect of what happens whenever I move my lips and sound emerges.

On Thanksgiving morning, I was sitting in the opulent lobby of a downtown LA hotel, my residence for approximately ten more minutes unless I could persuade my rat-scum attorney to swoop in and save me from the evildoers who'd canceled my AmEx card. As it was a holiday, I'd been on hold for more than twenty-five minutes.

The posh hotel smelled like a heavenly conglomerate of turkey and garlic with a slight undertone of lavender potpourri designed to cancel out an even slighter hint of lemon furniture polish or possibly carpet cleaner, all of which momentarily distracted me from approaching snickers and female gossiping voices. I could have sworn I heard my name resonate off those impossibly high ceilings, though Fee has always insisted I have an overactive imagination. Nonetheless, I slumped in the overstuffed chair I sat on to avoid being discovered.

Having already seen the *Mina Borsalino Flips Out* headline blasted across a major tabloid cover, and having clenched in my hand a restraining order barring me from the set of my own production company until the case of Borsalino vs. Borsalino could be "amicably settled," I was plenty sick and tired of seeing and hearing the Borsalino name.

When the chattering voices and click-clicking of Manolos faded, I sat back up and made a cursory glance around the place. I caught the eye of the stuffy concierge who gave me a little wave, a forced polite reminder that he was still there and that my two overstuffed bags were still on his trolley. I gave him the one minute sign and turned around in the high-backed chair for some privacy.

As I listened to Brahms play down the phone line for the zillionth time, I thought about the name Borsalino and the Great Surname Debate years earlier—whose name we'd take post-nuptials. I'd offered that it might be nice to go the way of Cher or Mr. Ed and use only our first names. But Fee's a traditionalist, so three years ago when we got hitched, I was effectively saddled with her last name, and enough with the horsy references. Now I figured I'd best hold onto that name because at last tally in our deadlocked divorce proceedings, it was apparently the only bit of joint property that I could actually use.

As for my half of our sweet Malibu home, a couple of fast cars, and some postmodernist frog art, those fates are presently in the ever-loving hands of Judge Samuel Swift. Our round one performance on the divorce court circuit resulted in Judge Swift deeming Fee levelheaded enough to avoid taking a chainsaw to literally enforce his "half of everything" proposal—I'd been joking, I swear—thereby allowing my ex to look after the aforementioned house and cars.

She's probably laughing that off now, too, or so I'd like to believe. Being furious with Fee would make it easier to swallow the news that my company AmEx had been canceled, causing me to be evicted from my hotel suite when I'd slipped out for complimentary coffee that morning wearing the same well-worn velour track suit I'd slept in. The morning had significance to me, not because it was Thanksgiving, but rather it marked the one hundredth day I'd awakened in the hotel suite without my wife and lately, with my fingers inside of me. Oh, the depravity.

"Good morning, Mina." The rat-scum—a.k.a. Attorney Susan Wendell—came on the line at last. "Sorry to keep you waiting. Frankly, I wanted to defer your rant, give you a chance to calm down a little before we begin."

In fact, I had prepared a terse salutation, but her opening statement caused it to quickly peter out. I hoped her closing argument in the courtroom was just as good. I sighed, wondering when my reputation for being a hothead had begun to precede me. I also wondered when I'd become such a hothead in the first place. I'm really a very good person.

"So Mina, how can I be of assistance on this fine, double-billing holiday?" Susan's performance of an overpaid, thoroughly bored lawyer deserved an Oscar. She droned on, "Was it the headlines? The frozen bank account? The canceled AmEx—"

"That one," I interrupted. By then, the rest of her words had sunk in. "Wait…there was more than one headline?"

"You've got to love TMZ," was all she said. I heard her soft groan. "Mina, we talked about this. Neither party can spend a dime of the marital bank accounts, or enter into or otherwise alter joint investments until we either lay the proper groundwork or actually finalize the divorce."

"Then lay some groundwork, already!" My voice echoed off the high ceilings this time. I turned to look at the concierge, gave him an artificial grin, and turned back around, cheeks ablaze. My harsh whisper substituted nicely for the yelling I really wanted to do. "How am I supposed to live with no money, no place to stay and no job!"

"You should have thought about that when we were trying to settle some affairs up front. Remember the day Fee's attorney offered an interim settlement? A cold day in hell, I believe you said." She quickly added, "Surely you have a friend to stay with."

My silence answered her question. My friends are more like network opportunities, and the few worth having were safely in Fee's custody, just like the house and the fucking frog art. I put on my game face and injected a nice little smile in my tone. "How can we expedite this process?"

"Look, you married in a state that performs gay marriage, and you're divorcing in a state that only recognizes gay marriage, thank you Prop Eight and all that hullabaloo." A groan came down the line that reeked of sarcasm. "It just takes more time."

"Wait a minute." I mean, why hold up the show now? Fee had filed for dissolution, she'd barred me from the set of our show—clearly my wife intended to divorce me.

By all tabloid accounts, Fee was heartbroken about the divorce, but bravely moving forward relatively unscathed. I, on the other hand, was reported as being utterly miserable, mad and sad without mention of any bravery. Sometimes I guess that's just the way it goes. Of course, heartbroken and surrounded by everything we own seems better than being miserable and homeless, like me.

"Are you saying since we married in Iowa, I could file for a quickie divorce in that state and get some of my life back?"

Crickets.

Finally, Susan said, "You could do that, but I wouldn't go overboard with the term 'quickie' as there is a successful business at stake and an exorbitant amount of joint property. That takes time, no matter who you marry."

"But you're saying this could possibly take less time in the state where we were married?"

"I *was* saying be amiable, but you've already blown that."

It sounded like she was eating. I envisioned her on the other end, scarfing down roasted chestnut and sage dressing or some other holiday delicacy, and my stomach growled. Then again, she was a lawyer. Perhaps she was eating another human.

In any case, for five hundred clams an hour, you'd think she could put that off for a measly five minutes, or $41.67 worth of my time, especially since I'd already been on hold to the tune of $208.34. That's the kind of stuff you obsess about when you're used to minding the details. I heard her swallow and she spoke again.

"Look, we can do this in California by utilizing a little patience and resolve. About Iowa, I'd have to check the state's residency laws. Probably a year to establish. Then again you did marry there and you were both born there. This stuff is tricky to navigate. But I can tell you that if you choose to go there, I won't represent you."

The thought of going back to Iowa for any reason made my stomach hurt worse than being hungry. The concierge impatiently cleared his throat behind me. I made a quick calculation of funds. I had roughly four hundred bucks cash on me, about eight hundred dollars less than my nightly rate at the Plaza. I could probably swing three nights at a cheap airport hotel where I could wake up with my fingers inside me and bedbugs. Cab fare would bring that down to two nights...

Dollar figures rolled around my brain until I felt dizzy with anger. I reacted the best way I knew how.

"Susan, you're fired." I punched the off button and dropped the phone into the pocket of my track suit.

I slipped out of the chair and looked around before slinking up to the front desk. I needed to go somewhere. I needed to collect myself, get a new attorney, begin again. I forced a smile at the concierge. "I need to go to the airport."

"We can certainly arrange a car for you, Ms. Borsalino."

I lowered my chin and practically whispered, "I'll need a courtesy car, if you know what I mean."

He did seem to know, and immediately trilled to the doorman clear across the lobby, "Please assist Ms. Borsalino in catching the free shuttle bus to the airport."

"Will do!" the doorman cheerfully reported back, saluting the concierge. He made a grand sweeping gesture toward the revolving doors. I tried not to notice the people around us or any reaction they may be having pertaining to the gleeful staff practically evicting me from my quarters or my request for a free ride.

"This way, madam," he went on.

I expected the concierge to follow me with my bags. Instead, he hefted them off the trolley and practically dropped them on top of my sneakers.

I swear it wasn't my imagination that even that little jerk was elated. My suspicion that he was the *National Inquisitor* mole rapidly firmed up. It had been reported that I'd been "making the Plaza staff's life hell," which is as much of an exaggeration as his delight toward me when he chirped, "Good day, Mrs. Borsalino!"

I picked up my bags. "That behavior is going to seriously hamper your tip."

"Shameful," he purred, grinning like the Cheshire cat.

I heard Fee's voice in my head begging me not to add to an already bad situation.

"Screw you," I told her, only in reality it came out to the concierge's face. That would certainly be hard to argue in the tabloids. I straightened and marched toward the revolving door, muttering under my breath along the way, "Screw them all."

***

The quirky driver operated the shuttle bus like Mr. Toad's Wild Ride. We made half a dozen stops to collect enough passengers that some were seated on the laps of others. I made myself as narrow as possible, kept my head bowed, and shielded my eyes with plate-sized sunglasses.

I was—*am*—half of the production company for the highest-rated live sketch comedy show on television. Before recently, the biggest problem I had with the press was when the *LA Times* landed on the sidewalk instead of the doorstep. But thanks to the high-profile personalities in the cast of *Viva Friday!* and the crystal-clear quality of a mobile phone video cam, anyone with the slightest temper in the remotest position of power can become an overnight pariah, God bless YouTube.

My tiny rant, although amplified via a bullhorn, went viral. Funny, but nobody had a problem with my biting sarcasm when I was one-half of the Fi-Mi Production team writing their weekly checks. How quickly they forget, the vultures. I made a mental note to ban all phones from the set upon my return—assuming I would return.

"Last stop!"

The driver had introduced himself as Rajah. It's interesting that Indian people, with their upturned inflection, always sound so damned happy no matter what they're saying, which is probably why they man so many collection agency phone lines. *"Yes, indeed! Your car is being repossessed! Dat is good news, no?"*

The bus doors burst open and the passengers shot out like we'd been spring-loaded into the vehicle. I remained seated until Rajah looked at me, grinned, and repeated in the same up-swinging voice, "Last stop!"

I lowered my dark glasses to read the airport signage posted outside the bus. "I'm waiting for the hotel, thanks."

"Last stop!" To clarify himself, he emphasized each word, smiling all the while, "Dis. Is. De. Last. Stop!"

I grumbled every swear word known to humankind as I scooted across the bench seat toward the door. A man around my age offered me his hand for assistance with the big step down from the bus. I deflated his ego with a death glare and he backed off in a hurry. For being a slight, very feminine woman, intimidation is my superpower.

I scrounged around the luggage mountain that Rajah had created and plucked out two authentic Chanel carpetbags from a stack of knockoffs. An unseasonably chilly breeze caused me to shiver as I stood there, contemplating my next great move. A digital airline departure sign blinked yards ahead. I lugged my bags toward it for a closer look.

"How can I help you?" The counter woman's squeaky voice caught me off guard. I'd drifted inside, out of the stiff breeze, and the next thing you know I was leaning against the counter at the AirWay terminal.

When I didn't answer her right away, she tipped her head to one side, causing her blond ponytail to bob like a cheerleader's. Her nametag read "Britney," of course.

"Ma'am, do you need help?" she prodded.

"Do I ever," I muttered. I eyeballed the departure list again. Since I had no place to be in LA, it wouldn't be the worst idea to get out of the city and out of the way of the evil press. Someplace I could lay low until this whole mess blew over, or at least until I had the cash to return to one of the most expensive cities in the world.

I mentally ticked through a series of friends' faces on a quest for loyalty until I came to my old friend, a college professor who happened to live in Iowa. Having already been lectured by Susan about my not-so-Constitutional Rights, perhaps if the divorce dragged on too long, Iowa could help me.

"Anything to Iowa City?" I asked.

Britney's perfect acrylic nails clicked and clacked against the keyboard for a few seconds. She pursed her lips, and raised and lowered her eyebrows several times. Clearly the mental work was taxing Brit.

She finally announced, "I've got Des Moines."

That was a few hours away from Iowa City. Surely the professor could fetch me from the airport and put me up for a few days until I could iron things out with Fee's attorney and be properly reinstated. Perfect.

"How much?" I pulled out my wallet and ran my fingers across half a dozen pieces of useless plastic.

"Carry on or check in?" she squeaked. Her nails clacked some more. "If you can do carry on, I've got a flight leaving in thirty minutes. Can you run?"

"How much?" I repeated.

"Gate C7." She looked thoughtful, more pursing lips and eyebrow wiggling. "You'll have to run quite a little bit."

I stared and blinked. "I meant how much is the fare?"

"Last minute, one way..." *Clack, clack, clack.* "Low volume flight, middle of nowhere..."—you can't make this stuff up— "three hundred seven dollars." Her bright gaze flicked my way. "Which card will you be using?"

I counted out the exact amount in cash. She stared as if I'd given her Monopoly money. I pushed it across the counter toward her. "Go ahead, it's real—touch it."

Britney's eyebrows made the ultimate plunge, and then she clicked and clacked some more. She ended up calling another attendant over to process the cash order. In moments, I held a ticket for a one-way aisle seat to the middle of nowhere.

"Go straight to security and run," she reminded me.

I collected my bags and hobbled toward the corridor.

Britney stepped around the counter and called behind me, "Don't dawdle. You seriously need to run!"

She sounded the same way my mom used to. I largely ignored her, the same way I used to pay no attention to my mom.

"If you don't make it through security, it's a nonrefundable flight!"

I ran.

\*\*\*

I finally got the day's first coffee at two p.m. It was not fifteen-bar pressurized espresso, but lukewarm instant. Only a douchebag would put coffee in a teabag. In place of froth, there was crystallized cream. An airline sample-sized bag of pretzels constituted Thanksgiving dinner, which I ate while we taxied the runway for two hours thanks to a bad snowstorm somewhere over Kansas. So much for all my running.

On the bright side, I'd lightened my load thanks to the fact that security insisted I pare down to a single carry-on or pay extra. There is some irony in ditching a thousand dollar bag to save fifty bucks. I bequeathed it to the grateful woman behind me in line. It split up the set, but I figured I'd be pretty good at splitting things up by the end of the divorce.

When the plane landed at five o'clock local time, I tried for three hours to get my professor friend on the phone. No luck there, damn the holiday. A splendid Thanksgiving it had been for me so far—so much to be thankful for.

I stood beneath a snow-covered awning outside the tiny Des Moines airport. Blasts of arctic wind sliced through me like a razor and made the cool breezes of California seem like a summer memory. Two cabs idled in the arrivals lane, puffing the place up with blue fumes. I took one of them to the only place I could possibly go given my current limitations. I wasn't sure I wouldn't get the door slammed in my face there.

Twenty-eight miles later, I arrived at my parents' old house in Landon, Iowa. I forked over the last of my cash to the cabbie for his fare and trip back to the city. When he quickly left, I realized there was no turning back.

A yellow security light illuminated sparkling, fluttering snowflakes as I shuffled up the poorly shoveled brick path, snow caking around the hems of my velour track suit. My teeth chattered nonstop from the biting cold, but also from nerves, I admit. I sighed and rolled my eyes, got every possible reaction out of my system, and then lugged my single overstuffed bag toward the porch.

I poised my finger in front of the doorbell of the cedar shake shingle cottage, but paused. I turned a generous half circle, giving everything I remembered most about Landon a good look. I couldn't help but recall the last time I'd stood in that very spot, what was said, and how adamant I'd been about never returning home.

Shielding my eyes from heavy, wet snowflakes, I strained to get a look at the highest peak of the little old barn in the distance behind me. The full moon hung low and fuzzy beneath a jumble of billowing gray clouds chock-full of nasty weather.

Although I could not see them, I felt confident that somewhere in the vicinity of that John Deere weathervane, pigs were flying.

# CHAPTER TWO

"Well, I'll be…"

Tina stood in the doorway looking dazed and downright confused at my presence. I had not spoken to, e-mailed, or in any way contacted my sister in five years. She blinked and stared at me a second longer before taking a step backward and waving me inside. She hurriedly closed the old door behind me. I looked around. Though I couldn't see much in the darkness, it felt like the same old drafty place. Considering the weather I'd just come in from, I didn't dare complain about it.

"Come in," she said, a delayed verbal accompaniment to her motion.

"I am in," I said, grinning at her dumbfounded expression. We stared at each other for a moment, and then awkwardly started to come together: left, then right, then we hugged with half-hearted, unsure affection before standing back again. By most standards, it was a horrible reunion between siblings—identical twins, no less.

My sister bit her lip and smiled, same as I was doing. I saw this by the dim glow of the outdoor security light filtering through the windows. As they say, it was like looking in the mirror, only my mirror was considerably thinner and paler.

In my typical non-filtered style, I heard myself blurt, "Are you well?"

She just stared at me.

"I'm sorry, that was rude," I said, looking down at my snow-caked sneakers, now melting into ice pools around my feet. "And I'm getting water everywhere…"

"It's okay." I felt her eyes on me, and when I looked at her again, her face wore a slowly growing smile. "It's been a while for us, that's all."

Her Midwest accent was pronounced. Mine was watered down from years of living around Valley girls. "It has been. Yes."

She carefully looked me over, taking in my track-suited, shivering glory. "They don't have coats in California?"

"Nope," I told her. I felt a glimmer of familiarity and found myself smiling. "Just wine, women and sunshine." Not that Tina would be interested in the women, just one of the many things she got right in the womb, at least according to my father.

She started for the adjoining great room. "Come on in and sit. I'll start a fire."

From memory, I knew the place was big and drafty. I thought it seemed like a pretty lonely way to spend Thanksgiving. Tina tossed a few logs in the fireplace and adjusted the damper, and soon the friendly blaze brought the darkened room to life.

In the orange glow, I saw that the place looked different than it had when it belonged to my now deceased parents. Now it was a sort of shabby chic. The once dark overhead beams had been whitewashed and so had the paneled walls. I sat down, carefully guarding the couch skirting from the damp hems of my sweatpants. My sister noticed, disappeared, and returned in moments carrying a fluffy robe.

"Here. Slip your pants off and we'll let them dry by the fire."

"Thanks," I said, taking the robe from her. I wrapped its softness around me and wriggled out of my baggy pants, then laid them out on the hearth to dry. I reseated myself and ran my hand along the cotton blossom fabric of the couch. "Wow, is this the old couch? I almost didn't recognize it."

"One and the same," she said, taking a seat in the library chair facing me. "I got a home-ec student to sew the covers. Took a bit longer than I'd have liked and the backs are twelve inches shorter than the fronts, but that part goes against the wall anyway, right?" She chuckled.

"Then I take it you're still teaching?" I leaned forward and clasped my freezing hands together, trying not to outwardly tremble.

"Hot chocolate?" she asked, rising.

"If it's no trouble." Since I had no idea what my sister had been up to, and since the hour was late, a new and very embarrassing thought occurred to me. "Are you alone? Am I interrupting anything?"

"Yes and no," she said.

I assumed she hadn't run off and gotten married like me.

The wall between the rooms had been removed, and now the great room and kitchen were part of a wide open floor plan. I watched her run water from the tap into a copper kettle, and then fan the gas burner to help start the stove—all things unheard of in California, particularly drinking water right from the tap.

"And yes, I'm still teaching," she added.

"Good." There was a spell of uncomfortable silence. I looked around again at the familiar but significantly improved furniture. "The place looks great. And I love the covers."

I wondered if she was thinking that I could have easily replaced such items in my own home, or perhaps even in hers. But the silence had nothing to do with furnishings or covers. It meant more than that. Here we were, estranged for five years, making small talk without addressing the elephant in the room.

I found myself stammering just to fill the void, desperately attempting to connect with my sister on some level. But there wasn't much I knew about her nowadays other than apparently, she was still the music teacher at our alma mater Catholic K through eight. I decided to go with that.

"So how is good old Sacred Heart anyway?"

"Times are tough." She poured two steaming mugs, went to the refrigerator and poked around. She emerged with a can of Reddi-Wip, sprayed two perfect dollops on our hot chocolates, and brought a mug over to me. In the firelight, I saw she was rail thin, her gaunt elbows pointing through her sleeves when she moved. I wondered if her job had actually gotten so tough that she couldn't afford to eat.

I tried my best to avoid gaping at her emaciated appearance or the dark circles underscoring her eyes. She saved me from myself, sort of. "How's the show?"

"Times are tough," I echoed.

She carefully sipped around her dollop of whipped topping and tipped her head slightly. "That can't be. I watch every Friday night. Really talented people you've got there. The reviews are always great."

It was the most enthusiasm she'd displayed so far during my unexpected visit. I smiled appreciatively. "Thank you. Let me rephrase. The show is fine, maybe it's me."

She seemed to take it in and nodded slowly. "I see. Is there trouble with Fiona?"

I hated to deliver the news, especially because I'd been so adamant that together, Fee and I could conquer the world. Still, if Tina had seen a tabloid lately, she already knew better.

"She left me. We're in the process of settling things. Meanwhile, she's got custody of the house and the show." I considered it for a moment. My voice dropped to a near whisper when I confessed, "It's really more like she made me leave her."

"I appreciate your honesty," Tina said, a steely look emerging in her navy blue eyes. She scooted aside a section of long blond bangs similar to my own, except her hair was thinner and lacked its former luster. I wondered what the hell had happened. Her voice was firm. "I understand now."

And like that, I suppose she figured me out. I was there for a free stay until I could negotiate a settlement with Fee's lawyer. Suddenly, I wasn't feeling nearly as demanding with my side of the legal terms as I had been in recent weeks. Sitting in my parents' old home, across from my waif-like, sickly-looking twin, I have to say that getting custody of the frog art didn't seem that important.

I was prepared to tell her that my stay—if she'd even have me—would be as short and sweet as possible. I was mentally formulating Plan B in case she refused me when she gave me the surprise of my life.

"So you've come to collect your half of the house."

"Do...do what?" I stammered. Realizing the breadth of what she implied, I quickly swung into damage control mode. "God, no! No."

"Uh-huh," she said, eyeing me with mistrust. "Why else would you come back after all this time? When the tough get going, so does good old Mina." She set her mug on the table between us, as this had apparently turned into a conversation about a will and real estate. But an even odder notion was on my mind.

"Wait...Mom and Dad left me something?"

"Half of everything. I sent the paperwork to your management agency when I couldn't get you on the phone." Her tone was decidedly defensive. "No forwarding address, no phone number—nothing. I wasn't even sure you knew about Daddy until I saw your *thoughtful* flowers at the funeral. It was just like having you there."

That was an ice-cold slap that I probably deserved. What a record fast segue from real estate chat to family therapy. I rubbed my forehead. Coming home may have been my worst idea yet.

"I'm so, so sorry," I mumbled. "And for the record, let me be very clear—I don't want the house."

"Good." She picked up her mug, but her eyes never left mine. "Because I can't afford to buy you out. I can barely afford the taxes on this place these days."

"I can help with that..." But my voice trailed off when I realized that I couldn't currently help with anything. If I could, we both knew I wouldn't be in Iowa. "I *will* help you, as soon as I get back on my feet, when these affairs of mine are settled."

"Not necessary." My sister's voice quieted, her features softened, and she appeared to be letting go of her anger right before my eyes. A modicum of warmth returned to her tone when she got down to business. "How long will you be my guest?"

I looked at my lap. "Just a few days. I hope it's not an inconvenience."

"Stay as long as you need." She took another sip. I wondered if she'd dosed her own drink with something that allowed her to suddenly appear so serene despite our near-argument moments earlier. "You can sleep in our old room. The twin beds are still there."

"Thank you, Tina."

"That's what sisters are for." She gathered our mugs and stood. Appearing to have fully let go of our terse conversation, her voice took on an almost storyteller's quality. "You know, I've had the nicest, quietest day. I put the car in the barn and used candlelight to fool everyone into believing I was gone on some great adventure. I ducked out on the world on Thanksgiving. Isn't that awful of me?"

Not nearly as awful as ducking out on your sister for five years. I mustered up a little smile, stood and stretched. "No, I don't think it's awful."

"It just seemed like a good day to count my blessings." Tina spoke with genuine gentleness, not at all holier-than-thou sounding, like it had when my father would say similar things years ago. Despite her thinness and hollow eyes, I have to say she looked happy. "I hid out like a child and made and ate peanut butter fudge for dinner."

I didn't know anyone else who made fudge. It made my smile even bigger.

"I hope you left some for breakfast," I quietly told her. She grinned so hard, her eyes twinkled. I started for the hallway. It had been a long day, no matter the time zone advantage I should have been enjoying. "I'm wiped out. You care if I head up?"

"Actually, I was already in bed," she said. I watched her check the stove pilot light, the fire—everything, just like my mother used to do. She stopped me in the hallway before we parted ways. "Welcome back, Mina."

"Happy Thanksgiving," I told her. There was something else I had to say. "Thanks for not rubbing the divorce in my face."

"Oh, you're getting divorced?" she asked in pretend surprise. "I didn't even know you'd gotten married."

I dared not budge or breathe as we stood facing each other in the darkness.

"Relax, I'm kidding," she said. "I'm sure my invitation just got lost in the mail."

"Ouch," I whispered, exhaling at last.

She didn't say anything, but I could feel her smiling in the dark. Her ice-cold hand wrapped around mine and she squeezed it tight. "Good night, little sister."

Since I was eleven minutes younger, she'd been saying that since she could talk.

Our large upstairs bedroom was mostly as I remembered it. The ceiling was barn-shaped and low on the sides, uninsulated and as frigid as ever. On one side, a blackboard hung over my old desk and typewriter, and on the other, bookcases overflowing with Tina's books and stuffed animals. Two pairs of ice skates dangled from hooks where we'd hung them years ago. On the far end of the room, twin beds were made up with the same pale yellow comforters, accented with colorful new throw pillows. My old guitar still lay across the foot of my bed. Everything was clean and dusted like a museum, as if my sister had attempted to preserve a gentler time from our former household.

I picked up the guitar and silently strummed my thumb across strings far out of tune. I set the instrument carefully in the corner and turned toward the prettily made bed. With a sweep of my arm, half a dozen dainty throw pillows were strewn across the floor. I crawled beneath the covers, robe and all, and drew my knees up so close to my chest, I could have fit back inside the womb. I was really that cold.

I lay there listening to nothing. At the hotel in downtown LA, I'd dearly missed the sound of the ocean crashing against the shore outside my bedroom window. Here in Landon, I missed the white noise of the city as I'd grown accustomed to it at the hotel. It had become part of the fabric of my nights, and without it, I knew I'd never get to sleep.

Of course, when I woke up a full ten hours later, I discovered that was just another thing I'd been wrong about. Less than a half hour after that, I learned that my mistakes hadn't vanished with a good night's sleep. Also, as it turned out, that whole firing-my-lawyer thing might not have been one of my finest moves.

# CHAPTER THREE

Fee's divorce lawyer was a bitch on wheels.

I got my first dose of attitude from her main receptionist, who transferred me to a department secretary who, in turn, transferred me to her personal secretary. As I got the same haughty tone from all three, it crossed my mind that it was the same woman slightly altering her voice for the sake of intimidation. I'd heard crazier things about Jane Silvia, the most powerful lesbian attorney in Hollywood.

At last, Jane came on the line and asked me how I was doing, but of course, she didn't wait for my reply. "I can appreciate your hands-on approach, but I don't want to talk to you, Mrs. Borsalino. You see, I'm a lawyer, and I like to communicate with other lawyers. Like minds working together, solving the problems of the lesser people. That's how I roll."

"I no longer have a lawyer."

"What? What's that? I can't understand you?" Her throaty chuckle could be heard down the line despite our crackling connection. "Ah, that's right. Because you're not a lawyer and you don't speak the language."

"I said I fired my lawyer."

"Of course you fired your lawyer, and do you know why?" She jumped straight to her answer. "Because you're not a lawyer. It's that simple. A lawyer would not be stupid enough to fire her own lawyer because she understands that a certain course is required to achieve certain goals. In your case, those goals might be, oh, say, shelter, food, electricity…stop me when I'm making any sense to you whatsoever. I can go on for about five more billable minutes, an invoice which I'll send your way when you get a lawyer, of course."

"I only have one question, that's all," I sounded like I was begging. The phone reception was poor at best. I stepped closer to the kitchen window to try to improve it. "You wanted to discuss an interim settlement the other day."

"Yes, we did." Jane Silvia sighed. "But alas, what's a good offer one day has expired the next. Sorry, Chiquita."

"Wait!" I opened the kitchen door, still trying for better sound quality. A treacherous wind whipped past me to assault notes and a calendar clipped to the front of the refrigerator. They fluttered and tried to escape their magnets. I hurriedly stepped outside in my thin jeans, blouse and socks so the whole house wouldn't blow away. My hair whipped around my face, tangling in my lashes and flying into my mouth. "Just talk to Fiona, would you? I have a situation here."

"Do you, now?" Jane Silvia mockingly said. "I, too, have a situation. Your almost ex-wife most certainly has a situation. Everybody has a situation, Mrs. Borsalino. It's called life."

"I *need* this—"

"Needs, yes, another favorite subject of mine. I need a new Porsche. A ruby red metallic 911 GT2 with five hundred-thirty horses, the finest automobile on the market. I *need* that car, Mrs. Borsalino. I need it like a priest needs an altar boy. We all have needs." She went silent for a millisecond. "And what's with this shit signal you've got going on? Where are you calling from? Bumfuck Egypt?"

The brisk wind swished ice crystals past me, dusting the top of a deep carpet of snow. Frozen cement steps had long ago permeated my socks and I could no longer feel my toes. In fact, I could very well be in BFE. Jane seemed to sense my defeat.

"Chin up, Chiquita," she said in her chipper power voice. "You go and get yourself a brand-new, shiny lawyer and have her give me a buzz, how's that?"

Before I could answer, she said, "And make sure she takes you on your word for credit per section four, paragraph eight, line two of the financial paperwork."

Either the connection was lost, or she'd hung up. Probably the latter. I punched the off button to make it official and started for the warm indoors, but the door didn't budge.

"C'mon, get serious!" I said to no one, turning the doorknob a few more times. Thanks to my sort of conversation with Jane Silvia, I'd actually worked up a nervous sweat, and my hand stuck to the icy doorknob. "No way! Shit!"

With my unstuck hand, I beat on the door until every brittle window in the old house wildly rattled. "Tina!" I called, feeling like Fred Flintstone. "*Ti-na!*"

My sister's wide eyes appeared in the window. She quickly sized up the ridiculous situation, and unlocked and carefully opened the door with my hand still frozen to the knob. I looked foolish without a coat, only socks on my feet. She spared me a lecture and instead handed me a plastic dishpan.

"Hold this with your good hand."

"They were both good hands a minute ago," I said through chattering teeth. At least my aching feet were now firmly planted on the wooden floor of the foyer instead of the outside steps. Tina ran the sink until the water was warm, and then poured a big cupful of it over my hand. The runoff went into the dishpan below it.

"Don't go tearing your hand off," she instructed me as she would one of her students. "Be patient and wait for the water to work."

With the wind still at my back, it was tough to refrain. At last, I was able to gently wriggle my hand free. I waggled frozen fingers and stared at my red palm, now minus at least one layer of skin. "Thanks."

"I'll take this," she said, whisking the plastic tub away from me.

While we look alike in a sort of dainty, girlish way, I am every bit awkward as she is graceful. Left to my clumsy control, the dishpan would likely have made splashdown.

She shut the door behind me and quickly moved onto a different subject. "You had breakfast?"

"Not even yesterday," I told her. I followed her back to the kitchen where the stove was already fired up and replenishing the kitchen with warmth.

The snow outside and the warmth of the oven inside triggered memories of us as kids, perched on high stools at the center island wooden chopping block, eating bowls of steaming oatmeal and bolstering ourselves to walk the half-mile to the school bus stop. The place felt haunted.

"Oatmeal with walnuts and brown sugar?" That Tina seemed to be reading my mind meant we'd not grown as far apart as I'd feared. "Maybe a dash of maple flavor?"

"I don't want to put you out," I said, knowing full well that I actually did.

Tina knew it, too. She smiled as she pulled out my mother's old cast-iron pot and filled it with water and milk. Within minutes, the kitchen smelled sugary and good, and I was sipping coffee with too much cream and refined white sugar. Go figure.

Tina slid onto the stool across from me and sipped her coffee. "So what were you doing outside, or shouldn't I ask?"

"Trying to get cell phone reception," I answered between delicious bites of oatmeal. "You have problems with it out here?"

"Don't know," she said, chuckling. "I don't have a cell phone."

"What?" I practically dropped my spoon and dove into an unplanned lecture. "You can't trek around the freaking north in wintertime without a cell phone! What would you do if you got stranded somewhere, huh? What if you had an emergency?"

I resisted referring to her obvious illness, whatever its nature. Her condition had become frontrunner in the elephant-in-the-room contest, leaving my family abandonment issues in the dust.

"I've got Ma Bell over there," she said, nodding toward the wall near the sink. The ancient, harvest gold, landline phone with a spiral cord was where it had always been. I shook my head when she went on. "Nobody really has cell phones in Landon. Too expensive. This has become one depressed little town."

Still, not having one seemed like a terrible idea. My phone buzzed as if on cue, saving her from further interrogation.

"We've got to fix that," I said before punching the phone on. "Hello? Hello?"

Through the static, I heard a faint digital voice, but could just barely make out the recorded message, something about paying my account balance. I started to press zero for customer service to argue the point, but quickly realized that perhaps my phone was no longer on auto-pay, thanks to good old attorney Jane Silvia.

I sighed, pressed the off button, and forced a smile. "Wrong number, I guess."

There was no need to bring her current on my miserable situation, given that I suspected she had one herself. I couldn't take it any longer. I had to ask about it.

"Tina, are you sick?"

She calmly sat there, self-editing before answering, just as she has always done. I pressed her. "I saw all the pill bottles in the cabinet when I got a glass of water this morning. I wish you'd tell me about it."

"I have been sick," she finally answered. A small smile touched her lips. "But my doctor says I'm getting better now."

"Sick with what?" But judging from medication labels with names that rang vaguely familiar and her skinny appearance, I figured I already knew.

"I was diagnosed with breast cancer over summer break." She leaned back slightly in her chair and appeared unwavering. "They removed my left side in July. I'm doing much better now."

And like that, we were no longer mirror images. I felt a lump in my throat. My mother had lost her life to the same hateful cancer eight years ago. The thought of losing my only remaining family, no matter our estrangement, made me want to cry like a baby.

I contained my emotions and whispered, "I wish I'd known."

"Hon, you wouldn't have wanted to be here then any more than you do now."

I leaned across the butcher block table and laid my red, chapped hand on top of hers. "I want to be here now. I'm sorry for my spastic behavior. I get very…impatient."

"No way," she said, teasingly. We both laughed, and then we both sighed. "You're here now, Mina. That's what counts. Let's make the most of this time."

I certainly didn't like the way that sentence made me feel. I swallowed hard, blinked back my tears, and hurriedly changed the subject. "I have an idea. Let's take a ride around town and you can tell me how everything's changed."

"I'd love to, but I'm a little tired today." She smiled at me and tossed her hand in a casual wave. "You go on ahead, though. I'll be fine by tomorrow. We'll do something then."

I didn't know if I should leave her, or if she needed me to leave her so she could feel good about resting. "You sure?"

"Yes. Take the car. It's in the barn so you'll have to open the big door." She stood and collected our mugs. She returned and set car keys on the wooden block in front of me. "You better let it warm up first or the engine will stall later." She drew her robe around her even more tightly, revealing her ribcage right through the plush fleece.

I tried not to stare and asked, "Do you need me to get anything while I'm out?"

She looked thoughtful. "Will you stop at Hy-Vee? Pick up a nice loaf of something we can have with the soup I'm going to make this afternoon."

"Sure," I said, and then suddenly remembered giving every last dime to the cabbie. "Oh, jeez, I—"

"There's some cash in the console," she interrupted, doing a pretty good job of pretending she didn't know that's exactly what I was going to say. The kid can really read my mind, I'm telling you. I started to speak again, but she softly laughed.

"I know, you'll pay me back after you reupholster my furniture, pay my taxes and get me a cell phone. I'm going to start a list. I'm sure you're good for it."

I was pretty sure she was joking, but even me, the Queen of Cynicism, could not tell if she was being sarcastic. I hoped not. Suddenly, I really wanted her to believe in me.

On my way out, Tina followed me to the door, warning me to stay away from several old main thoroughfares and certain neighborhoods. I thought she was exaggerating until I got in the car and started my tour of Landon.

The place was nothing short of utterly miserable. Graffiti tagged virtually every flat surface, like the kind you'd see in bad LA neighborhoods. Kids in hoodies gathered on corners around broken bus benches, or cruised the streets in cars with thud-thudding stereo systems, eyeballing everyone. Including me, having apparently pegged me for an outsider even behind the wheel of my sister's old Pontiac with local plates. It was more chilling than the weather.

I drove up a pothole-ridden Park Hill toward Landon's historic district, sad to discover that the sweet Victorians had mostly fallen into disrepair. Old five-and six-bedroom homes had been split up, and for-rent-by-the-week signs lined their cracked windows. Porches had collapsed and shingles were missing. Tarps were spread across the tops of some of the decaying buildings for lack of a roof at all. The district was a historical architect's worst nightmare.

I rolled the Pontiac to a stop in front of the single remaining lovely home. I knew it well. It belonged to Fee's parents.

The mansion stood in its bright, painted lady glory, seemingly oblivious to the town's poverty, a feat that was made easier by Fee, who made sure they were taken care of in every way. It would be a real war of daughter-goodness if ever Fee and Tina were pitted against each other for top honor. My brain conjured up images of them in wizard capes, wands clashing, only instead of invoking dark skies and lightning strikes, gumdrops and puppy dogs would rain down from the sky for everyone. I felt a twinge of guilt knowing their righteousness was even more pronounced when compared to me, the world's worst daughter. Funny how things had changed. When I'd marched away from my last visit five years ago, I'd felt like I was the righteous one.

I studied the impeccable three-story home with holiday garland and lights already wrapped around the banisters of its wide, sweeping porch. A candy cane wreath the size of my whole body hung between the highest windows. Even in the afternoon light, an orange, comforting glow emanated from inside. It looked like something out of a Thomas Kinkade painting, only I knew it was real. As real as the love I'd shared with Fee. No matter how mad I was at her, I missed my wife.

As for the Borsalino residence, I hadn't been there since my last visit to the town, the same fateful day I'd forever walked away from my father for calling me a filthy, sinful lesbian. But it certainly hadn't been the last I'd seen of the Borsalinos as they'd been frequent visitors to our Malibu house.

Nobody made a house smell like garlic and olive oil like Mrs. Borsalino. I would sincerely miss their loving compassion. The only thing I wouldn't miss was Mrs. Borsalino's pained look when she repeatedly, sweetly pressured me to speak to my father, the old miserable widower. That she'd been convinced our argument was one big misunderstanding was the real misunderstanding, and I certainly wouldn't miss defending my abandonment to her.

It wasn't like she and my father had ever been on friendly terms anyway. Not even the church connected our families since the Borsalinos had always attended a later Mass designed for hipper, new age Catholics, while my father was on his knees at the crack of dawn with the rigid traditionalists, praying for the sinful likes of myself. So separate were our families that I hadn't even heard rumors that my sister was sick.

I figured I should leave the curb before anyone saw me spying on them. I crossed my fingers that the car wouldn't stall. My eyes were watery when I drove away.

As I'd promised my sister, I stopped at Hy-Vee grocery store before heading back. By now, the building showed its age. The shoppers and workers were largely Latinos wearing tired, untrusting expressions. People dressed shabbily. Most of them clutched food stamp cards and other government vouchers.

A small girl in line ahead of me stared at me as if I was a foreigner. I'm sure to her, I did look funny. She had holes in her coat and no mittens to protect her little red hands. Her untrimmed bangs hung down far enough to stick in the snot dried around her tiny button nose. I smiled at her, but she ducked behind her mother's pants leg. Her mother was arguing with the clerk about something or other. I quietly stepped into the next line, paid and quickly left.

Landon certainly had changed. Its depressing atmosphere seemed to support my own rotten mood of late. I felt a pang of guilt about being so incredibly anxious to leave my sister in such a miserable place.

# CHAPTER FOUR

"What in the hell happened to this town, anyway?"

I blurted the question as we were settling ourselves for dinner that night. Tina's illness had already won top spot in a competition of woes, but other issues were leapfrogging their way up the chart, surpassing my measly divorce.

Tina set the soup tureen on the butcher block between us and dropped the potholders on either side. She slid onto her stool and handed me the silver ladle. Mom's ladle. I held tight to the handle for several seconds, lost in a memory of my mother dishing up soup or chili on a cold winter's night. I noticed Tina watching me. I smiled.

"Smells fantastic."

"I hope you haven't gone vegan on me because this broccoli cheese soup is the real dairy deal."

"For ten years, I've been an aspiring vegan. I guess if I haven't fully crossed over by now, it's hopeless." I accepted the piece of warm, crusty bread she offered me. "No red meat, though."

"Me neither," she said.

I looked at her, surprised. She'd always been a meat eater. "Is that what your doctor advised?"

"No." She tore off a small chunk of bread and dipped it into her steaming soup. "I've just never really liked it."

"Wait...you always ate whatever Mom put in front of you."

"I was being agreeable, that's all."

"Being agreeable?" I smirked. "It's called being agreeable when you go to your second choice movie or make lame chit-chat about the weather. Putting something in your body to make someone else happy is not being agreeable."

"You're making it sound like a bigger deal than it was."

"It's a form of peer pressure, dear sister," I chastised her. "Why not just do drugs to be agreeable with the street people? Or drink yourself blind to be sociable with the folks at Barney's Bar?" I shook my head. "That's not being agreeable, that's being a big wuss."

Her silence made me notice that she was giving me the same look my mother used to. It's the look that says she's not engaging in such a juvenile argument. Come to think of it, it was also the same look Mom used to give Dad.

"What?" I said, unable to take her silent stare any longer. "Fine. Sorry I'm not as agreeable as you are."

"Mom was sick, but she still wanted to cook," my sister finally said. "She was a traditional chef—meatloaf, chops, ham—you know her."

I watched as she dragged her spoon along the edge of her steaming bowl, and I realized the irony of her words. Tina also liked to cook. Apparently, my sister was also quite ill. I, on the other hand, was thoughtless enough to argue with her over a good meal she'd prepared for us. I felt a knot in the pit of my stomach and my throat felt tight.

"I just wanted her to be happy," she finished.

We ate in silence until I circled back to my earlier inquiry. "So tell me what happened to Landon."

My sister blotted her papery thin lips on her napkin and set it aside. I could tell she was settling in for a story. And a story I got.

"It started with the big strike at Buchanan's about six years ago. You remember it, right?" she asked.

I did. The meatpacking plant made national headlines when its workers calmly closed shop and staged a sit-in to protest poor working conditions and inadequate cost of living increases. I remembered seeing the picketers during my last visit to Landon. Fee, the do-gooder, had insisted on taking them all coffee and doughnuts, of course.

"Six months pass and Buchanan's is losing contracts right and left," Tina continued quietly. "They ordered the workers back on the line, and when they refused, Buchanan's fired them all and had the police haul them away."

"Wow."

"Wow is right." She wore a sympathetic expression. "Then the plant brought in nonunion replacements—scabs, they called them. Fast-forward through car fires, and threats, and cinder blocks thrown through windows, and most of those replacement folks gave up and quit. They said it wasn't worth it."

Bad story so far. "I feel like you're going to tell me nobody got their job back."

"I am. So the company recruited migrant workers to do the work instead. Moved them here by the truckloads, set them up with work visas and apartments. All of this solved Buchanan's problems, but created tons of them for Landon."

I pushed my empty bowl ahead of me and leaned on the block, thoroughly enthralled by now. "What happened?"

"Some of the fired townsfolk moved away and were able to get new jobs. Others couldn't get work and went on government assistance." Tina shook her head. "Some turned to doing drugs or even selling them. Theft and robbery went through the roof, and people started taking the law into their own hands. Everybody's got a gun nowadays to protect their families."

I thought of her living on the outskirts of town, unarmed, un-everything. "Oh, Tina…"

"No incomes meant no spending, which meant all the local businesses folded. Only Walmart and a handful of small stores or restaurants survived. Then came the housing collapse and the recession. People got cynical, shifty and downright mean." She sighed deeply and her eyes went glassy. "In the midst of it all, here we are trying to teach their children something. Trying to give them hope in a hopeless situation."

"The school was hit hard?"

She raised her gaze to me and looked away, effectively answering my question.

"How bad is it?"

"Enrollment is down and many of the students we do have are on scholarship. I don't know how much longer the school can last. Most of our school population is ESL."

I was confused. "I don't know what that is."

"English is their second language. They interpret student conferences for their parents, if the parents bother to show up, that is." She rubbed the tiny lines that had cropped up on her forehead. "Sacred Heart may not even be in business come spring, and that means all those kids will go to the public schools, which are already stuffed to the gills and dangerous."

"What kind of danger?"

"Gangs." She looked utterly disconsolate. "We've had shootings, suicides, you name it."

"I had no idea." I reached across the block and touched her hand. "I wish there was something I could do."

She started to shake her head, but stopped short. "Actually, there might be."

Gone was my ability to simply write a check for guilt alleviation. I couldn't imagine what else I could possibly do, and wondered what I'd set myself up for. I can tell you this, I'm not a hands-on sort of girl.

"I'm sick, Mina." She looked me square in the eyes.

"I know. We'll get you better," I said, probably more for my sake than hers.

Tina didn't look quite as confident. "I talked to my doctor again today. I had some tests done before Thanksgiving. It looks like I'll have to have my other breast removed."

Tears sprang to my eyes. I hadn't seen her for years. I'd turned my back on her…I forced myself to remain calm. "What can we do? How can we fix it? Who can we get?"

"Stop, Mina," she firmly, sweetly ordered me. She proceeded to lay out her medical plan with the same calm authority of someone planning their week. "I am having surgery on Tuesday followed by a round of radiation. Whatever it takes, I'll try it."

"You'll beat this," I told her in a ragged sounding voice.

"I hope so," she said. "About that favor?"

"Anything," I told her. "You name it."

"You say that now," she whispered, her expression sincere. "Would you take over my music classes?"

I was stunned. "Anything except for that."

"Mina, please. The kids have been working toward the holiday concert and I'll be too tired and sick to help them now." She looked hopeful, and her hands tightly clasped mine. "I just want to hear them sing at my last Christmas concert."

Tears came freely now, anger sweeping right behind my sadness. "That's a fucking morbid thing to say, Tina."

She looked momentarily put out, realized what she'd implied, and moved to correct it. "No, no—it's their last music concert at Sacred Heart. The music program will be cut after December."

I wiped my eyes and sighed with relief. Sort of. "So you're unemployed for the New Year?"

She nodded. "Just like everyone else."

I was stunned into silence. A million things went through my mind. At the top of the list was a selfish wish that I'd never returned to Landon. I wasn't a teacher. I could barely tolerate adults, let alone their pint-sized versions. About music—I can't even operate a slide whistle, let alone hammer out anything resembling a tune on a piano!

"No. I'm sorry." I shook my head so mightily, I swear I heard my brain rattle. "Ask me to do anything else, but I can't do that."

"I just thought since you were going to be around for a while…" Her voice trailed off and she got very quiet.

"I don't know how long I'm hanging around. I don't know what's going on with my divorce case or my job," I sputtered. "I still have a show to run in LA. Or at least I did have, and I have other commitments that need to be taken care of."

None of this seemed to make a dent in my attempt to explain why I couldn't help.

"I see," she calmly said. "Well, then, could you do me a favor?"

I blinked a few times. "First you tell me the favor, then I'll decide. We know where that already got me."

A small smile touched her lips. She looked paler than ever, making it difficult to conjure up any resistance to whatever she might ask me. "Would you talk to Diane on Monday and tell her about me? Then pick up my last check, please?"

Diane Reeves had been the principal at that school since we were students there.

"You know she'll try to talk me into staying on," I told her.

"She'll try to talk *me* into staying on!" Tina burst out, half laughing. "The woman is relentless."

"Can't you call her?" I pleaded.

She shook her head. "I wasn't really square with you about my phone situation a while ago. I don't exactly have service at the moment," she quietly admitted. "I had it disconnected early in the fall."

I sat up straight, resisting chewing her ass for neglecting this very basic utility—a safety requirement. "You have no phone at all? Period?"

"Pay cut."

"A pay cut and now you're fired?" I looked up at the ceiling and shook my head, almost speechless. "This is some great school system. We need to get you a lawyer. I'm sure you have some sort of case here."

I felt helpless because I'm a fixer. It's what I do. I've been minding the details, including legal nonsense, since Fee and I established Fi-Mi Productions years ago. Why, I've worked alongside the very attorney who'd verbally bitch slapped me on the phone that morning. I guess Fee got temporary custody of her, too.

Anyway, Fee's a University of Iowa theater major and a creative genius. I'm a U of I grad too, only my major was business, since my parents would never help pay for a frivolous education like theater. Hence, I am the organizer. The fixer. I'm generally quite good at it, or at least I was. My sister's next words brought me back from my own weird wonderland.

"No attorneys. Besides, the school didn't really do me wrong, they just fired me because of budget cuts." Tina gave me the same wide-eyed, innocent look she'd always given Mom to get pretty much anything she wanted. Very effective. "As for the telephone, what did you want me to do? My other option was to cut my bit of cable, and then I wouldn't be able to watch your show."

"Ah, Christ." I rolled my head, cursing everyone and everything internally. A little seeped out to my listening audience as well. Super—just pack my bags and send me on a first-class guilt trip. When I quit shaking my head, muttering swears and uttering "no, no, no," I looked at Tina and made my stern announcement.

"I'll tell Principal Reeves and I'll pick up your check, too. But I'm not—so help me Jesus, Joseph and Mary—I'm *not* going to fumble-bumble my way through teaching a bunch of snot-nosed, rotten-tempered kids to do-re-mi. Never! Period. Do you understand me?"

Tina nodded, smiled and politely thanked me. I figured I'd made a good case for myself. But I should have known it wouldn't be that easy. I was quickly learning that nothing ever is.

# CHAPTER FIVE

On Monday morning, my sister insisted on going to her pre-op doctor's appointment alone. I didn't like to see her get on a city bus, but she demanded that I take her car, repeatedly reminding me that my day's mission was to tender her premature resignation, and collect her final pittance and anything else she had to show for twelve years of a teaching career.

My first clue as to how much Sacred Heart had changed came when I attempted to yank open the front door and nearly broke my wrist. The thing was solidly locked. I moved on to the next in the row of four doors, but it was also a no-go, and same with the next and the next.

I peered through one of the slim rectangular windows and saw the short, waddling, round form I'd know anywhere. Principal Reeves gave me the one moment gesture, and after much fumbling with keys while I froze my gloveless, coatless butt off, one of the doors swung open. She ushered me in from the cold and went to work relocking the padlock on the clanging strip of chains that secured the doors.

"Are you keeping someone out or someone in?" I teased her.

"My Mina." Principal Reeves ignored my smart opener and drew me into her tight midget's embrace. She patted my back and whispered, "I knew you'd come through for us."

I pulled back slightly and looked at our old principal who had always been a good foot shorter than me, and who was now about half again as wide as me, too. I knew what she thought I was coming through on, and I was there to make it clear that I was not at all a comer-througher.

"I can only stay a minute," I said, providing her with a little foreshadowing. "I came to update you about my sister's illness and pick up her check."

"Mmm-hmm, I stopped by her place the day after Thanksgiving," she said. She tossed her blue-gray bob and marched down the hallway. "Right this way, honey."

"Wait…you already talked to Tina?" Something fishy was afoot and I am no sucker. Still, I followed her to the tiny closet that she had the nerve to call an office. "Funny, she did not mention that to me."

"She told me the good news about you being back in town for a while. How wonderful. Your sister really needs you, you know, though she'd have my head for telling you as much." She motioned toward a chair, frowning upon seeing that it was piled high with folder files. Though the tiny office had been in the same cramped chaos for as long as I could remember, she still seemed surprised at its condition, as if it had happened overnight. "Oh, dear me."

"It's okay, I can't stay long," I said, dispensing hint number two. "Anyway, it looks like Tina's not going to be back through the end of the year."

Principal Reeves tsked and looked down at her paperwork-strewn desk. "Yes, so she told me. I was thrilled when she suggested you as a pinch hit teacher to get us through the holiday program. You understand our system and our very limited budget."

"I'm not a teacher. I'm not qualified—"

"Nonsense. It's only a temporary position so the Board can vote you in. That's me—I'm the board. I already voted." She grinned at me. "You're in!"

"No, no." I chuckled. "Tina misspoke if she said I'd do this. That or you heard her wrong."

"I didn't." Principal Reeves was off again. For a moment, I lost a visual on her behind those tall mounds of overstuffed manila folders. She reappeared near the door and motioned for me to follow her. "We'll walk and talk since we can't sit."

"I really have to be going. If I could just collect Tina's check and anything else she may have here—"

"Right this way," she said for a second time, grabbing my arm and giving me no choice but to follow her. It was either that or shrug free of her hold, which is rude, and in truth, perhaps not possible. She had a hell of a grip for a little lady approaching seventy.

"I remember when you girls used to sing at the Christmas program here. How those heavenly twin voices filled the church. Beautiful!"

"Principal Reeves, I'm in a bit of a hurry," I told her, casting a wary eye toward the chained front doors as we bypassed them. She led me up the stairs of the two-story, K through 8 school. "I'd love it if we could have a nice talk over tea one night. I'll be in town for a bit. Why don't you come out and see us?"

The woman carried on as if my voice didn't register with her on even the smallest level. "Of course, these children don't quite have all the musical gifts you children had. Good heavens, some of them barely speak English."

"That must make it difficult."

"For me, somewhat. I'm learning the language, but not as quickly as I'd like." She stopped abruptly on the steps, causing me to nearly trip right over her. She turned and smiled. "Lucky for you that Spanish is your specialty."

"That is incorrect," I told her, acutely aware of the hog-tie she was trying to perform on me. I stepped up my exit strategy. "A single course in high school to satisfy a graduation requirement hardly qualifies as a specialty. Nowadays, I can't even order at a Taco Bell."

"And gifted musically! My, we couldn't luck into a better music teacher replacement, could we?" She blinked, her fleshy cheeks rosy from hefting her short, wide body up so many steps. She took off again, finally stopping on the top floor. She turned to me, her voice whisper soft. "Now, you shouldn't run into any problems, but if you do, Mrs. Duffy is next door and she can certainly come over and bellow the appropriate directives. She's really got a holler on her, that one."

"I can't stay, Principal Reeves," I firmly told her. I found myself raising my voice and refusing to budge a step further, even as she gave me a gentle shove in the general direction of the music room. "I came here for two reasons. One, to tell you about my sister, which apparently you already know about, strangely enough. And two, to pick up Tina's check. I have no desire, nor have I ever had the desire, to teach music. To teach anything, for that matter."

Principal Reeves stared at me blankly for a moment. "Well, why didn't you say so?"

"I did. Or I tried to, or I wanted to." I stammered. "I'm sorry, but I'm not the person for the job."

"Very well, then," she said, turning around and heading back toward the stairs. "Be a dear and do me a favor?"

I was getting tired of people asking me for favors. Lately, I couldn't even do myself a favor. I loudly sighed. "What?"

"Run to the music room and dismiss the children waiting there."

Now that, I could manage. "Done." I started to go, but stopped short. "Should I send them to study hall?"

"Just send them to the parking lot."

I spun around.

"Wait a minute, hold up," I said, halting her on the top step. "Why can't they go to study hall? It's twelve degrees outside."

Principal Reeves turned around to face me, holding tight to the banister. She sweetly whispered, "We lost our study hall last year, dear. We rent it to the city to store their parking barriers and other equipment."

"Why did you do that?" Though I figured I already knew that every answer was going to center around economics.

"It was a nice little trade-off," she said, her eyes twinkling. "We're survivors at Sacred Heart School. We make ends meet wherever we have to."

She turned around again, but again I stopped her. "Then how about the cafeteria?" I glanced at my watch. It was still plenty early. The lunch ladies would be preparing the food, but not near ready to serve it yet. "I'll tell them to bring a book and stay out of everyone's way."

"We lost our lunchroom, dear," she told me.

"Let me guess—the city's storing a bulldozer in that one?"

Principal Reeves only gave me her same sweet smile. "It's the science wing now. We had a little Bunsen burner incident a year ago for which we were apparently underinsured. We had to relocate our future scientists."

I was puzzled at both her optimism in referring to these kids as future scientists and that there was no longer a cafeteria. "Where do they eat lunch?"

"In their homerooms."

I tipped my head to one side. "And where do you prepare it? Over the Bunsen burners?"

Principal Reeves beamed. "We pay to have public school lunches trucked over now. It was significantly cheaper to do that than keep the lunch ladies or the food prep staff—all of them had to go."

"Along with your music program," I quietly added.

"Yes, that too." With that, Principal Reeves looked crestfallen, proving she wasn't optimistic about everything. Her body heaved with a deep sigh. "And believe me when I tell you that I will surely miss those angelic voices trailing down the hallway."

I looked out the window just over her shoulder above the stairwell landing. Large, fluffy, beautiful snowflakes would not be nearly as charming after forty minutes spent standing ankle deep in them. I sighed and glanced down the hall toward the music room.

"Look, what if I just stay in the room with them? Just for today, understand? No music—none of that." I emphasized my last sentence. "I could just sit in there with them so they don't have to go outside. They can do their homework or something."

Principal Reeves smiled and slowly spun on her low heels. She headed downstairs, her orthopedic shoes shushing along the old cement floors. Her voice sounded in a echoing sing-song that bounced off the high ceilings of the stairwell. "Whatever you like, dear. I certainly don't want to twist your arm."

I rolled my eyes at no one.

My feet automatically took me toward the old music room. The place smelled like floor wax, glue and sweat, your standard grade school-middle school smells. I glimpsed into the window of each classroom as I passed and saw children reading, giving presentations or being otherwise productive. The silence gradually gave way to noise that became louder and more rambunctious with each step I took until I reached the music room. I leaned my forehead against the door window to see what I'd gotten myself into, if for only an hour. Inside, it was total chaos.

Rap music blared from the class stereo. Judging from the Spanish words I did recognize—of course I remembered the swears—I was pretty sure my sister hadn't given its vulgar content her teacher's stamp of approval. The only chairs that weren't overturned served as platforms for dancers in a style I'd never witnessed from a nine-to twelve-year-old age group. Girls were jiving and catcalling the boys, and the boys were eating it up, responding with howls of approval.

As I was in a Catholic school, it seemed appropriate to cross myself before pushing through the door, which felt heavier that I remembered, probably because I'd never entered it as an unwilling babysitter before.

I held a faint hope that the atrocious music would cease the moment an adult entered the room, that the students would scramble to organize the room and themselves. Instead, my presence seemed only to exaggerate their dance moves and add volume to their inappropriate and very un-Catholic rapping, because now they had an audience.

I made my way through the small, hearty throng of jiving bodies, found the stereo, and killed the electronic portion of the noise myself. Of course, the student portion of the noise raged on as they continued to rap at the tops of their lungs. I thought about Principal Reeves' conversation in the hallway. Angelic voices, my ass.

Only when I pressed two fingers to my lips and expelled a shrill, taxi-halting whistle did they mumble their protests concerning my presence. I suddenly understood why most substitute teachers are bad asses when I shouted my first order: "Put this place back together. *Now*."

About fourteen kids jumped down from windowsills and seat tops, and begrudgingly dragged their chairs back to form a lazy half-circle. I started to take my jacket off in a show of authority, figuring I'd drape it over the back of my chair just like they do in the movies. I quickly thought better of it. The room was cold enough that the windowpanes were frosty outside and in. Little fingernails had carved hearts and symbols and initials into the frost. I shivered as I surveyed the art from the podium.

I heard snickers directly behind me and turned to address it, but saw nothing untoward. I lowered my gaze. A small group of students with their heads together had formed a cover over something I could not see. I prayed it was not drugs. Surely things had not gotten that bad.

I stepped off the platform and headed their way. "What gives, guys?" I asked. A few of them scampered back to their chairs. By the time I reached the place, only one boy remained. He was a small, mixed-race boy, and thankfully, he was dealing cards, not drugs. My shoulders collapsed with relief.

"Back to your seat," I ordered him.

Deep-set brown eyes looked up at me. A grimace came over his face. "Shit, lady, you're busting up my business here."

A pile of pennies was center of the action. I quickly pieced together that the kid was the a bona-fide Catholic grade school hustler.

"What is your name?" I asked him.

"What's yours?"

"I asked you first."

"I asked you last," he said, leaning back and folding his arms across his narrow chest. Untamed, afro-like hair lopped over one eye. We had a silent standoff. I hoped he couldn't see that I was a little nervous. Finally, he rolled his eyes and collected his pennies. "Forget it, I don't give a shit. I already know who you are."

He filled the pockets of his well-worn navy blue uniform pants with the money and gathered his cards before sauntering over to join the half-circle. "You're the new teacher, Ms. Smith's sister. Only you're fatter."

Helpless to my own reaction, I glanced down at my five foot six, maybe one-thirty pounds of a frame, and looked back at him. I'd never considered myself fat. I'd never considered anything. Of course, compared to my sickly sister—all ninety pounds max of her—I probably looked like Mama Cass. I shook off the insult and went back to the podium.

"I am not your new teacher," I declared right away. My gaze fell across an attendance book on the stand before me. I opened it to the class roster. "I'm only here for this hour, but we will conduct this hour with some civility. Which includes not speaking unless I give you permission to speak, understand?"

Nobody said a word, so either they were following instructions or ignoring me.

"Good. Then we'll call roll." I checked the list of largely Hispanic names that I was going to have some trouble pronouncing. I started in anyway. "Carlos Sanchez?"

"Yo."

"Luis Cristobel?"

"Yep."

"Juana…Guillermo?" I mangled that one.

"Uh-huh."

The next name on the list I could pronounce, and I'm sure my voice reflected some degree of relief when I announced, "Steven Weitrich?"

"Present," came the cool answer.

I raised my eyes to see a blond, clean-cut boy wearing the best version of the school uniform I'd seen so far. He moved his arm and I saw that contrary to the dress code, his crisp white polo bore an oversized pony and rider, a tactic employed to set him apart from the rest if the bright white shirt and pressed slacks failed. I recognized him, or some incarnation of him anyway. I smiled.

"Are you Thomas's son?"

"I am," he answered in a bored tone.

My mind rolled back to the days of high school and Thomas tooling around in his swank little convertible. TW, as he was known, captain of the high school football team with a solid place in society.

His son Steven stared me straight in the eye, unafraid of anything—especially me, and intimidating everyone in the room—especially me. My momentary joy at being able to pronounce his name was replaced by my dislike for his apparent family endowed snotty attitude. I went back to the class list.

"Emanuel Diaz?"

"Yo."

The tiny voice came from the boy with the pennies. I tipped my head slightly. "Ah, the resident card shark."

"Spic." The single whispered word floated through the air and assaulted my ears, causing me to look up from the attendance book. I studied the students, face by face, until I came to the smirking, half-smile on Steven's face.

"You'll refrain from such remarks as long as I'm in this room." It was as stern a voice as I could conjure up. I locked eyes with him for several seconds, an intended intimidation tactic that didn't even scratch the surface with this kid. Hatred surged through me, which is ridiculous. I've never hated a kid in my life, not that I have spent time around a lot of kids.

I lowered my eyes again, scanned the column, and realized it would take me fifteen minutes to sound out the remainder of the list. Instead, I counted the names, cross-checked against a headcount in the room, and slapped the book shut.

"We'll use this time to study or read today."

I started to step off the podium but the children only stared at me. I swallowed hard and tried to put the words together. "*Estudiar o leer*, I think."

"They know what you're saying, lady." Emanuel, the card shark, rolled his eyes. "They just don't have no books."

"They don't have any books," I corrected him.

"I just said that." Emanuel looked thoroughly disgusted with me. "Can't we watch some television or something? That's what Ms. Smith does when she doesn't feel like teaching us."

I looked around the room, wondering about that, but figured if my sister could do it, so could I. "I suppose so. But no talking or I'll turn it right off. That's a promise."

An ancient TV set sat in the corner. I dragged the rickety, wheeled cart to the center of the room and turned the set on. The poor reception was good for five channels. One was a show about rap star "cribs," and another was about cribs of an entirely different nature and teenage parents. There was the reality show called *The Shore* about early twenties kids partying/drinking/puking/screwing around, and another reality show about a family with twenty kids—about nineteen too many, if you ask me. Toss in some Jerry Springer for good measure and it was inappropriate-as-hell programming for preteens. I turned the set off again, much to everyone's dismay.

"This sucks," Emanuel loudly muttered.

"You're not watching that crap. It will turn your brain to mush," I told them. As I'd already heard their music, I wasn't about to let them offer that as an option. I flipped open another folder on the podium, one containing sheet music. "Why don't you just practice whatever you've been working on."

"You play the piano?" Emanuel asked me.

"No," I confessed.

He shrugged. "Then you'll have to get Roddy to do it."

I furrowed my brow. "Roddy?"

"Rodriguez," he clarified. He turned in his seat and ordered the boy behind him, "Roddy, hit us up with some tunes."

A tall, lanky Hispanic boy in taped glasses, wearing a yellowed uniform shirt, made his way to the front of the room and took a seat on the piano bench. In moments, he played a rather crude, but passable rendition of Pachelbel's *Canon*, only with lyrics. The class was singing along, hitting and missing—mostly missing—notes all along the way.

I let this go on for a few minutes, and finally couldn't take it any longer. Though I'm not a teacher, I tried a tactic that Fee always uses when directing a show that's not quite living up to her expectations. Emphasize the positive first, and then slip in the correction. It worked on full-grown divas, and I hoped these kids weren't wise to my trick.

"That was great. Now let's switch things up a bit." I flipped through the music. "Let's start with page two."

"We don't get copies of the music. We rememberize it." Emanuel again.

"Memorize it," I corrected him. Jesus. Maybe it was too much to think these kids could read music; but we had at the same age at the same school. I didn't know what to make of his ignorance. "How on earth can you sing the music without actually seeing it?"

"It's okay," he said. "Some of us don't read for shit anyway."

I didn't get a chance to correct his grammar or his swears, thanks to the smug Steven, who sat there with his legs crossed, coolly picking imaginary lint off his slacks.

"Many of *them* can't read simple English," he said.

I sighed loudly and muttered, "Christ."

"Amen," said a girl seated in the front row.

Caught off guard, I mustered a half-smile for her. "Naturally," I mumbled, desperately seeking my second wind. "Okay, let's pick it up from the first rejoice."

Thirty minutes and a thousand Merry Christmases later, the bell rang. I was thoroughly wiped out and more than ready to go home. I felt sorrier than ever for my sister, and any fool in this chosen profession, as I picked up the in-room conference phone and dialed the office. Principal Reeves answered after the fourth ring. At the same time, new, slightly younger students were filing into the classroom.

"I'm done. That's it for me. Send up relief," I told her. I wondered if my sister kept alcohol at the house. I wondered if there was enough money in her car's console to at least buy a quart of cheap beer at the gas station.

"I don't have anyone else, dear," Principal Reeves sweetly said. "Just send them to the parking lot."

# CHAPTER SIX

"You are thoroughly in trouble for what you did today," I informed Tina as soon as we sat down for dinner that evening.

She ladled steaming soup into bowls.

Antique wooden spools held flickering candles that had been placed between our settings. Even our water sparkled from my parents' anniversary crystal wineglasses—tons of nice ambience designed to sidetrack me from my intended tirade, I'm sure.

I stared her down. "I'm only going to defer my rant until after you've told me about your doctor's appointment, lest I should appear narcissistic."

I'd already read that narcissistic business about me in a tabloid. I couldn't help it, the thing was lying on the empty seat next to me on the plane, almost as if God intended that I should see what the world—or at least Hollywood—thought of me.

Tina shot me a smile, and then slid onto the stool next to mine. She shook out a cloth napkin with pristine crocheted borders and tiny Christmas trees stitched in the corners. As she laid it on her lap, I reached for my own napkin and gently rubbed the linen material between my fingertips.

"Are these Mom's no-no napkins?" I quietly asked her. It was a name my mother had given them years ago because we were never allowed to use them. Same with the crystal.

"They are." She raised her glass of water for a toast.

"You just use these for everyday?" Since I'd only ever seen them behind the glass doors of the china hutch, I figured Mom was surely turning over in her grave.

"Yes. But what were we waiting for all those years, right?" Tina shrugged and smiled. "I'm here now, and I want to use a pretty napkin."

My insides sank and once again, my throat felt tight. Of all the things I tried not to think about, missing my mother was at the top of my list. I wasn't prepared to miss my sister too, as she'd repeatedly hinted I might be doing in the near future. All that time I'd stayed away from her, and for what? To return home to say goodbye? And would I have ever come home had it not been for my failure at being a wife? I blinked several times and hurriedly raised my water glass to silently change the subject.

"Here's to the no-no napkins."

"To the no-no napkins!" she cheerfully echoed me.

We clinked glasses and drank up, me wishing all the while that my glass contained something stronger than water. Apparently, Tina read my mind. She stood and retrieved a bottle of Merlot from the cupboard.

"It's cheap," she warned me, filling my glass. I tossed back a grateful swig and even held it in my mouth for a second, savoring the bleached out, bitter flavor. I glanced at the unfamiliar label and twist-off cap. Seems like winemakers can slap "Reserve" on any old thing these days.

"It's delicious," I told her. "Don't rush to put that bottle away."

"Deal." Tina set it on the table between us. We ate in silence until she was ready to talk about her day. "The appointment went well. I'll have a mastectomy tomorrow. They'll remove a few lymph nodes under my armpit just to be sure they've got it all. The procedure will take about three hours."

She listed the steps in the casual tone one might utilize when delivering instructions for making a pot roast. It felt like my soup was steaming up my eyes. I took another drink of the bad wine which was, by the way, improving with each sip.

"Inpatient surgery?"

She shook her head. "No. I'll be home by evening."

"Then what?" I closed my eyes tight, unable to keep my memories of my mother's struggle with the same cancer at bay any longer.

In my mind's eye I saw her lying in bed, too sick to get up, too tired to unwrap Christmas gifts, the front of her gown yellowed from her lightly weeping sutures, the only evidence that she'd had her breasts recently removed. She'd been as frail and pale as Tina looked right at this moment. I'd come home to hell and at the worst possible time of the year. I suddenly hated that house with every fiber of my being.

I swallowed hard, opened my eyes, and forced myself to smile. "How can I help?"

"You can go with me, hold my hand, and stay with me for a while." Her expression turned worried. "You can stay with me for a while, right?"

I wanted to run so far away.

"Yes, I can." I reached across and patted her hand, adding, "It's not exactly the way I wanted to get out of your teaching gig, but it will do."

"How did that go, anyway?" She brightened significantly. "I can't believe you stayed all day. Did you sing for the kids?"

"You knew I'd stay all day, and no, I didn't sing for the kids," I admonished her before pouring more wine. "But that was a pretty tricky trick, dear sister."

She smiled. "They need a teacher."

"I'm no teacher," I clearly told her.

"You were always pretty good on the guitar and you carry a nice little tune. Remember that song Mom always had you sing for us at Christmas?"

"No," I lied.

"'Song for a Winter's Night,' the Sarah McLachlan version." Tina's eyes sparkled in the candlelight. "God, I loved it when you'd play it. So did Mom."

I aimed a serious expression at my sister and heard my own voice crack. "Please, Tina. I can't talk about Mom."

"Okay," she kindly told me. She'd obviously made peace with Mom's death long ago, causing me to wonder if she'd gotten my share of decent mental health in the womb.

"And I'm no music teacher," I said, putting Mom-shaped thoughts out of my mind. My tone rapidly gained strength. "And then I found out you had already talked to Diane. You two are sneaks. You shouldn't even be allowed to teach at a religious school, you're both so deceitful."

"Can't blame us for trying." She made a little dismissive shrug. "It was worth a shot."

\*\*\*

The next morning, I delivered Tina to the hospital in her comfy clothes and listened to the surgical nurse's instructions. Tina calmly took it in, nodding when appropriate, not at all looking the part of a woman who was about to lose her other breast.

"What about reconstruction?" I asked the nurse. "Will they do that at the same time?"

She glanced at Tina, and then back to me. "Your sister has elected not to undergo reconstruction."

"Why not?" I turned to Tina and repeated the question. "Why not?"

Tina looked suddenly embarrassed. "My insurance doesn't cover enough of it." She rushed to comfort me. "It's okay. I'm fine with it. Now I'll have a matching set."

She grinned, but I didn't. I wanted to throw up. Leave it to my sister to try and comfort me in her most uncomfortable time.

She handled the situation with an amazing calmness, which of course, reminded me of our mother in her day.

The nurse gave her a bonnet and a flimsy hospital gown. I turned away so that I could avoid seeing her skeletal body in any true detail. I helped get her settled on a little bed while the nurse loaded her full of IV drugs. Tina was loopy within minutes.

I sat on the metal chair next to her bed, freezing my ass off in the subzero surgical bay. I clasped her hand through the side rail of her bed. She smiled.

"I'm glad you're here," she told me, a drugged little slur in her delivery.

"I'm not, Tina," I leveled with her since she was under the influence anyway. The familiarity of the entire setting had caused my internal panic to reach outstanding levels. My voice trembled with my confession. "I don't want to be here. I don't want *you* to be here. I can't stand this. I don't want to lose you like we did Mom."

My doped-up sibling wasn't fazed. "Mina, this isn't the same as with Mom. She didn't catch it early enough, that's why."

I supposed that could be true. My mother was solidly religious and modest to a fault. The idea of exposing herself for a simple mammogram probably horrified her. It just pissed me off.

"But they already operated before…" My voice trailed off, leaving her to fill in my obvious blanks.

"They'll get it," she told me, and then she closed her eyes. I thought she'd fallen asleep when she surprised me by speaking again after several minutes. "Tell me what happened with you and Fiona."

I felt my eyes reflexively widen. "You don't want to hear that now."

"Yes, I do," she quietly insisted. "I've got time."

"Okay. Oh, boy, so many things…" I thought it over, making edits to a story I'd not even made a peep about at this point. I'm a talker, but not about these things. I decided to go with the legal description. "We had irreconcilable differences."

"Bullshit," Tina muttered. I arched an eyebrow at her uncharacteristic swear. She tiredly pressed on. "Did you cheat on her?"

"No," I quickly answered. Wow, people were really under the solid impression that I was a well-rounded bad person. "Why would I be the one to cheat on her? I'm a good person."

"Did she cheat on you?"

I slumped slightly in the hard chair. Fee was, and would always be, a much better person than me. I wish she had it in her will to actually do something awful to make me hate her. I sighed. "No."

"You love each other?" She would not quit, this kid.

"I have no problem with loving her." I thought it over. "She probably loves me still, I think. Look, it just wasn't working anymore. We have too many different ideas."

"Like what?" she asked in a childish tone. "Lay it on me."

"Everything." When I saw from her expression that my answer hadn't satisfied her, I rolled my eyes. "Everything from thread count, to where to eat, to kids."

Tina moved her head to the side to get a good look at me. "You want them? Kids, I mean?"

I really didn't want to go there. I offered her a very abbreviated truth. "Let's just say she might have wanted them a little more than I did."

Tina seemed to accept my explanation. She closed her eyes. "I mean, really, who argues over where to eat, right?"

I nodded though she couldn't see me. "Right."

In a few moments, she said, "You should have some."

"Jesus, Tina. Every time I think you've gone to sleep, you're yakking again. Even the drugs won't shut you up." I chuckled softly. "You're a pushy broad, you know that?"

"I would have some." She smiled and nodded without opening her eyes. I assumed she was talking about the kids again. "I can't, but you should."

"Of course you can have kids," I told her, assuming she meant because she'd yet to find a suitable man. "You don't have to have a guy to have kids, I think that goes without saying. How'd you think we were going to do it? Duh."

"Actually I can't," she lazily muttered in her drug-happy tone. "They took all my parts last year. My baby-making career was finished before it even started."

Her sweetly voiced announcement broke my heart. Things were bleak.

I quickly reconsidered the tabloid's narcissistic accusation. I suppose I'd grown so self-centered, I'd never considered what Tina wanted for her life. I quietly leaned my forehead against the railing on the hospital bed. This sister of mine was in bad shape, a truth I was only dragging out of her little at a time. I didn't want to hear anything else. I couldn't stand to know any more. I struggled to breathe.

"Can I ask you a personal question?" Tina asked.

I lifted my face to see if she was serious, and forced a playful smirk to lighten the dark mood. "Oh, only now you want to get personal? That was some foreplay. Jesus, you should be a police interrogator."

That caused her to laugh. She quieted and furrowed her brow. Her eyes remained closed, her voice groggy. "Why did you take Fiona's last name?"

I'd wondered how many years it would take for anyone in my family to ask that question. Maybe I was waiting for every last one of them to die off so I'd never have to answer. Maybe I almost did. Anyway, you'd think I'd have been prepared with an answer. I was not.

"Were you really that angry at Dad?" she pressed.

"Tina…" I rolled my eyes, but I knew that as drugged up as my sister was, she'd never remember the conversation anyway. "It was just easier."

Tina's eyes opened wide and she looked at me incredulously. "Borsalino was easier than Smith?"

She had me. I smiled and so did she. She closed her eyes again. You can leave your home, your town, even your last name behind, but I guess you can't leave everything. Like now, I desperately wanted to leave, if only this room and this conversation. I forced myself to remain seated and speak.

"Fiona wanted to hyphenate. It wasn't her fault. She wanted our kids to have both our family names."

"Thought you didn't want kids."

I stammered around and Tina let me. I appreciated her sparing me a lecture. I knew I owed her the truth, but it didn't seem like the appropriate time or place. I gave her the abridged version. "We actually did try to have kids for a few years. For all the things I can do right, that's apparently not one of them."

Tina was quiet. I laid my hand on her cheek. She was asleep. I hoped she would have long forgotten our conversation upon waking. I felt utterly helpless in a battle she was fighting alone. I fished my cell phone out of my pocket and headed for the hallway.

I'd yet to hear anything from Attorney Jane, and I was pretty much done dicking around with her. I wanted to appeal directly to Fee for release of funds. Angry as I was at her for banishing me from everything, I had to admit that my soon-to-be ex was generally quite reasonable. I'd offer to expedite the divorce process, anything she wanted, anything to give my sister the smallest bit of comfort, if only financial. I pressed the autodial for Fee's cell phone, and in moments an automated voice came on the line telling me my services had been interrupted for nonpayment.

"What? Hell, no," I muttered. I hammered my thumb against the zero a dozen or so times until at last a real voice came on the line. "There's been a mistake. There's no way my service has been disconnected. Impossible."

The woman identified herself only by employee number and told me I had a past due balance in excess of seven hundred bucks, and would I be paying by Visa or MasterCard? My dammed up emotions finally found their outlet—fury—and I released it right down the line.

"I am a very good customer to your company. My employees are walking around right now with about eighty of your fucking walkie-talkies in their back pockets. As for me, *I'm* stranded in the middle of a goddamn cornfield and I need my goddamn *phone!*"

The line went dead. I threw the phone down hard. The shattered parts went in every direction. At the same time, something roughly poked me in the shoulder blade.

Turns out it was an index finger attached to a hulking nurse who looked like her name should be Helga. She pointed to a sign posted in front of me. I watched her mustache writhe above her fat upper lip to accompany her thunderous, well-rehearsed announcement.

"The use of all electronic devices is prohibited in the ICU."

I glimpsed down at the mess I'd created and shoved the bangs out of my face, forcibly composing myself. "Looks like that will no longer be a problem."

\*\*\*

That night, I practically carried Tina into her house and to my parents' bedroom. Had there not been fourteen agonizing stairsteps separating us from our old room, that's surely where I would have put her. Powerful, painful memories flooded me as I assisted her, even tucked her into my mom's side of the bed which she used to share with my father. It felt like I was living that hell all over again.

Seeing the old intercom system on the bedside table, I turned it on so I could hear her if she needed anything.

My father had built the system into the house years ago, I suspect so he could hear if Tina and I were talking about boys. I guess he wanted to know what he was up against and arm himself with appropriate Bible passages to steer us back to the path of righteousness. Of course, he didn't hear any such whispered conversations out of me.

He must have hated what he did hear because before I'd barged out five years ago, I'd always told my sister absolutely everything for as long as I could remember. Thanks to his not-so-covert spy system, he was spared no detail. Since we all knew he listened to our every word, perhaps I'd just wanted to torture him.

I started to leave the room, but I heard Tina stir. I went to her bedside to ask, "You need anything?"

"No, I'm good," she said, smiling in the dark. Her body was so small, she barely made a bump in the covers. "Thanks for taking me."

"Don't be ridiculous," I softly chastised her.

"Do me a favor?"

I eyed her warily, helpless to do anything but listen. She stated her case tiredly, yet succinctly. Of course, it was about my taking over her class.

"Tina, I appreciate what you're trying to do for this hapless, hopeless bunch of kids. But I can't go back there. I'm sorry, I just can't." In the darkness, I couldn't tell if she'd already fallen asleep or not. "I'll do anything else, but please don't ask me to do that again."

I left her and slowly trudged upstairs, bone weary. I sat on the edge of my old twin bed, picked up my old guitar, and strummed and tuned, strummed and tuned.

I missed Fee. More than the physical exhilaration I felt whenever our bodies were near each other, I craved her sweet reassurances and gentle touch. I'd been craving it since the day I'd stormed out on her. By now, I'd pretty much established that I was gifted at storming out.

What happened to me? Could I blame the seventy-hour work weeks, or had I simply turned into some kind of organic asshole, like my father? I'd deserted my family, copped out, and clung to the safe shelter that was Fee.

My Fee, earnest and grounded, and beautiful through and through, and now thoroughly sick and tired of me. I wondered what she'd ever seen in me in the first place and I hoped I hadn't ruined her. We used to talk for hours. Now there was a lawyer even handling that. I set the guitar aside and lay down, drawing the covers around me in the freezing upstairs room. My ears rang with the dull headache that had become the background music to my life of late.

I heard my sister's soft breathing over the monitor next to me. My eyes burned and welled with tears. I'd been a bad wife, a horrible sister, and despite my nutty, mean father, I'd been a piss-poor daughter. I was the worst possible candidate for the job of music teacher.

It felt as if God had crafted a penance for all my wrongdoings and cleverly dealt it through the sick sister I'd estranged myself from. I knew I would be conducting Sacred Heart's final Christmas program, God help us all.

# CHAPTER SEVEN

"Hey, Granola Lady, thought you chicken shitted out on us."

It was a special sort of greeting from Emanuel-the-gambler. I closed the music room door behind me and sighed. I walked across the room that had been called to semi-order in advance by Mrs. Duffy, the yeller from next door. Since everyone knew about my sister's illness, I guess the staff had figured I'd had a rough night.

I shrugged off the coat I'd borrowed from Tina, and set my bag on the desk chair. Sans the music, the room was pretty much the noisy chaos as it had been on my first day.

"You hung?" Emanuel persisted.

"Beg pardon?" I arched an eyebrow at his strange inquiry.

"You know, brown bottle flu?" He made a little bottle tipping mime.

"What? No. Jesus."

"Sure," he remarked with obvious disbelief. He climbed on top of his chair and cupped his hands around his mouth. "Listen up! Get your asses back in your seats, *ándale*! Pronto!"

I guess Emanuel sensed the lack of fight in me. That or he really thought I was hung over. He repeated his order. I watched disgruntled students return to their chairs. Then it was quiet, just me standing on the podium watching them watching me. I soon discovered that having their undivided attention was almost as nerve-wracking as enduring their chaos.

I opened the attendance book, started to pronounce the first foreign name, and then stopped and went with the head count again. I slapped the book shut, hoping I had the right set of fourteen pupils.

I opened the folder I'd brought with me, which was limp and damp with illegally copied, sloppy purple sheets of the score of Pachelbel's *Canon*, an arrangement with some nice Christmas lyrics. I passed the soggy things around without a word. When I returned to the podium, I noticed they were all nose down on their papers.

"Granola, you tryin' to get us high?" Of course, Emanuel was the first to speak. He had a purple smudge on his nose. "I think I'm getting a contact buzz off this shit."

"You've got a little…" I waved my hand in the general direction of my nose, but he didn't get the hint. A dozen students looked up at me with the same purple smudges on their noses. I shook my head. "Never mind. Look, don't smell it. Read it. This is the actual music for the song you were singing last time. I want you to see it because the symbols will help you know what notes to hold and which ones to cut off when you're singing them."

"What symbols?"

I skimmed my own sheets and felt a little guilty for having the clean, original version. I couldn't believe the inkjet copier in the office was broken. How can a school function without even the most basic office equipment? I'm sure I was the first one in decades to fire up the purple mimeograph crank-style machine. Even the bottle of ink was long expired. I found an example in the music and started in.

"Look at the top of page three, see the dots over those single notes?"

"The periods?" It was Rodriguez—Roddy, as I'd come to know him the first day, the sort-of piano player.

"It's called a staccato, imbecile." The rude answer came from the overly confident Steven.

I'd already come into the school with a hurting head and an aching heart for having left my sister alone. I quickly realized there was some room inside me yet for a different emotion. I felt hatred creeping up on me, and right behind it, shame that I felt such a thing for a twelve-year-old kid.

"It's called a staccato," I said to Roddy, trying to ignore Steven. "It means short and sweet, very light. Like *dat-dat-dat.*"

"Nice," Roddy said, nodding.

"Even the notes tell a story about how they should be sung," I continued. "For instance, one note alone can be…" I found my unrehearsed explanation trailing off. I was tired, and in truth, I didn't feel like teaching music to kids who probably didn't feel like learning.

"What up, Granola? You distracted?" Ever-loving Emanuel. "You want we should take us another day to watch TV?"

"No," I told him firmly. I looked at the rest of the class, and then back to Emanuel. I cringed. "Please, stop calling me Granola." I cleared my throat and started over. "If we refer to the single notes as a sound, like *ta*, then the two notes together would sound like *tee-tee*. Can we just talk along to this line right here?"

I started ta-ing and tee-ing. Though their hearts clearly weren't in it, the class chanted along with me for the duration of one page. I guess they probably had it by then. I ignored the asinine looks dealt my way by Steven, who chose not to join us in the exercise. Big surprise.

I clapped my hands together. "Good. Now, there are other notes, like the hollow-looking one at the bottom of page six, last row. See it? That means you're supposed to hold the sound out for four counts."

Emanuel sighed loudly. "Just tell us what it should sound like and we'll do it. We're not idiots." He turned in his seat to face Steven. "Contrary to the popular belief of certain smug douchebags."

I felt my temples already beginning to throb. "Emanuel, I've had it with your language. Do it again, and I'll have to ask you to go to the office and speak with Principal Reeves about it."

"Chill, Granola." He bobbed his full head of wild hair in a move that I'd previously found kind of cute, but was quickly getting over. "Not like you've got such a honey mouth on you yourself. I read the stories."

I felt my cheeks burn as I forged ahead. "Let's start from page two."

"Spoiled California chick with a bad temper, freaking out on her own TV show, and that's a quote," he stated. "Everybody knows it. My grandma showed me."

Well, at least he didn't see the YouTube version since he probably couldn't afford the Internet. A smiling little girl with tight braids sweetly spoke up.

"My mom said you got kicked out of California."

"And you're a homo, just like Rodriguez," Steven said. He looked at Roddy, and then at me, clearly pleased that he'd silenced the room with his announcement. "Ms. Smith's sister isn't wanted by her own people, so now she's here with us. How fortunate are we?"

Roddy was three shades redder than he should have been. He glared at Steven and appeared to be employing every bit of self-control not to jump out of his chair and pulverize the arrogant jerk. My own self-control was running dangerously low.

"That's rude. You should be ashamed of yourselves." I leaned over the podium stand and stared them all down. "What kind of moron would read such tabloid trash and believe it?"

One by one, everyone but Steven raised their hand. They didn't even have the sense to be insulted by my assessment of them. Steven stared at me, a smile slowly growing on his snarky face. I suppose he figured he'd broken me; or worse, I suppose he figured he'd reduced me to his level of insulting behavior.

"They're twelve years old, twelve years old, twelve years old tops, " I muttered under my breath. I pursed my lips tight, smiled, and started over. "Let's sing this."

"Miss Teacher?" A small girl's hand went up in the front row.

"I'm not a teacher," I impulsively corrected her.

"Miss Not-a-Teacher?" she started over. I let her error slide. Her big brown eyes were wide and sincere. "Can we sing something else?"

I glanced down at the sheet music I'd made such a tremendous effort to put in front of them. "What's wrong with this song?"

Her tanned face lit up. "We need something we can wiggle to."

She stood and began gyrating her four-foot-tall body in ways I hadn't seen since the days of The Fly Girls on *In Living Color*, before Jennifer Lopez was a household name. Though I felt a small amount of relief that she wore navy blue cable-knit tights to prevent a full preadolescent reveal, I was shocked by her bump and grind.

"Oh, my God," Emanuel said over the classroom snickers. He slapped his forehead in an exaggerated move. "Mercedes, sit your wiggly ass down right now." He appeared as exasperated as I felt. "She does this all the damned time."

"Mercedes," I said, finding my voice at last. "That is inappropriate. Please, sit down."

She gave a few final hearty Mae West-type bumps, and then took a bow. A smattering of applause and a few whistles followed.

"My momma's a famous dancer, you know," she told me, shooting me an air kiss and a wink on the way back to her seat.

"Famous at the Kit-Kat Club," Emanuel clarified, as if I hadn't already guessed.

"You're just jealous because you don't have a momma, that's all." Mercedes' high-pitched voice and tiny stature had me curious about her age in this class full of middle school kids.

I couldn't resist asking, "How old are you?"

"Ten." She proudly added, "Momma says I have a dainty frame."

"She probably said you had a dainty brain," Roddy spoke up at last. Everyone giggled. His anger toward Steven had dissolved. He smiled when he reached over and rubbed Mercedes' head in a playful way. She took it well.

Emanuel said, "Sit down, kid. Pronto."

My gaze returned to the sheet music for a few rare, quiet moments. When I glanced up, the students were staring at me again. "Well, what do you want to sing, then?"

"What do you mean?" Emanuel lowered his chin and looked at me suspiciously.

"We have little more than three weeks to put together your Christmas show. Is there anything else the class is working on?" I dumped the folder on top of my stand and riffled through it, finding typical religious carols and nothing more. The class seemed taken aback that I had asked for their input. I was pleased I could surprise them at all, given everything they'd dished my way so far. "If you were going to a Christmas show, what would you like to hear? What would you like to see?"

Everyone remained silent. I considered that I should have entered the classroom with such questions and things might have come to order more quickly. I stepped off the podium platform, headed toward the old blackboard, and picked up a piece of chalk. I turned to face them.

"Look, we all know that the music program is gone after December. This is your last hurrah, your last chance to do something great. Something imaginative. What do you want to do?"

"Sing...songs?" The delayed response came from a little girl with tight braids.

"What is your name?"

"Maria," she sweetly told me.

"Maria, think bigger."

"Well, what else would we do at a music program?" She looked like I'd given her the trick question of the century.

I shook my head and felt creative gears creaking back to life inside my tired head. "No. It's a show. *Your* show. What do you want to do?"

"Dance!" Mercedes' enthusiastic answer prompted more giggles from the class.

"Okay, there should be dancing," I said as I made a note on the blackboard. I turned to shoot her a cautionary glance. "Regulated dance, understand? None of that business you just showed us."

More giggles. I felt them loosening up, saw them wriggling around in their seats.

"Poetry," said Roddy. Okay, so maybe he was a teensy bit gay. His eyes were bright as he went on. "Some readings of poetry, or stories between songs, or something."

"That's a stupid idea," Emanuel said. "It's a music show, Chrissakes."

"No, I like that idea," I said, writing it down. Not that I really knew how we could work poetry into a music program, but I wasn't about to further demean Roddy in front of the class by questioning him. "Remember, there are no bad ideas. We'll write them all on the blackboard and vote on them."

"Instruments too," a slim, exotic-looking, mixed-raced girl in the back row spoke up. I noticed Steven giving her the eye and my stomach turned. "We've only had piano in the past. I would love instrumental music."

"Do you play an instrument...I'm sorry, what's your name?" I asked hopefully.

"I'm Brenda, and no, I don't," she said softly. Her eyes brightened when she went on, "I'd like to learn. I'm a quick learner."

I looked around the room. "Do we have instruments?"

"Over there under that cover is a bunch of shitty instruments," Emanuel said. Upon seeing my reaction, he rolled his eyes and corrected himself: "*Crappy* instruments. They suck."

I strolled over to the cover where he'd pointed and found old xylophones, both wooden and metal, many missing bars and with broken or altogether missing mallets. There were also a few dented brass instruments and woodwinds without reeds or keys. It didn't look promising. I picked out a trumpet and held it up. Steven loudly laughed from across the room.

"Face it, you drew the losing card." He shrugged when I looked at him. "Don't waste your time making this pathetic lot your cause. Assign us a few songs and let's close this program down."

"Shut up, douchebag," Emanuel fired back. I didn't correct him.

"I have a say in the matter since I'm one of the only ones who pays real money to attend this wretched, indigent institution," Steven droned. "We even pay for the spics with our family endowment. You surely don't expect us to kick in for instruments, too, do you? Look how horridly they treat the things they do get."

"Steven, that's it. I'm sending you to the principal's office." I pointed toward the door. "Go there, now."

He stared at me, unblinking.

"Go," I repeated, snapping my fingers. "Now."

"She'll just send me back to class. Why don't you call her and save me a trip downstairs? I'm tired this morning." He wore a conniving grin.

I went to the class phone and did just that, only to have Principal Reeves verify his claim. Apparently, there were no repercussions for rude behavior when you're one of the only ten paying students. I hung up without a word and went back to the blackboard.

"Told you," he muttered behind me.

I ignored him and instead wrote "play instruments" on the blackboard before turning around to face the class. "Anything else you'd like to do for your last concert?"

Emanuel sat up straight. "You mean like lights, and props, and pyrotechnics, and stuff?"

"No to the pyro stuff and maybe to the rest."

"Killer," he said, sitting back in his chair and looking thoughtful. "Yeah, I'd like all that."

"Me, too," I said, wishfully thinking aloud. I clapped my hands. "Okay, so does Sacred Heart still have an art class?"

"Pay for these losers to paint?" Steven jeered. "That would be a solid no."

It was the kind of colorful answer I was beginning to anticipate from this twit. I ignored him, something I'd obviously have to get used to in a hurry or I'd be bursting blood vessels left and right.

"Your assignment for today is to write down five songs you'd like to sing and bring the list to class tomorrow. Then we'll vote on them and decide what to sing."

"Any song?" An obese African-American girl in the middle row shook her head. "I don't know about that. We never get to pick our own songs."

"Well, you never had props and instruments either," I said, warily eyeing the pile of brass and percussion destruction across the room. I swallowed hard, hearing my voice squeak with uncertainty. "But things change."

"Who's going to teach us to play the instruments?" Mercedes looked as skeptical about the situation as I felt. "I don't have much use for instruments."

"You can beat a drum, right? Shake a tambourine?" I smiled. "It doesn't take long to learn that stuff."

The bell rang, saving me from having to explain how on earth I'd teach anyone to play a broken-down woodwind when I could strum a few chords on a guitar at best.

"Class dismissed." I watched them file out of the room. They were noisy, but for once, the noise was about music. Amazing. The next class filed in, a good head shorter, a few years more restless, but at least not as jaded as their predecessors seemed to be.

"Good morning, class," I said. "We're going to wrap packages today."

My odd announcement was greeted with enthusiasm and curiosity by the younger set. I'd been thinking about those battered instruments, which had me thinking about Mrs. Bernard Fontaine, one of the wealthy Malibu wives always calling around for donations to her music charity. She was in the business of restoring old instruments for use in poor schools. Though I'd never actually seen one of her charity schools, I felt that Sacred Heart surely qualified.

I was partially hopeful that my plan would work, as Fee and I were—or had been—gold star donors. Of course, the other side was that as a gold star donor, Mrs. Fontaine knew I had money, even if I couldn't presently touch it, and might not deem my cause to be a charitable candidate. Still, it was worth a shot.

Worse-case scenario: she'd reject us or the instruments could be lost in shipping. I took a gander at the pile again and figured that the latter might be considered a godsend.

At three o'clock, I called UPS and arranged pickup for my heavy boxes, packed tight with cellophane tape imprinted with the fingerprints of every five-to eight-year-old in music class. I included a note to Mrs. Fontaine briefly explaining my situation, and sent the entire works COD.

I'd already thrown myself at the feet of the snootiest society woman I'd ever known. What would begging a little postage matter at this stage in the game?

I got out of class later than usual. It was dark when I drove toward my childhood home. I felt a little better that I'd gotten a call at school from Mrs. Wellman, my sister's neighbor, who reported that Tina was doing well and had eaten something. As she was already sleeping, Mrs. Wellman warned me that I might want to stop somewhere for dinner on the way home to avoid making a ruckus in the kitchen. It was a wise idea, since I think I mentioned my gracelessness.

With a fond memory of a greasy tuna melt and fries, I scrounged through Tina's console for enough cash to stop at Barney's Bar inside the old Plaza Hotel. The place was just as dark and anonymous as I remembered. And dead, too. Thank you, economy. I ordered my sandwich and sipped the cold froth off a beer.

"Pick a card, any card. Bet you a buck I can tell you what it is, and this ain't no top of the deck scam. You hide it."

I looked over and saw Emanuel standing beside my booth. We recognized each other at the same time.

"Shit," we both said simultaneously, and then, "It's you."

# CHAPTER EIGHT

I shot a bit of beer out my nose, coughed, and quickly wiped the spray with my napkin.

"What are you doing here?" we asked each other in another chorus.

"Okay, me first," I sternly told him. "What are you doing here?"

Emanuel quickly pocketed his cards and started to scram, but I grabbed his scrawny arm and steered him onto the vinyl seat across from me. It was dark outside and getting late, and downtown Landon wasn't exactly an idyllic safe haven.

"Do your parents know you're here?" I asked.

He shrugged. I guess he hadn't expected to see his music teacher—gulp—in a bar.

I, on the other hand, hadn't recognized him quickly as he'd suppressed his wiry locks beneath a handkerchief instead of a hat. His thin, obviously hand-me-down parka was held together with safety pins in lieu of buttons. He looked like a street kid. I wondered if he was.

"Emanuel, do you have a home?" I softly asked him.

"Of course I have a home," he said, waving his hand as if to dismiss me. "That's a stupid question. I live with my grandma."

So nice a home that he was scamming for dollar bills inside a bar? My line of questioning was interrupted by Barney, the owner of the bar. I was surprised to see he was still alive—the man had to be a hundred years old. He quickly proved himself to be as loud and spry as ever.

"I told you to stay outta here, you lowlife!" He aimed his cold words right at Emanuel. The boy slid to the front of his seat and prepared to split a second time. I held his coat sleeve, making it impossible for him to go. As worn as the material was, I hoped it wouldn't tear right off.

"That's no way to talk to a kid," I told Barney. "What's the problem here?"

"The problem is this kid, who is always coming around here scamming my customers out of their tip money." Barney nodded and pointed at Emanuel, frowning. I thought that in his age, he'd grown to look a bit like Mr. Burns from *The Simpsons*. "Get out of here. For the last time, get out of here!"

"Calm down, he's just a little boy," I said, rising out of my seat. The only other patrons were seated at the bar, but they had turned on their stools to observe the commotion.

"It's bad enough you people have to come here and ruin my town. Now you want to ruin my business?" Barney continued to address only Emanuel.

"That's very much enough!" I harshly whispered. "Leave this table or I'll leave too. Then you'll have one less meal to sell."

Barney glared at me for several seconds. Suddenly, as if the ice around his hard façade melted with this economic realization, his anger lines relaxed. He smiled. With some delight he asked, "Are you saying this young man is a paying customer?"

"That's what I'm saying," I said, sitting back down.

"And what will he be having today?" Barney was really testing me.

I was acutely aware of my limited—and borrowed—finances. "I just ordered him a tuna melt and fries. Please bring him a water with lemon to drink."

Barney looked as though he was certain he'd been conned, but wasn't exactly sure of the nature of the con. He barged back to the bar and conferred with his only waiter. The fellow nodded and filled a glass full of ice and water. In moments, the glass sat in front of my impromptu dinner guest.

"Where's my lemon?" Emanuel demanded.

"Be nice," I scolded him. I watched him suck the juice out of four tiny lemon slices after they were delivered to him. He downed the water, stifled a burp, and looked around. I swear he was eyeballing the ketchup. I hoped they'd hurry with that sandwich.

"I'll ask again. Does your grandmother know you're here?"

He shrugged. "Dunno. She's busy."

"Does she work?" I pried, dying for a sip of my beer, but hesitant to imbibe in front of a student. "I mean, does she get home in time to make dinner?"

"She's busy, but she don't work." It was hardly an explanation.

The waiter returned and slid a plate in front of him. After he left, Emanuel guiltily slid the plate toward me. "I don't want your dinner."

But I knew he did. "I'm not hungry," I lied. "I just didn't want to look like a lush by just ordering a beer."

We smiled at each other. He hungrily dove in, chewing each bite slowly, savoring every last morsel like he was a restaurant reviewer. In turn, I sipped my beer. I wondered what anyone would think about seeing a teacher in a bar drinking a beer with her student at the same table. I looked around at the few patrons with their chins down, their eyes forward, and put the worry out of my mind.

"You do this often?" I asked, eyeing the pocket where he'd crammed his cards. "What's your game?"

"Everything," he said. "Poker is good. Blackjack is for suckers. I've got some card tricks, but they don't pay well for the trouble."

I ran my finger along the rim of my glass. "You make much money in your line of work?"

"I do if I can get a good poker game going with some sucker grownup. Kids don't pay for shit," he said, then corrected himself. "Don't pay for nothing."

"I see."

"You get an oatmeal cookie or pennies," he said, shaking his head as he polished off the last of his fries. "Not much worth nothing."

"Does your grandmother like you hustling people?"

"Only suckers get hustled. If they a sucker, then so be it." He licked every finger despite the fact that I held a napkin out to him. He pushed the plate aside. "You want me to show you a card trick?"

He pulled his cards out when I nodded and had me pick one. I'd seen it a million times—guy places the card on top of the pack and ta-da! It magically resurfaces. But Emanuel didn't play it that way. He buried the card, didn't look at the surrounding ones, yet produced my ace of spades moments later.

"How'd you do that?" I asked him, slightly baffled by his technique.

"A good hustler doesn't give out his secrets," he said, and then he shrugged and added, "I count them."

"That's pretty good," I said, nodding. "You good at poker?"

"Want me to show you?"

"No," I said. "You do that good in math?"

"No money in math," he said with a frown. "Besides, bookwork sucks."

I was getting a very clear picture that a lot of things in Emanuel's life sucked.

"That's a pity. You could get yourself a scholarship, go to college, and get yourself out of this town."

"And go where?" He looked dumbfounded, as if the idea never crossed his mind. "Go to California like you and get kicked out? I think California's for suckers."

I considered it. "Maybe." I stood up and dropped enough money on the table to cover our bill and a tip. "Can I give you a lift home?"

I could tell he was prepared to say no, but when we stepped outside, the freezing wind and dark night quickly changed his mind. "Yeah, that wouldn't be so bad."

I followed his directions to a nearby neighborhood, one that my sister had specifically warned me to stay away from on my first day back. I figured if a little kid like Emanuel could live there, I could drive through it one time, no problem. I pulled the car to a stop in front of a little ranch tract home. All the lights were on inside.

"I thought you said your grandmother wouldn't be home."

"She ain't. We live here with a bunch of people."

I had to wonder how many people allowed this child to roam a dangerous neighborhood in a safety-pinned coat to hustle a buck for his dinner. I shook it off and smiled at him.

"Did you think about the songs you want to sing?" I asked, changing the subject. He looked momentarily caught off guard. I reminded him. "You know, for the music program?"

"Does it matter?" He sat in the cold of my sister's car, looking at me.

"Sure it does," I said half-heartedly. Fee's favorite phrase rolled through my mind and I heard it coming out of my mouth. "Everything matters."

"Whatever." He opened the door and got out. He turned to say, "The food was good," before shutting the door.

"I'll see you tomorrow, Emanuel."

I watched him disappear around the back of the ramshackle house. I wondered if anyone would notice him slip inside. I wondered if anyone had noticed he'd slipped out in the first place. I drove away.

I felt lonelier than ever as I exited the shabby neighborhood and headed for the main street. I stayed too long at a stoplight that was probably on a timer, since I was the only one in the area. Up ahead, I saw the neon flashing arrow sign of a movie rental store boasting three dollar Christmas rentals.

I scrounged around the console for change, came up with that much, and figured it was a good investment since another dinner was now out of reach. If I know anything about my sister, it's that she loves Christmas movies. I stopped in the store and picked up an old copy of *The Preacher's Wife* before heading home. It was musical and a little corny, my sister's favorite recipe.

I found Tina slowly moving around the kitchen making herself a cup of tea.

"I got this, sit down." I shrugged out of my borrowed coat and took the kettle from her to finish what she'd started. "How do you feel?"

"I'm fine. Did you have a good day?" she asked.

"I'm frozen clear through," I told her. I fished around the cabinet for the teabags. "I'm considering making three cups of this stuff. One for you and one for each of my feet."

I heard her chuckle. "You'll get used to it."

"Thank you, but I really won't," I said. "I don't want to, no offense to you."

"None taken," she said, sitting down at the butcher block. I tried not to notice that she was obviously in pain when she moved her arm near the surgical site. "This lap of luxury isn't for everyone, I know."

Her comment triggered a memory that I'd sooner forget. My father and I used to have a war of words regarding why I felt I needed to leave Landon. In these arguments, he'd paint himself and the other townspeople as mere peasants, saying I had high-and-mighty ideals that were too good for Iowa. He called me The King, and though I'm nowhere near a butch dyke, he apparently felt all dykes were the same.

"You hate Landon," Tina said when I returned to her one-sided conversation. I spun around to look at her.

"I don't hate Landon. You sound just like Dad. Jesus Christ, what is so wrong with not wanting to live in Landon?"

"Mina, I wasn't—" She started, but I cleanly cut her off.

"Wasn't what? Trying to remind me about how I busted my ass to get out of this place?" I pointed toward the door. "You could have gone, too, you know. You could very easily be teaching in some better place without a superinflated crime rate, with actual salary and benefits! So don't act like I'm the one who bailed on you."

She folded her arms gingerly across her chest and studied me. "So I'm the stupid one for staying, huh?"

The kettle whistled behind me.

"Yeah, maybe." I turned around and plunked two teabags into two cups. My hands shook as I poured steaming water over them. I handed her a cup, but she didn't take it right away. I set it in front of her on the butcher block. I sipped my tea too quickly and scalded my tongue.

"I stayed, Mina, because Mom and Dad needed me. Mom was sick," Tina began her case. "When she passed, Dad got sick. What was I supposed to do? You weren't here."

"I was out pursuing the lap of luxury lifestyle, isn't that what Dad always said?" I leaned against the counter and stared her down. "Let's get down to what we've been avoiding ever since I walked back into this house. You think I'm a lousy daughter because I wouldn't put up with Dad's shit."

"Dad was very stubborn, you know that," she defended. "He wasn't educated. He was a simple man who wasn't good with words."

"He found a few when he told me what he thought of my lifestyle. Did you expect me to keep coming back to be treated like some kind of pariah? Do you know how hard that was to listen to?"

"Do you know how hard it was to watch him die? *Alone?*" She had me there. Her voice dropped a level. "It was the hardest thing I've ever done. Real hard work there, Mina. You got a pass out of this place because you were angry, and I got to watch him die because I wasn't."

My guilt did not deter my defensive nature. "I didn't run off without reason."

She was quick to answer. "Nope, but you sure did run."

We stared at each other.

"Well, I'm here now, aren't I?"

"Because you want to be, or because you have to be, just like I had to be?" She clearly had me there. I took too long to answer her question. She nodded. "Just what I thought."

I set my mug aside. "Don't do that to me. Don't make me feel like I'm arguing with a ghost, like Dad and I had a simple, lifelong misunderstanding when there's nothing I can do about it now." I heard my voice rising in volume. "And don't you dare tell me he was okay with me because I know better."

"Dad didn't have a problem with you being gay!" Tina spat. "He was a farmer. He had a problem with you being creative. Mina, he didn't know what to do with you!"

"Bullshit!" I burst out, and then forced myself to calm down. I walked to the center island where she sat and looked her square in the eyes. "Don't discount my instincts. It's really all I have left."

Once again, we stared at each other for several long seconds.

"Tina, I…I'm sorry," I stammered at last. What was I thinking, arguing with my sick sister?

"No, it's true," she said at last, slumping slightly on her stool. She looked utterly defeated and tired. "Dad was a staunch old hateful asshole. I guess my making excuses for him didn't die with him."

We were quiet in the wake of her revelation.

"I'm sorry I left you to put up with him," I finally whispered. "I should have been a good sister to you even if I wasn't a great daughter to them."

She raised her glassy eyes. "That's not true. Mom loved you very much."

I heard my voice crack when I said, "I hope so."

Tina reached across the butcher block and rested her hand on mine. "She told me once that Fiona was the best thing to come along. That's pretty good for a little old Catholic woman. She adored you both and admired what you'd done with your lives." She softly chuckled and looked away. "I actually felt a little left out for having the unexciting career."

"Unexciting, my ass." I smirked and hurriedly wiped my wet eyes on my sleeve. "That school teacher business is not for wimps, I can now attest to that."

"That part might be true," she admitted.

"Might be?" I pretended to bow to her. "You're my fucking hero."

I put my arm around her and gently pulled her toward me, carefully guarding the general area of her stitches. Tina laid her head on my shoulder.

"Tina, what are you going to do come January?" I asked.

"I honestly don't know," she said. "What about you? What are you going to do with your life?"

I pulled back from her and shook my head. "I honestly don't know, either."

I went upstairs to bed that night, grateful that Tina hadn't seen the mess I'd left the bedroom in. Not one for early rising, I didn't make the bed at all anymore. Plus, I liked the way the covers looked all messed up like that when I came in at night. Like someone had been there already. It made things a little less lonely, if only for a minute before I crawled into bed alone. I slowly undressed and did just that.

I did not know what I would be doing come January. I didn't know what I'd be doing ever again. Despite what Tina had told me, I really wasn't the creative side of the partnership. I was pretty sure there'd be a buyout of sorts and I would never see the inside of a studio lot again. I'd probably take an apartment in the city, probably some pre-fab condo looking thing, where I'd probably raise cats. It wasn't an attractive prospect. I wondered if I'd had too much California bullshit, but in truth, I simply couldn't see myself there without Fee.

Fee was not my first love, but certainly she was my best. We became friends in high school, though prior to that I'd seen her at church. I always thought she was beautiful even if she didn't show the slightest bit of romantic interest in me.

We discussed attending the same university, as friends will, and as soon as those small-town constraints were lifted, we fell into each others' beds and subsequently in love. It was fast, but it seemed like the most natural thing in the world. Fee was my security. With her at my side, I felt invincible, utterly untouchable by the unkind words of others, particularly my father. Her smart words and gentle touch made me feel like there was no other love but ours.

Fee could do amazing things to me. She touched me beyond a physical way. Our bodies seemed to react to each other even without our permission. Of all the sex-related things I've heard of killing perfectly good relationships; our problems were opposite. Long after we'd begun to clash in public, we could still mesh in private, pleasing each other with our soft touches and loving kisses everywhere.

I fell asleep with these things on my mind, which is probably why I drifted out of one erotic dream into another, all starring Fee. I awoke for good in the throes of passion involving one of those aforementioned deep south, sultry kisses. Nice as it was to greet the day that way, disappointment quickly came over me at the realization that the fingers inside me were my own. This had happened before, of course, but I don't even remember the last time I came in bed by myself. In addition to my tabloid bitchiness and my current state of poverty, it was affirmative: I was utterly sexually depraved.

There wasn't much I could do about my reputation or my depravation, but I intended to fix the money situation pronto, as Emanuel would say.

# CHAPTER NINE

I checked on my sister, then grabbed the unwatched movie on the way out the door the next morning. Three bucks down the drain. No way was I going to add to that tab by not having the movie returned by the four o'clock deadline.

I arrived to find that the movie rental place hadn't opened yet and there was no drop box, of course, which added to my already cranky mood from not yet having my coffee. Tina didn't drink the stuff and the only thing they sold ready-made in Landon came in the form of vending-style crappucinos. I suppose it was just as well since I didn't even have pocket change at this point to buy one of those.

I arrived at the school early and beat on the front door until Principal Reeves waddled into view and unchained everything. I went straight to her office and used her telephone to dial the studio.

"Good morning, Fi-Mi Productions," a voice squeaked down the line.

"This is Mina Borsalino. Put me through to Fiona, please." Somebody in the production company was a dirty tabloid rat. No sense in fanning the storytelling fires. It was necessary to pull out every please and thank you in the book.

"Hi, Mrs. Borsalino. Mrs. Borsalino isn't in right now. Could I take a message?"

She was far too chipper for this early hour. I looked at my watch and realized I was on Iowa time. Just after seven my time was still only five hers. I'd only reached the after-hours answering service. I hung up without even a goodbye and dialed Fee at home, but there was no answer. As only a select handful have our private house number, when it rings, we always answer it no matter the hour.

"Damn it," I muttered, slowly punching in Fee's business cell next. No way would she answer it so early. I'd probably have to leave a message and hope like hell she called back. I was considering what I'd say when I heard a click.

I arched an eyebrow and mumbled, "Hello?"

"Production office. This had better be good." The tired sounding voice practically croaked the greeting. It was not Fee. I was momentarily stunned into silence. The strange woman said, "Hello?"

My surprise was quickly replaced by anger. I snapped, "Who is this?"

"Who is this?" she countered in a smooth, low rasp.

"I asked you first." It was beginning to sound a lot like my first exchange with Emanuel. I shook my head. "Never mind. I need to talk to Fiona right now."

"She's not available," the voice droned.

"Sure she's available," I said, my voice rising. "So just roll over and wake her up, or whatever the hell you have to do, and put her on the phone, *now*."

"Just who do you think you are?" She had the nerve to sound offended? Please.

"This is an emergency!" I bellowed down the line.

"And I told you, she's not available!" Mystery girl did not back down. "For the last time, leave me your name and I'll deliver the message. That's as good as it's going to get!"

"Well then, here's the message." I heard the sounds of children bursting through the front doors of the school and down the hallways. "Tell her to call Sacred Heart Catholic in Iowa. She knows the place. I'd say call my fucking phone, but it's been fucking disconnected."

"That's a lot of *fucking* to be calling from a Catholic-anything, isn't it, ma'am?" she remarked. Bitch might be as sarcastic as I am, and this early in the morning—her time?—I would have applauded her, but she was probably sleeping with my wife. I actually heard her writing down my message. "Since I'm sure you're not a fucking nun, would you care to leave a name?"

"This is her wife."

"Oh, my…" The realization in her voice rang loud and clear—it usually does for the guilty party.

I slammed the phone down before she could utter an excuse or an apology. I picked the handset back up and slammed it down several more times just for good measure. The old-fashioned appliance jingled loudly with each crash.

"Tramp!" I hollered. I heard a gasp and spun around, only to discover that I had an audience. A six-year-old girl with ponytails sprouting like water fountains on each side of her head stood staring at me from the doorway. I recognized her from my second class. Still, my patience left something to be desired. "What do *you* need?"

She promptly scampered out of the doorway.

I immediately recognized my foolish and immature error. I started after her, but hit a slick spot and went down hard on my ass. I sat there while the first bell rang, the heels of my hands resting in a puddle that I'd initially assumed was melted snow, but it was warm. I sniffed it. It was pee. Six-year-old girl pee, to be exact. I swore to anyone who was listening as I alternately slid and lumbered to my feet.

I heard high-pitched squeaking. In moments, the omnipresent Principal Reeves steered her galvanized mop bucket right next to me. She calmly stepped over the puddle and dropped a heavy, industrial string mop into the mess and swished it around. She even hummed a little tune as she did so, making me wonder if she was altogether right in the head after so many years of smelling glue, floor wax, and apparently, sometimes bodily fluids. She turned toward me with her usual unwavering smile and soft voice.

"Get something out of the spare uniform wardrobe behind you, would you, dear?" she asked, pointing. The wardrobe turned out to be a small cardboard box filled with ratty uniform pieces.

"Thanks, but I don't think anything here's going to fit me," I muttered.

She dumped the mop in the rolling bucket and squeezed it out. "Not you, dear. The little girl with the wet britches."

I started to sort through the wrinkled, yellowed things. "What size am I looking for?"

"First grade size," she said, re-mopping the same spot.

I rummaged around for a minute, and then dropped all the pieces back into the box. "This stuff is in terrible condition. In fact, most of the kids' actual uniforms are in terrible condition."

"It's not about the quality of the uniforms, dear," she said, dunking the mop head back into the bucket. "Sacred Heart is not about fancy uniforms and hi-tech equipment. We're building good, bright children with spirit."

"Spirit?" I headed for the door, made a little leap over the wet spot, and turned to share my disgusted expression with my old principal. "Spirit won't keep you warm when you've got no knees in your pants."

I bolted toward the front doors of the building, loudly chastising her all the way. "And I challenge you to print fourteen copies of sheet music using nothing but *spirit*!"

It was freezing outside. I went to Tina's car and got a pair of sweatpants out of the backseat. I'd been meaning to bring them in after her surgery and kept forgetting. Thank God for my poor memory now. I started to go, but caught a glimpse of the movie I'd been unable to return. I grabbed it, too. No sense letting it freeze and break, adding to my growing list of IOUs for things I needed to replace and/or repair.

Back inside, I was greeted by the same pandemonium I'd come to expect from my nine-to-twelve year-olds. Thirteen wild hooligans were jumping, jiving, leaping and anything else you can think of that requires the accompaniment of laughter and catcalls. The fourteenth student, Steven Weitrich, ignored their antics, deeply involved in a text conversation happening on his fancy little phone. I thought of my own shattered phone and was actually jealous. I clapped my hands loudly.

"Return to your seats!" I called to them. When that didn't work, I grabbed a pitch pipe off the podium and blew into it so hard, its high-pitch squeal probably set dogs on high alert for a two-mile radius. The kids covered their ears and squinted, and with much grumbling about how immature I was—go figure— they returned to their seats. I chucked the splendid pitch pipe into my sweater pocket for future use.

I counted fourteen heads and called it attendance before walking back to the blackboard to finish what we'd started the day before.

I asked, "So, what kind of music did you come up with?" I turned around after several seconds of silence. The class looked dumbfounded, though admittedly their ears could have still been ringing. "Nobody knows what they'd like to sing in your last Christmas show at Sacred Heart?"

"I know!" Mercedes' hand shot into the air. I nodded for her to continue. She stood up and announced, "My all-time favorite Christmas song is 'Santa Baby'!"

In a split-second, a full montage of everything that could go wrong with that sex-kittenesque, materialistic, ungodly song wound through my head. "No," I firmly told her.

Her brow furrowed. She crossed her arms over her thin chest and dropped back onto her chair.

I turned back to the blackboard and made a new column, addressing the class as I did so. "And before we go any further, I'm going to post a list of singers whose music we will never perform, starting with anyone whose name contains MC, P-anything, Big, Lil', Daddy, Mack, Wayne or Madonna. Not even Eartha Kitt." To prove my street smarts, I further elaborated, scribbling madly as I went on with the verbal list. "Nor will we be singing songs containing the words bling, shiznit, grind, pimp, ho, mo-fo or anything in the fo-shizzle family."

I heard groans all around and was secretly pleased to be responsible for them, as bad a mood as I was in.

"Eartha Who?"

I turned around, and brushed the yellow chalk off my fingers and all over the black sweatpants I'd put on. Smooth. The heavyset African-American girl from the middle row had asked the question. She looked like I'd referenced a Martian.

"Eartha Kitt," I repeated. Her eyes didn't hold even a slight glimmer of recognition. "You know, Catwoman?"

"That's Halle Barry." It was the first thing I'd heard from Emanuel that morning.

"A poorly done remake, but me-*ow*," I muttered under my breath. I cleared my throat. "Eartha Kitt is an…" I nearly choked on my next word, "old singer who did a rendition of the song Mercedes referred to. It was nice, but not Catholic school appropriate."

The girl nodded and coolly stated, "I'm down with that."

"With what?"

"You know, the old singers," she said. "My grandma introduced me to them. We sing that stuff around the house all the time."

"Really?" My interest level was ramping up right along with her enthusiasm. Perhaps we were getting somewhere. "Like who, for example?"

"You know, Donna Summer, Tina Turner, Whitney Houston. All the greats."

I stood staring and blinking as I quickly calculated that her grandmother had to be all of forty years old to consider those singers, "the greats."

"They're nice," I said, sighing. "But I'm talking about Ella Fitzgerald, Etta James Billie Holiday."

"Never heard of 'em," she said, and just like that, her interest vanished.

"Excuse me?" Mrs. Duffy, the next-door teacher, stood in the doorway. "I heard a loud whistling sound from this direction. Is everything okay?"

"Yeah," I assured her, embarrassed. I felt the pitch pipe burning a hole in my pocket. "The kids were just picking songs for the Christmas program."

"Oh, my," she said, looking surprised or horrified, I wasn't sure which. "You're letting the children choose the songs?"

"We're coming up with a pretty good list so far," I casually lied.

Mrs. Duffy briefly scanned the blackboard and her eyes widened. Her voice sounded squeaky and funny when she said, "Should be...interesting."

She said a quick goodbye and ducked out of the classroom. I turned toward the blackboard and only then realized that our "list" so far appeared to consist of only those words and singers I'd vetoed. Mrs. Duffy must have thought I was off my rocker. I hurriedly erased the evidence. When I turned around, my gaze landed straight on Steven. He wore his typical snarky smile. I quickly looked away.

"I hope you committed that list to memory," I told them. "Now let's come up with some actual songs."

"Who cares?" Emanuel said, deflating the very last of my mood.

"You should care." I scanned fourteen blank faces. Their collective interest appeared to be solidly negative. I gasped. "All of you should care. It's your responsibility to give a crap about what you do in this world."

Emanuel rolled his eyes. "Shit, lady, just assign us some Christmas carols and let's get a move on, already."

"Emanuel, you I *can* suspend," I harshly told him. "And if you don't knock that crap off, I *will*."

"Chill, Granola," he said, making a yielding motion with his hands. "You are one high-strung teacher."

"I'm not a teacher!" I felt myself losing it. "I'm just here trying to help you put on your stupid Christmas show so that my sister can feel like she's actually achieved something with this hard-headed, inept, trash-mouthed, ignorant, rotten bunch of kids that she cares about for some reason I can't fathom, because I want to just walk right out of here *right now*!"

"What about the dancing?" Mercedes asked, looking deeply troubled.

"Yeah, and now we don't have any instruments," Roddy put in.

Emanuel counted the facts on his fingers. "We've got no songs, no dancing, and now you done mailed off our only instruments. Good going so far, teacher."

I gave up.

"Yep, I sent them away." I walked to the podium, collected the music folder, and dropped it into the garbage can on my way to retrieve my coat. I pulled it on en route to the classroom door. "You can add one more thing to that list of things you don't have—me. Goodbye," I said. For the Spanish speakers, I added, "Adios."

I skipped downstairs and toward the solidly locked entryway. Principal Reeves heard me jangling the chains and quickly waddled my way, wearing a puzzled expression.

I am sure I looked mentally unstable as I laid out my demand. "Let me out of this godforsaken school right now, or I'll go through the fire window."

She unlocked and unchained the doors faster than I'd ever seen her move. I pushed through the door and almost skidded down the snow packed, steep steps outside. I regained my balance and went to the car, which refused to start.

"Piece of shit!" My words were muffled in the snow-insulated parking lot.

I slammed the door and headed toward downtown. My fingers were already frigid. I crammed them into the pockets of my thin sweatpants where I miraculously found a dollar. Twenty minutes later, I employed it to take the city bus to the stop nearest my sister's house. Inside two measly weeks, I'd gone from private car to public transportation.

I was met at the house by the neighbor, Mrs. Wellman. She was fraught with worry as she ushered me into her car and drove me to the edge of town. Tina had taken a strange turn after her radiation treatment. She was in the hospital.

# CHAPTER TEN

The flu is never pleasant. Add to that recent surgery and a radiation treatment, and my sister had concocted a splendid recipe for nausea and pure exhaustion. Tina slept and IV hydrated in the hospital for two days before that same good neighbor showed up to return us home. Once there, I made her soup and tea, performed all the motherly-type duties I had on my very limited roster, and then I helped her into bed and took enough money out of her purse to catch a cab to retrieve the car still parked at the school.

Over the course of forty-eight silent bedside hours, I'd decided that I was going to open a new line of credit—divorce rules be damned—and get my sister the healthcare she deserved. It was time to get her to a specialist or something somewhere else. I wasn't going to have her dying of the flu or pneumonia on me after she'd pulled through surgery for cancer. I was also going to get her car fixed, get some groceries, get her a goddamn phone, and firewood, and anything else we required, thereby thoroughly destroying the "bonds of trust" I'd been warned against breaking by Attorney Jane Silvia. That "matrimonial bank" was half mine, damn it.

Armed with my formal resignation letter—a courtesy only, as I'd never signed an actual employment contract, since apparently Principal Reeves operates Sacred Heart by rules created on the spot—I had the cabbie drop me at the school.

It was dark outside as well as inside the school, and the doors were locked. I spun a slow circle in the parking lot and saw the soft glow of candlelight emanating from St. Mary's several yards in the distance. I hoped there would be a nighttime janitor there with a very big ring of keys.

St. Mary's Cathedral had been built sometime around the turn of the century. It had a stone exterior and high gothic pinnacles that appeared to point right to heaven no matter how much the town at its base had changed.

I pushed through the doors and was ambushed by immediate welcoming warmth. I entered the sanctuary and wandered around a bit, but didn't find a janitor, just a handful of scattered faithful parishioners lighting candles or kneeling in prayer. I recognized a kid or two from the school. I ducked out of sight into one of the last pews, habitually signed the cross, and went to my knees like everyone else while I formulated my next move.

It had been ten years since I'd been inside St. Mary's, or any church for that matter. I lifted my eyes to the crown of stained glass windows along the ceiling. Despite the upsurge of crime in Landon, the church was revered. I was glad to see that no one had dared graffiti a wall or take a stone to a window.

Even in the darkness, the church was spectacular, and brought back memories of growing up in this town where everything gentle had seemingly vanished. As I was on my knees in this warm, heavenly place, I dropped a line on my sister's behalf.

"Heavenly Father, Christ, Our Lord…" It was an awkward beginning at best. I trudged ahead anyway. "I'm sure You're in no mood to hear from me after all this time, but I'm here for my sister. She's in pain and she needs help that I can't give her."

I suddenly felt myself getting jammed up. I blinked my eyes clear and let a wavy curtain of blond hair swing forward to shield my face in the event anyone noticed me. I felt downright guilty to be in the company of others, showing up after all this time and asking their God for help. I swallowed hard and tried again. This time, I got right to the point.

"Please don't take her from me." My whisper sounded as worn out as I felt. "I'm asking You for a miracle. Please send us *something*."

"Mina?"

My eyelids sprang open like cartoon window shades. I'd know the voice anywhere. I didn't turn around right away, but remained kneeling. My prayerful voice rose and was somewhat tinged with sarcasm. "That's not what I had in mind, Lord."

I crossed myself anyway, wiped my eyes clean, slowly stood, and turned to address the interrupter.

"Mina?" she repeated. "My God, what are you doing here?"

I lowered my chin and dealt my best intent gaze toward familiar, deep-set dark eyes. Wispy ends of an auburn pixie poked out from beneath her knitted winter cap and tangled in her long eyelashes, and her cheeks were pink from the cold. Her smile, though guarded, was stunning.

I mustered up my best possible greeting for the woman who had ruined me. "Hello, Fiona."

I silently followed her into the grand church foyer where our voices would not disturb anyone who was actually there to pray without the worry of running into their exes. We took a seat on a bench. Fee peeled off her cap, playfully batting down static in her hair.

"Iowa winter," she remarked smiling, as if nothing was wrong between us. It reminded me of a kinder, more playful time in our relationship, and triggered other feelings within me as well. I actually felt my nether regions surge at the notion of having her so close, depraved as I'd been feeling. Angry or not, in the midst of a divorce or not, I craved her. The body wants what it wants. So does the heart. Fee also seemed uncomfortable, but it was now impossible to know if our reasons for discomfort were the same. I wondered if I still knew her beyond her physical curves.

She jarred me from my reverie. "I was just lighting a candle for Papa Borsalino."

We both crossed ourselves at the mention of her deceased, dear grandfather.

"So when did you get here?"

"Thanksgiving," I answered flatly.

"I'm so glad you got to spend the holiday with Tina. How is she?" Her eyes had the nerve to twinkle.

"Actually, we didn't share the holiday, I came in late that night." Even I could hear the coldness in my voice. "I couldn't stay in California because I had no money."

Fee furrowed her brow. "What do you mean, you had no money?"

"No. Money." I figured it didn't get much clearer than that, but just in case, I added, "No house. No car. No job. No money."

"Didn't you take the temporary support settlement?" she asked. I shook my head. Her eyes went wide. "Why would you refuse to take that? How did you expect to live?"

A good question. "I didn't take it because I didn't think you were serious about the divorce."

"You never take our problems seriously," she said, and then hurriedly closed her mouth as if she was worried something more might slip out. She quietly said, "I was serious. I am serious."

"I know that now," I said, softly chuckling. "I got the Jane Silvia memo."

She squirmed a bit. "If you're back in town on Monday, I'll have a check waiting for you. After all, it's your money, too." She started to rummage through the tiny messenger bag slung around her shoulder. "Meanwhile, I've got some cash on me…"

"Can you just have your pit-bull lawyer wire some dough to me here?"

Fee stopped rummaging, closed her bag, and looked at me with an incredulous expression. "You're not staying here."

"Why should you care, really?" I asked her. I leaned against the hard back of the bench and folded my arms across my chest. "I believe your last instruction to me was go to hell."

"I didn't mean literally," she whispered, looking around to make sure no one had overheard. "Book a flight and get out of this poisonous town as fast as you can. You don't need one more thing bringing you down. *Not* good for your fragile psyche."

Nice. "I can't."

"You and your stupid pride," she admonished me, looking disgusted. "Rise above it, all right? Just forget about that stupid *National Inquisitor* and rise above it."

I didn't get a chance to tell her that wasn't the reason why, as the sound of the sanctuary doors swooshing open caused our conversation to cease. We watched as a woman and little girl came into foyer and bundled themselves in preparation for the cold outdoors. The woman adjusted her daughter's scarf. When she moved, I recognized the kid as the hallway pee-er.

"Oh, boy," I muttered under my breath. I started to turn around and hide my face, but the kid had already recognized me and was running toward me. I wondered if I should run, too, before she or her mother caught up with me. Another thing to add to my list of accomplishments: I'm the mean teacher who inspires kids to pee their pants.

"Teacher!" To my surprise, she threw herself into my unprepared arms. I awkwardly moved to half-hold her and pat her on the back. "Are you coming back to school tomorrow?"

"How are you?" I quietly asked, an obvious subject change that didn't go unnoticed by Fee. She arched a suspicious eyebrow as she watched. I looked toward the sanctuary and struggled to make conversation. "So did you pray?"

By now her mother stood in front of us too.

"I prayed and lit a candle for my daddy." She plainly announced, "He's dead."

I didn't have words for that. My voice quieted when I said, "I'm sure he would like that very much."

She asked me again, "Are you coming back tomorrow?"

I was locked in the kid's gaze. At last, I gave her a little smile and nodded if only to pacify her. "I am."

"It's late, Suzette," her mother quietly prompted. At least now I had a name to attach to the kid's face. I silently vowed to never raise my voice to her again. Suzette gave me another hug goodbye, and I put a little more effort into that one. Apparently, all was forgiven between us.

I whispered, "Good night, Suzette."

She waved the entire time she left the building and went down the steps, and until I could no longer see her. Little kids get excited about funny things.

"What was that about?" Fee asked when we were alone.

I had to give some answer, but I knew what Fee would think. "I'm kind of volunteering in my sister's classes."

"That's nice," she said, though clearly befuddled. She returned to our earlier conversation, a subject I was anxious to hear more about—the money. "I won't be back to the city for a few weeks because the show's on winter hiatus. Well, you know that. Anyway, I'll convince Jane to lift the AmEx and cut you a check on Monday. Can you swing by her office to pick it up?"

Funny, but she made it sound like a pleasant business transaction and not the end of our lovely marriage.

"Actually, I'm staying around here for…for a bit," I stammered. But far be it from me to turn away money, so I asked again, "Could you tell good old Jane to wire-gram that check to Landon?"

"There's no point in you staying around here. You belong in California as much as I do. Buy a plane ticket with the AmEx."

Boy, oh, boy, did that sound good. Still, my sister needed me.

My voice cracked when I said, "I'll hang around awhile."

Fee chuckled. "You hate this place. And the last thing you want to do is hang around school-age kids, wiping snotty noses."

"That's not very nice, and it's not true."

"I'm not so sure…" Her voice trailed off.

The door swooshed open again. The African-American girl from first class, middle row, was buttoning her coat to go. She spotted me and her face lit up. "Hey, Ms. Not-a-Teacher, what up?"

I felt ashamed that I didn't know this child's name either. I half-smiled and mumbled, "Hey there."

"That was some good movie you made us watch," she said.

"Movie?" I had no clue what she was talking about.

"Yeah, all that good music in it," she said, beaming. "I've got all sorts of ideas for songs now. I didn't think you knew what you was doing in our class, but I gotta hand it to you, Teach, you might not be so dumb."

"Thanks, I think." I grinned slightly. "See you tomorrow, then?"

She gave me a wave and went out the door. I watched through the window as she adjusted her collar, shielding her face from the wind and snow flurries. She walked down the sidewalk and disappeared. I hoped she didn't have far to go.

"Teacher?" Fee's voice sounded funny and she suddenly looked very nervous. She stood up. "I hope she didn't really mean teacher, because I can tell you that's the *last* line of work you need to be in."

My smile disappeared. I stood up beside her, momentarily forgetting we were in church. "What the hell's that supposed to mean?"

"It means no." She shook her head. "No, no, no—you can't teach kids. It's not a good situation, no offense."

"How can I not be offended by that?" I heard my voice pitch awkwardly. My sudden anger reminded me of something I'd almost forgotten about. "You're no more entitled to give me your opinion about that than I'm entitled to tell you how tacky it is that you're already dating!"

"Dating?" She spat. "How'd you—"

"Yeah, I talked to her," I said, pleased to have busted the case wide open. "You didn't instruct the bimbo not to answer the phone. I won't tell you how stupid that was."

She looked stunned. I knew I'd hit a nerve. She slowly recovered and even smiled. "Well, then, don't tell me."

"I won't!" I snapped.

"Good! And in turn, I won't tell you that you are a professional at keeping full-grown adults on the brink of nervous breakdowns, and how cruel it is that you now want to inflict that brutal talent of yours on innocent children!"

"That's ridiculous." I realized how loud our voices had gotten when I saw a janitor coming toward the double doors to see what the commotion was about. I whispered, "You're being ridiculous."

"I'm just going to say it. You have no business being in charge of kids and nobody in their right mind would let you—period." She shrugged. "That's the truth."

"You certainly didn't used to feel that way!"

"Well, maybe I was wrong."

I stared at her for a moment. "I don't need this. You know what? Keep the money. Keep your check and your stupid AmEx, too." And though I had no idea how I'd do it, I said it anyway. "I'll wait until the divorce settlement is finalized, thank you very much."

"You won't make it," she said, her lips forming a stubborn line.

I'm stubborn too. "Oh, yes, I will. You're going to the cleaners!"

The janitor pushed through the door and politely said, "Ladies? Please?"

"It's okay, I was just going," I said, turning toward Fee. "Because I am a teacher and I have a class to teach in the morning!"

I stormed out of the church and down the steps, almost forgetting that it was about ten breathtaking degrees outside and it was blowing snow. I plunged my hand into my pocket to retrieve my keys and pulled out my resignation letter. I wadded it up and chucked it back in my pocket. I was inside the car with the keys in the ignition before I recalled why I'd come here in the first place—well, aside of tendering my resignation—to call a tow truck for the stupid car.

"No, no, no, no." I tapped my head on the steering wheel with each "no" and heavily sighed until the windows were completely fogged up. Good, then nobody would see me crying. I got control of myself, glanced skyward, and filed a request with The Big Guy. "Please?"

I turned the key and heard the same slow, groaning whine I'd heard mornings earlier when I'd tried to escape this place. Miraculously, the engine turned over.

"What?" I said, sitting upright. I jammed my toe on the gas a few times, causing the engine to roar angrily about being disturbed in such cold. I looked up and laughed. "Thank You! Not that I doubted You, but thank You!"

I let the car run a bit to warm up, per my sister's warning. I prattled all the while.

"I mean, after that back there, You did kind of owe me one, right? Not to be a holier-than-thou, which I suppose is impossible because nobody is holier than Thou…"

Given the mindless quality of my yammering, I figured The Big Guy might stall the engine again at any moment. My gaze flicked to the rearview mirror where I looked into my own blue eyes. "Mina, stop it."

Gone were my marriage, dreams of AmEx, and cars that started without relying on the Grace of God. I'd have to establish my own line of temporary credit to help my sister. I could do it—I had a job, after all, though not quite as glamorous and high paying as my former position. And I felt like I had something else. Something good.

I did, I guess, if only a few kids who didn't abhor me—as the readers of the *National Inquisitor* apparently did—and a sister who wanted me to stick around a while. Tomorrow, I might wake up with a high-spirited hangover, but tonight, I had spirit enough to crank the radio and loudly sing along to Christmas music all the way home.

# CHAPTER ELEVEN

It was a morning for miracles.

It began when I found my sister in the kitchen first thing. She had some color in her cheeks when she presented me with instant coffee and steaming oatmeal. I gladly accepted both. Then the car started. I shot a thumbs-up to the sky. Anyone watching me would think I'd lost my mind, and maybe I had. I certainly felt a little light and nutty.

Miracle number three happened when I went to unlock my classroom and found an envelope taped to the door with my name on it. I slid my finger along the flap and pulled out a paycheck.

Although I couldn't figure out how in the world any human could survive on such a pittance, I grinned and quietly said, "We eat tonight."

I dumped my coat and bag on the desk and went to retrieve the music I'd thrown in the garbage can days ago, but it was gone.

I thought that might be a problem until I reached the podium and found the folder there, stuffed full of the blue copied songs. I froze, contemplated the nature of my seemingly good luck, and the cynical side of me figured that when the other shoe dropped, it would be a doozy.

My kids came in, all fourteen of them. I started to stumble my way through the class name list with Emanuel's help—and snide laughter, let's not paint too rosy a picture here. I made it to name eight before giving up, which was about four better than usual. I resumed my headcount method of taking attendance, shut the book, and clasped my hands together on the podium.

"My sister was sick." It was an abbreviated explanation and nobody inquired further about it. I moved forward. "So we've got about three weeks. Did anyone come up with any song ideas?"

"I did," said the African-American girl in the middle row, the same one I'd talked to the night before in church. She wore an ear to ear grin on her fleshy face. "From that movie you gave us."

I know I looked utterly dumbfounded. "I'm not following."

"Well, we had the one song on our list from before, anyway. We want to funk it up," she happily reported.

I didn't feel good about funking anything up. I frowned. "I hope you remember everything I wrote on the board."

*What movie?* She kept referring to it as if I'd left a bona fide lesson plan and not run out of the classroom like a madwoman, vowing never to return.

The next thing I knew, she was on her feet, swaying and snapping her fingers in an energetic gospel version of "Joy to the World". Whitney Houston's "Joy to the World", to be exact, from *The Preacher's Wife*. Holy shit—pardon the pun—I'd left the movie on the desk in my haste to get out of there.

Her voice was deep with an imposing vibrato that gave me chills. I wondered if my sister knew there was a candidate for *American Idol* sitting middle row in her first class. By about the sixteenth bar, the class was nodding, clapping and stomping along with the girl. I was ready to send her to the final round. A knock on the door interrupted the impromptu jam session. I held up my index finger to pause her.

"Wait…what's your name?" I asked in pure astonishment.

"Gabriella Lavonia Constance Foster-Jackson-Hicks," she proudly exclaimed. She grinned again. "It's a long name because I've got a lot of people to honor."

"You sure do," I said, walking toward the door. I pointed at her, talking as I went. "You sure as hell do."

There were snickers all around regarding my use of inappropriate language. I opened the door. Two guys in brown UPS coats entered the room, pushing large boxes on low carts. They unloaded them and handed me a clipboard.

Confused, I signed an electronic signature and asked, "What is it?"

"Dunno, lady, but it's yours," one of them said. He tipped his head to the class and they left.

I stared at the boxes in the center of the floor.

"You gonna open those or what?" Emanuel impatiently asked.

I glanced around the room. Every face in the class wore the same curious expression as mine, I'm sure. Using my pen to slice through the packing tape, I tore open the flaps. Miracle number six—we had instruments. Not just the refurbished, crappy instruments I'd mailed off, but brand-new, shiny ones. We had bells, xylophones with mallets that weren't broken, a portable keyboard, two student guitars, a few brass and woodwinds, small drums, maracas…far more than I'd sent in for repair.

I carefully laid them out to the oohs and aahs of the students. When I finished, I sat cross-legged behind the glorious spread. Emanuel leapt out of his seat and grabbed for a piece of paper that had floated out of the box with the tambourines. He turned it over and read it out loud.

"To Mina's new friends from her old ones," he said.

I cradled my face in my hands and quietly cried. Nobody said anything for a long time. Emanuel finally spoke again in the softest voice I'd ever heard him use. "That's some friends you got to send all that stuff, teacher."

"I suppose so," I said, my voice further muffled against my hands.

"Well, then," Emanuel said, rising from the floor. "We got no excuses now. I guess this show better kick…" I parted my fingers to look him straight in the face and his voice trailed off. He rolled his eyes and reformulated his intended statement. "Better kick butt. So let's get a move on, y'all. Pronto!"

I stood up, dabbed my face dry with half a box of tissues, and clapped my hands.

"Now we've got us a show," I said when I was able to speak.

Roddy's hand darted into the air. I nodded at him. "Teacher, none of us knows how to play those things."

"I've got that figured out," I assured him, but that was not quite yet the truth. My brain was clicking and clanking with a lucidity I hadn't experienced for a long time. I knew what I needed to do.

*** 

As Sacred Heart dismissed an hour earlier than public school, I walked uphill to the town's high school after our last bell. I went to the main office, made my request, and was directed to a classroom on the second floor. The place looked shadier than I remembered. Thin coats of paint hardly masked the graffiti sprayed on the walls. Kids passed through the hallways, bumping around mindlessly while wearing raccoon eyes for makeup and clothes that would never have passed the dress code in my day. I was happy to quickly find my designated classroom, which turned out to be a home economics class. Only one girl was inside, hunched over a sewing machine. She stood up, slightly startled, when I entered the room.

"Hi, I'm Mina Borsalino," I said, crossing the floor and thrusting my hand out for a handshake. She regarded me with a fair amount of suspicion, her wide brown eyes peering at me from beneath a pretty knitted beret. She daintily shook my hand.

"Ricardo Martinez. Ricky." The voice, effeminate or not, was decidedly male. I tried not to look surprised. He gently shook my hand. "You lost?"

"No," I said. "I asked for a place to have an after-school meeting and they sent me here. Do you mind if I hang out and wait for the bell?"

He shrugged his narrow shoulders. Ricky was model beautiful, and his every move—even his shoulder shrug—was nothing short of completely graceful.

"They probably sent you here because nobody's ever in this class. Well, unless you count me," he said, looking away. He added, "And most people don't."

I looked over the shoulder of his slim fitting, white, military-style shirt jacket. "What are you working on there?"

"Oh, that?" He flipped his wrist toward his sewing machine. "I'm taking the ruffles off a jacket I did for Ms. Frazier, the math teacher."

He motioned that I should follow him and I did so, pulling a chair up in front of his machine. He held out the beautiful coral colored garment, which frankly, would rival anything a designer could dish out.

"Ms. Frazier's a real cutie-pie. She goes to Iowa City on the weekends to the clubs and she wanted a little va-va-voom for her wardrobe." He appeared to analyze the garment. "I guess I took this one too far."

I scrunched my brow. "What's wrong with it?"

"Too many ruffles, too short, too thin, too sexy, too New York for Iowa," he critically reviewed his own work. He dragged a finger along the front to demonstrate. "My plan is to remove this ruffle, create a faux collar that rides a little higher, then bunch the ruffles on one side to make sort of a flouncing corsage."

"Sounds brilliant," I said. Still, I was aghast. "I hate to see you cut that one up."

"You want to try it on?" he suddenly asked, his voice bright. "You're about a size four, right? I'll sell it for only what I've got in it. Fourteen bucks."

"You made that for fourteen bucks?" I gulped. "Jesus, you're in the right line of business, but the wrong town." I stood and picked another blouse off the table next to him. "You do this one, too?"

"Indeed," he said, clearly happy to have a captive audience. "I can do pretty much anything, but no knitting, that's for grandmas."

I looked at him and nodded. "You've convinced me."

"Better than what you can find around this sorry little town," he said, his mood suddenly taking a dive. He adjusted the thread on his machine and slid a pair of horn-rimmed glasses on his nose. I could easily understand—and recall—how it would be difficult for him to fit in a place like Landon. He went on. "I'm trying to get a scholarship for a design school and blow out of this place."

"Looking at this stuff, that shouldn't be a problem."

"Looking at my grades, it just might be," he said, his shoulders falling. He made his final offer. "You sure you don't want this before I tear into it?"

"No, go crazy."

I took a seat and he fired up the machine. The mechanical buzz was almost loud enough to override his loud, pitchy singing of a Diana Ross tune. Almost. I listened to both for a half hour, and then the pre-bell announcements began. There were club notes, sports scores and a plea for someone to return Hemmingway the Hawkeye—the bronze-plated mascot—to its rightful place in the schoolyard. My announcement came last.

"There will be a meeting for all Sacred Heart alumni in room 203 after school today. If you can attend, please do, and be sure to document your volunteer time tomorrow morning."

Good enough. The bell rang. I waited. Within the next five minutes, about twenty kids ambled into the room. For the most part, they looked just as bored, and had about as much attitude as the rest of the school population I'd seen. I'd harbored the smallest hope that the students who sprang from Sacred Heart would be more lively and engaging. I cleared my throat and started the presentation.

"First of all, how many of you were involved in the music program at Sacred Heart?" A few nods, a few hands, a few grumbles. I continued, "Good, then some of you are already familiar with my sister, Tina Smith." Same response, same level of disinterest. "She's been sick recently and I've taken over her class. I'm Mina Borsalino."

I started to pace, more nervous than I thought I'd feel. "This is the last holiday program because all music classes at Sacred Heart have been discontinued due to budgetary constraints."

I looked over the heads of my audience and saw Ricky listening intently. He nodded, the only support I felt in the room. I continued. "I know many of you are still in music and some of you play instruments. Frankly, I need your help, whatever your talent is. Together, we can help these kids put on the best Christmas show ever, something they can really be proud of." My voice softened. "It might make you proud to help out your alma mater. What do you say?"

Crickets.

I didn't let their disinterest deter me. I grabbed a stack of dry, wrinkled, purple mimeographed papers and stood by the door.

"I'd like to have a meeting tomorrow after school in the music room of Sacred Heart. It's only a short walk from here. I've got some information so that your parents will know where you'll be."

The first interest that flickered in their eyes came only when I announced they were dismissed. I didn't feel terribly hopeful when I handed the flyers to them as they filed out. Some rejected the flyers upfront or dropped them straight into the garbage can. A few mumbled something about the papers smelling like airplane glue.

"Thanks for coming. It will be a lot of fun, I promise," I called after them, and then they were gone. I looked at Ricky. "Wait and see?" I asked more of myself than him.

He shrugged. "You never know."

I dropped the rest of the flyers in the same garbage can and retrieved my coat. I was putting it on when I heard Ricky chuckle.

"I thought that was you, Mrs. Borsalino. You really need to let me make you something nice to wear to show off that tight little figure of yours." He pretended to spank his own bottom in reference to mine. I felt suddenly self-conscious, though I guarantee his study was only through a tailor's eye. "Wouldn't be something you could wear around here, but what a splendid reentry you'd make on the Golden Coast. Trust me. I'm really that good."

"I'm sure you are," I said smiling, my cheeks warm. "It was nice to meet you, Ricky."

He gave me a toodles gesture. I left feeling that aside from the ass compliment, the trip had otherwise been a complete waste of time.

Having allowed the car ample time to warm up—no need to push the heavenly envelope—I stopped by my old bank to resurrect my account and cash my check. Afterward, I drove straight to the phone company and arranged to have landline services restored at my sister's house. They promised it within an hour. I guess they only had to flip a switch or something.

I also stopped at the movie place and paid thirty bucks, about twenty bucks more than the going rate, for *The Preacher's Wife*. After hearing Gabriella Blah-blah-blah-big, huge last name's voice—I wouldn't have made it out of kindergarten spelling that name—I called it a sound investment. I'd give the movie to her. My extravagant day left me with half my measly check. God bless teachers everywhere.

My sister was making soup, her go-to dish, when I got there. She was looking better and better. I handed her a fresh loaf of bread that I'd picked up, and then promptly went to the phone and snatched up the receiver. I grinned and held it out for her to hear the buzzing dial tone. She grinned right back at me.

Usually, the Fi-Mi accounting department handled both our business and personal utility bills, so I really wasn't sure what those things were going for these days. When we sat down at the table, I asked Tina, "Where are your bills?"

"Pardon?" She seemed slightly taken aback.

"C'mon, Tina. We don't want to be living by candlelight in the coming weeks," I told her. I made a gimme motion with my hand. "Let's get those bad boys squared away."

She stared at me for a moment. I watched as her expression softened from nearly offended to a more grateful one. She smiled, looking a little smug when she said, "I already paid them. As soon as I found out I was losing my job, I paid myself up through February, excepting the phone bill, of course."

I had to hand it to her, that was smart. She grinned and went on, "You're not the only one who does a great job managing things."

"I never said that," I quietly answered back. I suddenly wondered if Fee had ever really needed me to do all the things I'd done for her—minding her appointments, being the barrier between her and the press, arranging calls and conferences. It made my half of the Fi-Mi name seemed unjustified. Tina must have known what I was thinking.

"It's a simpler life here," she sweetly explained. "Take a load off. You've got your hands full enough with those kids, right?"

I smiled, hardly relieved. "Yeah, I guess so."

My spirits lifted when I recalled the day I'd had. I enthusiastically filled her in about discovering Gabriella's big voice and receiving the new instruments. When I finished, Tina bowed her head and closed her eyes. Though my sister took her faith quite seriously, I hadn't seen her pray at the table since I was little, back when my father demanded it of us. I respectfully waited until she crossed herself and I did the same.

"Just saying thanks," she said, smiling.

"No kidding, those instruments..." I shook my mother's fancy napkin out and laid it on my lap. "What a miracle, right?"

Tina didn't move. When I looked her way again, she had tears in her eyes. "You're the miracle, Mina," she said. "That's what I was thanking Him for."

A lump formed in my throat. Previously, only Fee would say something so corny to me. I'm sure she did it so I felt like I had some small purpose in her creative, wonderful life. But this was different. This might be the first time in my life I actually did have a purpose. What a place to discover my worth, in Landon, Iowa.

Thinking about it gave me heartburn before I'd taken my first bite of soup.

# CHAPTER TWELVE

I listened to Gabriella belt out "Joy to the World" for the fourth time. The rest of the kids were getting restless regarding the time I spent on her song. It was time to move on.

"I'm giving this to you," I said, handing the DVD to her. She looked at me and I nodded. "Go ahead, it's yours."

She didn't move to take it. "We don't have a DVD player in our house."

Now that was a first. We didn't have one in California either. We had a top of the line Blu-Ray player inside a miniaturized surround sound theater with deluxe leather loungers. I walked to the TV cart, unplugged the DVD player, wound the cord around it, and lugged the ancient contraption to her desk.

"You do have a TV, right?" I asked her. She nodded. I set the thing beside her, almost straining my back with its outdated size. "Now you have a DVD player. Can you hook it up?" I figured what the hell—the music department would be nonexistent come January anyway.

"I can," she said, grinning wide. "I sure can."

"But Gabriella," I said, walking back to the podium. I stepped on the short platform and turned to look at her. "Don't copy Whitney. This is for inspiration only. People always make mistakes by trying to copy the greats. Make it your own, you hear?"

"Yes, ma'am. I will."

"Good," I said, clapping my hands. "What's next?"

"The instruments," Roddy spoke up. "You gonna teach us how to play that stuff, teacher?"

"Kind of." I didn't correct him for calling me teacher, but it still felt weird. "Later," I promised.

"When's later?" He raised his hands and made an exaggerated shrug. "We've only got a few weeks to get this show on the road."

"How well I know," I muttered. "Okay, we've got some music and that's a start. We've got instruments. We should do something a capella, and of course, throw in the dancing and the poetry. Did I forget anything?"

"What's a cappella?" Roddy again. Clearly his faith in me was wavering.

"A cappella is music sung without accompaniment. I like a four-part harmony, myself."

"Just what I thought," he said, sounding disappointed. He folded his arms across his chest. "No accompaniment. We don't have a piano player—"

"We've got you," I interrupted him.

"I'm not good enough to play in the church." He flipped his hand as if to dismiss the whole idea. "And now you're backing out on the instruments. What? Gabby gonna carry the whole show?"

"Have a little faith, man." To my surprise, Emanuel spoke on my behalf. Almost. "Just because she acts a little nutty don't mean you shouldn't give her a chance."

"Absolutely," I chimed in my agreement, and added a quiet, "I guess."

"What about the dancing?" Mercedes reminded me. She jumped out of her chair—as she was prone to do—and launched into another gyrating, hip-grinding dance inappropriate for audiences under thirteen. As the class was prone to do, they cheered her on. Emanuel threw his hands into the air with disgust.

I leaned my forearms on the podium to simply remain standing up and rubbed my temples. I figured if I was teaching at the high school instead, I might actually be able to buy something more powerful than ibuprofen to kick my headache. The bell rang, saving me from having to address Mercedes' dancing yet again.

"Dismissed," I airily told them. Emanuel started to file out behind the other students when I stopped him. "Wait, I need to see you."

"For what? I didn't do nothing," was his immediate defensive answer.

"You're not in trouble. Can you come in after the next class and help me put this stuff together?" I motioned toward the boxes of still unassembled instruments.

"Yeah. I only got hallway reading." Hallway reading was the term school administration had come up with to make it sound like something more than it really was. Just as it sounded, it was students sitting on either side of the hallway, reading. I guess it's what you do when there's no classroom to hold a formal study hall.

He left. Meanwhile, I hunted down Mercedes' home number and dialed from the classroom telephone. Almost immediately, I got an answering machine, so I left a message for a parent to call to arrange a meeting with me. I didn't know how else to dial down the multiple dancing mishaps we'd experienced in class lately. I hoped a conversation would help.

As promised, Emanuel returned during period three and began carefully picking instruments out of the boxes. "You know how to put this stuff together?"

I shrugged. "I know what it's supposed to look like."

He looked over the instructions for a particular xylophone. "You got a hex-key wrench?"

"I don't know what that is," I admitted.

He lowered the instructions and looked at me. "Level with me, Granola. Should we be worried?"

I shook my head at last, but I admit I probably didn't look terribly convincing. I watched while Emanuel laid out all the paperwork and smoothed it flat. "There's a hex-key wrench taped to this," he informed me. He tore it off and I watched him moving his lips, silently reading. He began laying out the rest of the xylophone as well, but I was focused on something else.

Each time he bent over, his shirttail rode up just enough to give me a glimpse at something on his back. It was only when he practically dove headfirst into the box to reach something that I got my best look at his scars. It looked like he'd been whipped repeatedly. He almost caught me looking when he abruptly turned around.

"You think you could help me out here?" He sounded disgusted that I hadn't already offered.

I quickly averted my eyes and nodded. I helped him dump the box carefully upside down until every last nut, bolt and washer jingled out. We collected them and made a nice little pile.

He noticed my silence. "What's wrong with you?"

"Nothing," I lied. "I was just thinking about Mercedes."

"It ain't entirely her fault," he said.

"Beg pardon?" I'd forgotten my lie that quickly.

"Mercedes ain't a bad girl. I don't think you have to kick her out of the music program. She wants to be on stage—it's all she ever talks about." He paused, sighed, and rolled his eyes. "Of course, I'm not sure what kind of stage she's got in mind, exactly. Brother."

I softly laughed. "I'm not going to kick her out."

I'd noticed from day one that Emanuel was painfully thin. I thought about the lunch I'd thrown together before leaving the house that morning. I casually went to my desk and reached into the oversized bag Tina had loaned me—teachers and their damned oversized bags—and pulled out my paper lunch sack. I made a dramatic sigh.

"What now?" He was busy with the hex-key thing.

"It's my sister," I pretended to complain. "Every day she makes me a lunch and every day I toss it out."

"What's wrong with it?" He didn't even look up, just continued twisting the wrench until he'd assembled a low stand. It looked pretty good.

"She sends me weird stuff, like chicken salad with cheese on a bagel and chocolate fudge," I said in my most sorrowful voice. "I feel so guilty throwing it out, but I don't want to hurt her feelings by taking it back home. She's been so sick and it makes her feel good to do something for me."

"Chocolate fudge?" He sounded like I was crazy. "Why would you throw that away?"

I held the bag over the garbage can. From the corner of my eye, I saw him watching me. "You probably don't want it, do you?"

He stood and pretended to amble casually toward me, but he was moving pretty quickly. "It'd be dumb to throw it away, and a sin," he said, taking the bag. He opened it, appraised the contents, and made a low whistle. "This is a good lunch. You're ungrateful."

"No," I said, watching him tear into the sandwich first. "I'm from California. We only eat granola, remember?"

He shot me a smile between bites. The kid ravenously ate the large sandwich, and by the time he finished the fudge, I wondered if his belly would burst. His mood had clearly lifted. I wondered what it would be like to be hungry all the time. We tackled the rest of the percussion instruments in record trime before the bell rang.

"You want I should hang around again tomorrow?" he asked on his way out.

I nodded. "It will probably take a few days to put them together."

"Then I could eat the lunch and your sister's feelings won't get hurt."

I appeared to consider the idea before nodding. "That's fair."

"I could come every day until we have the program, you know, in case you have other stuff to do." He looked hopeful.

"Actually, I demand that you do," I emphatically told him. "There's too much stuff to prepare all by myself."

"Bossy," he said, pretending to complain. It seemed our whole relationship was based on make-believe. He gave me a wave. "See you tomorrow, Granola."

***

The high school dismissed at three o'clock. By three thirty, not a single former Sacred Heart student had yet to make an appearance. At a quarter to four, I was preparing to lock up and leave when Ricky Martinez breezed in, and I mean literally breezed. The boy moved more quietly and gracefully than some dancers I'd known in my life. He wore a red trench coat and a beret—this time purple to match his shoes—and he took a seat in the front row of choir chairs. Ricky shrugged out of his coat and folded his hands before him in a display of excellent posture.

He looked around. "I see the gang's all here."

"Funny," I told him. We both chuckled. My gaze flicked to one side as I considered a sudden realization. "You didn't go to Sacred Heart, did you?"

"No, I didn't, but here I am." He looked around at the classroom and made an exaggerated grimace. "This décor…it's so institutional. It's what I've always imagined a prison would look like." He glanced at the handful of shiny instruments already on display. "Prison for pop stars."

"As long as you're here, tell me something." I crossed the room, snagged a chair, and pulled it front and center of the room to stare right into his face. He wasn't even slightly intimidated. "What do you think I should do with the Christmas program?"

"Cancel it and run for your life," he said flatly, and rolled his eyes when he saw I was serious. "You don't expect me to teach the little rug rats to sing, do you?"

"No thanks," I told him. "I've already heard your singing."

"Then I guess I'll just drape the tots in something fabulous so no one notices how awful they sound, or that they can't pick out a nursery song on a toy keyboard." He'd pretty much pegged us. I'm sure I looked surprised. "That was the rumor, but your expression just now confirms it."

"Is that what they're saying?" I asked him. He nodded. "What else?"

"That it's not just the music program, but the whole school is pretty much on its last leg." He shrugged. "I sit in the high school teacher's lounge during lunchtime. I'm under the distinct impression that they want to see Sacred Heart fail."

"Why would they want that?"

"Public school teachers always band together. Rumor says Sacred Heart giving all those kids scholarships has knocked down enrollment in public grade schools. Supposedly, that's why some of the teachers lost their jobs. But I don't believe that."

My interested piqued. "What do you believe?"

"Bad teachers get fired. But they'll find a way to blame it on anyone else rather than take responsibility for it themselves."

"Ricky, that's a horrible thing to say," I chastised him.

"Some people are just mean, and meanness is contagious in this town, Mrs. Borsalino. Can I call you Mina?" He paused. I nodded. "As far as I'm concerned, Mina, if it'll piss off the administration, I'm all for it. What have they ever done for me besides send me to lunch with the teachers instead of punishing the bullies who make my life a living hell?" He clapped his hands, apparently glad to have it off his chest. He smiled. "So how should we start?"

A female student appeared at the door, peeked around, and quietly took a seat behind Ricky.

"Welcome, thanks for coming," I told her. Three more students dragged in for a sum total of five. I checked the hallway to see if there were any other stragglers, and then I closed the door. "Thank you for coming. I'd like to get your names, your level of commitment and any special skill you can bring to the table."

I passed around the clipboard and talked while they scribbled away. "Does anyone play an instrument? Please tell me yes."

A boy in the second row raised his hand. His style of dress put me in mind of the Weitrich kid, and I prayed they weren't related or otherwise similar in nature. "What's your name and your specialty?" I asked him.

"Name's Chip Harris, and I play sax and clarinet," he answered and frowned. "It took me years to learn to play. I don't think I can teach a kid in a short amount of time."

"I no longer want you to teach them," I said, quickly processing the information Ricky had shared with me. There was certainly no reason to make a mockery of the school any more than it apparently already was. "We need a class act here. I'd like you to play in the show. Would you be willing to do that?"

He seemed to consider it. "Yeah, that wouldn't be bad."

"I'll have the music for you by the end of the week. You a fast learner?"

That earned a smile, and I could tell I'd presented him with a challenge. "I'm first chair band, jazz band and orchestra, high school, civic and all-state. Lady, I'm fast."

"That's what I want to hear." I smiled at the other students. "How about dancers?"

"You're going to have us dance too?" A blond girl spoke up next. I looked at the name she'd just written on the clipboard when she handed it back to me. Abby. "Are you going to have these kids do anything at all? Or just us?" she went on.

"They're working hard, trust me," I assured her. I got back to the subject at hand. "I need someone to lead them in some minor dance moves. Are you a dancer?"

She shook her head. My disappointment must have been obvious, since she added, "But I'm a cheerleader." I wondered how that could help, but before I could ask, she followed up. "I can do almost any tumbling routine, and I taught K through eight cheerleading camp last year."

"Good with children," I mumbled as I made the note by her name. That was certainly worth something. Though I wasn't sure how the rest pertained, I added, "Heck of a tumbler."

"I've got little brothers and sisters. I'm a good babysitter." That was Raul, according to the small list. As there were only two other boys besides Ricky, it was easy to figure out who was who. He looked as though he felt stupid for mentioning it, but said anyway, "And I guess I can draw a little."

"A painter?" I asked hopefully. He nodded, and I smiled and noted, "In charge of scenery. Good." I looked up at them. "The biggest challenge will be keeping the kids organized because I'm planning a lot of movement in this show."

"What about me?" The only other girl looked like I'd purposely excluded her. "What can I do?"

"Good question. Shivan, right?" She nodded. "Do you play the piano?"

She shook her head to that and a few more things I suggested. "Can you write poetry?" I asked in desperation.

"I do." Surprisingly, the statement came from Ricky. "I dabble."

"Good, then you can help with the adaptation of *The Christmas Story*, how's that?" He nodded. I still had to think of something for Shivan to do. "You a singer?"

"I play a little guitar. I taught myself." She shrugged. "Maybe I shouldn't have come. I don't think I can help."

I shook my head. "Hey, I taught myself to play the guitar. I've got two in that box right over there. I'm thinking mostly simple chords."

Shivan grinned.

"Okay," I said, rising from my chair. "We got a late start today. How about tomorrow we get here as soon as we can right after school?"

A knock on the door expedited the dismissal process. In strode a beautiful Latina woman in a full-length fur coat. Her luscious red lips looked like they could do amazing things, and her black hair fell in cascading waves clear to the top of her panties.

I knew this because once the children were gone, she shrugged her full-length coat onto the floor and stood before me wearing little more than a garter belt and stockings.

# CHAPTER THIRTEEN

I dropped to my knees, gathered her castoff coat lying in a careless heap at her ankles, quickly rose, and just as quickly handed it back to her.

"Christ," I muttered, shell-shocked. She was truly the best thing I'd seen in months—in Iowa—in Hollywood—anywhere. I gulped and tried not to look at her too much. "Ma'am, can I help you?"

"I can't make the meeting tomorrow," she said, as if I should know what she was talking about. She dropped the coat again and stepped on top of it with her tall spiked heels. "These things are best done during the evening anyway."

I felt a little drool pooling at the corner of my mouth and struggled hard to keep my eyes focused on hers, not on the full breasts burgeoning from the tiny demi-cups of a La Perla knock-off bra. "What do you mean these, uh, things?" I stammered like a fool.

"I'm Sofia Reyes," she said, extending her hand. When I still looked puzzled, she smiled broadly and clarified, "Mercedes' momma. Good to meet you."

I took her hand. She clasped mine for a firm handshake as if we were merely having a business meeting and she wasn't standing there in nothing but a bra and panties. I felt almost physical pain at having such an exotic creature in front of me.

I shifted uncomfortably and forced a smile. "Ms. Reyes—"

"Sofia," she declared, confident and beautiful. "I am understanding that there was a problem in the classroom and I am here to work it out. First, the ground rules. Look only, no touchy-touch. Lap dance okay and yes to the dirty talk. No to all kinky stuff."

I stammered, "C-could you put your coat back on? Please?"

"Ms. Borsalino, I am a businesswoman who believes in cash on the barrel," she declared, her tone insinuating that I'd somehow offended her. I stared at her with such wide eyes, they were actually burning. She didn't budge. Sofia was charming and her accent thick.

"How do you think I got my son Eduardo through the twelfth grade, hmm? He could have dropped out in the eighth, but no! Today he is studying at the Institute of Technology in the auto mechanics division." She folded her arms over her chest, smashing her voluptuous breasts together and causing them to jiggle when she spoke proudly of her son's accomplishments. She looked me over and quieted some. "I admit that this particular case is a little different. But the tabloids say you swing toward the ladies, so I'll swing toward them this time. Anything for my children."

I got the very clear impression that Sofia didn't believe she was degrading herself, not in the least. She was simply knee deep—and breasts and garter belt deep—in a formal business transaction. She released her bosom and reached around her back to begin unclasping her bra. I knew I would melt to the floor if she did. I forced myself to quickly turn around.

"Please, Sofia, put your coat back on. I'm begging you."

"You reject me?" She sounded genuinely offended. "What is wrong with you?"

"So many things, " I muttered so she could not hear. I raised my voice, "Look, can you tell me when you have your coat on? Please?"

"Fine. Go on," she said.

I turned around, and thank Christ, the full-length coat was back in its rightful place. Sofia was a drop-dead stunner with endless confidence to boot, but she seemed put out.

"Then how on earth am I supposed to have a rational discussion with you?" she asked.

"Let's give it our best try, okay?" I was almost breathless. I motioned for her to follow me to the student chairs because for me, it was either sit down or fall down. When I caught my breath, I realized I might not be able to make the point I had planned to about Mercedes' dancing, and frankly, it no longer seemed important.

"Mercedes is a wonderful girl."

"I know," she said, her beautiful face lighting with pride. "She gets that from her momma."

"I'm absolutely sure of that," I said, smiling. I mentally reframed the conversation I'd intended to have. "She is very free and expressive with her body, which is good. However, many of the children in our classes are not as free and expressive, do you know what I mean?"

"I tell my daughter to be proud of her own body."

"As she should be," I tried again. "Which brings me to the point of our meeting. We plan to have some dancing in our Christmas program—at your daughter's suggestion, I'll add." I glanced toward the ceiling, and then back to her. "I wonder if I could have you talk to Mercedes about toning her dancing down just a notch so that the others who might not be as proud of their own bodies will feel more comfortable."

Sofia scoffed. "That is ridiculous."

"Please, think of the other children," I implored her.

"I am thinking of the other children. What is wrong with the way their parents are raising them?" A different thought seemed to occur to her. "Wait a minute…are you saying the others are not as talented as my Mercedes?"

I gulped and ran with her explanation. "That's exactly what I'm saying. And it would be boastful to make them feel inferior because of their shameful upbringings. Do you know what I mean?"

"Not really, but okay."

"You're a businesswoman. You know there are different shows for different audiences. Like just now when you came in here, right? I am not your audience, so we tried a different approach. Now we're talking."

"Your audience is not so different from the audience of a red-blooded male, am I right?"

I wondered if I was really gaining any traction in this conversation.

"I'm thinking ballet," I blurted. I'd really pulled that one out of my ass. The idea was gaining momentum as I continued. "I'm thinking sweet pirouettes, nice little movement, very simple. Something every child can do. Nothing fancy."

"Interesting." Sofia seemed to consider it. She slowly nodded. "I like that."

"So if we could get Mercedes to tone down her wiggle, that would be wonderful."

"For the good of the other children."

"Yes, the other children," I heartily agreed. I stood up, anxious to end our meeting. "Thank you for coming in today, Ms. Reyes."

"Not a problem." She started to go, but stopped short and turned around. "I've never had a problem with my Mercedes."

"And I don't think you will," I said. "She's a good, smart kid. I'm pretty sure with this one, you'll be able to conserve your assets." My eyes went automatically to her breasts, curvaceous enough to be evident even through her heavy coat. *Your very, very nice assets,* I thought. I gulped for at least the fourth time since her arrival.

"You let me know if you need my help with the ballet program," she trilled on her way to the door. Oh, Lord, how I would loved to have seen Sofia bouncing all over the place. The woman rolled her Rs like an angel. I hardly noticed she was still talking.

"I will like to come and help any way that I can, as long as it's not after nine p.m., Monday through Saturday."

"That's just a lovely idea."

We shook hands, and she left, fully coated.

I plopped onto my chair, rested my head on my desk, and wondered if Sofia's visit would inspire me to wake up with my fingers inside myself again.

I was a basket case. After I restored myself, only vaguely recalling that I'd even conducted an after-school meeting besides the one with Sofia, I grabbed my coat and my mammoth teacher bag and went home.

***

My strange afternoon meeting had me feeling preoccupied and out of sorts for the rest of the day. That night as I lay in my old bed, I turned my face toward the live intercom and whispered, "Tina, you still awake?"

In moments came her sleepy response. "Yeah."

"I was wondering about Emanuel, that kid in first class."

"I know the one," she said after a moment.

So much to ask. "What do you know about him?"

"He's on scholarship, but then they all are." I heard her pause for a yawn. "Lives with his grandmother."

"What happened to his parents?"

"Drugs," she said, sounding regretful. "His father is dead and his mother is just...gone. She signed over custody to her mother, according to his enrollment records. We only get a snapshot picture of the kids' home lives."

"Okay." It wasn't much to go on. In a moment, I bugged her again. "Tina?"

"Yeah?"

"I thought I saw some marks on his back. Do you think he's being abused?"

I heard her shift in her sheets. "I don't know. But working for the school, you're a mandatory reporter. If you suspect something, you can turn it in to the Social Services division."

I considered it. "I'd have to gather more information first." Several minutes later, I still wasn't near sleep. "Tina?"

"Yeah?" She sounded even more tired. I figured I'd pulled her out of near-sleep yet again.

"What about that Mercedes girl?" God help me, but she—or rather her mother, Sofia—was also on my mind.

"Mercedes comes from a very well-adjusted, single-parent household," Tina said. I heard her chuckle. "Her mother pays their way. I understand she's quite a businesswoman."

"*Quite* a businesswoman," I echoed.

As much as I tried to fight it, Sofia's wondrous form was emblazoned on my sex-starved brain. I hoped she didn't come back to haunt me in my dreams. For a moment, I wished I'd never switched that intercom on. I clenched my eyes shut and tried to think about something else.

That, of course, brought me back to Emanuel.

# CHAPTER FOURTEEN

I made a seriously beefed-up lunch before work that morning, but Emanuel was absent from school. That worried me. I considered calling his house until Ricky showed up earlier than normal with an offer to help. He'd apparently gotten permission to leave his study hall for volunteer hours.

I was ecstatic. I let him oversee the vocal warm-ups while I worked with Gabriella for a while, and then the kids regrouped to brainstorm song selections. Even Steven seemed to be remotely interested, which was a half step up from thoroughly bored. It was nice to see everyone working as a group.

While the students were talking it over, Ricky returned to my side in front of the class. As we watched the kids working together instead of tearing each other apart, I seized the moment and whispered to him, "I need to ask you a weird favor."

Ricky peered out from beneath his hat selection of the day, a wide-brimmed fedora that shaded one eye. He had on more eyeliner than a runway model. Or a raccoon. "What can I whip up for you?"

"It's not about clothes," I said, eyeing Roddy while he engaged with the other students. "Level with me, Ricky. You're as gay as I am, no?"

"Every bit as gay, only better dressed," he replied without missing a beat.

"Let's not get catty." I shot him a look and continued whispering, "That boy over there, Roddy. Do you think he's gay?"

Ricky watched him for a moment, then shrugged. "Dunno."

"I've heard that rumor and he doesn't vehemently deny it." I sighed. "I'd just hate for him to feel as picked on as you do in school, you know?"

"So now I'm your gaydar?" Ricky giggled. "Never mind. I'll check it out."

"Use tact," I instructed.

I continued making notes in my book, very aware that Ricky had strategically planted himself right next to Roddy. They casually talked for a while and in a few moments, Ricky returned to my side. He slid into the chair next to me.

"No way, no how. The boy is straight," he said with much assurance in his tone.

"Really? You know that quick?" I sounded surprised, I'm sure. "It looked like you were hitting it off."

"Because he's a nice guy. Now and then you find one of those." He shrugged. "Open-minded too. But alas, our hero is straight."

I thanked him and mentally shelved the information for later review. I joined the group and together we tore apart a song list with much lively debate all around. By the end of the hour, we had a strong lineup and things were starting to feel better.

I put the guitars on display during my free time and refrained from assembling any more instruments without Emanuel's help. He'd worn such a look of satisfaction the day he'd put a few things together. I wanted to give him that. He was on my mind a lot these days.

A few girls in my older class had expressed interest—and more importantly, aptitude—in learning guitar. They returned on their own accord after school to learn a few chords with my new assistant music teacher, Shivan. Afterward, I armed the girls with the student guitars and sent them on their way. As for Chip, I'd managed to get to the post office to copy—on a copier from this century, no less—a few songs for him to work on. Then I paraded the rest of my alumni crew into the sanctuary so we could formulate ideas about a set and stage. In all, it was a fairly productive day.

It turns out that Ricky—who'd already turned eighteen—lived alone in a government-sponsored apartment. He briefly explained to me that he'd been thrown out of his parents' home and bounced around the foster care system for a few years. Now he was considered an emancipated minor and received a small government allowance that would stop once he graduated high school. So many of these kids had sad stories. I sincerely hoped he'd pull his grades together to get some kind of scholarship so he wouldn't become homeless at the end of the school year.

After rehearsal, I dropped him off at his shabby apartment building, and then drove by the hotel looking in vain for Emanuel. I didn't see him, but I did see a handful of familiar kids crouched around a Salvation Army bucket singing four-part harmony.

I slammed my sister's car into park so hard, I practically hurled my body over the steering wheel. I jumped out and raced over to them. Three of the four boys were in my music class.

I waited for them to finish before I stuffed a few dollars into the bucket, feeling rather guilty because the boys looked like they needed it worse than the Salvation Army.

"Do you know what you're doing?" I asked, my mouth agape.

"Our moms know where we're at," Carlos spoke up defensively. "We ain't doing nothing bad."

"No, no! Of course you're not!" I threw my head back and laughed. "You're singing four-part harmony a cappella. *That's* what I'm talking about!"

They looked puzzled. "We're just singing with no instruments."

"Yes! Yes, you are," I agreed, nodding and grinning. I turned toward the boy I didn't recognize. "I'm Mrs. Borsalino, the music teacher at Sacred Heart. I haven't seen you around."

"Rafael," he said. A brief introduction at best, made in an incredibly baritone voice. "I don't go to school."

I didn't ask him how old he was. I didn't want to know if he'd dropped out. I just nodded again. "Can you do that in our Christmas program?"

Rafael looked at me as if I'd lost my last marbles. "Sure, lady," he finally said. He chuckled. "You're goofy."

"I am," I said, laughing again. "Will you sing that same song?"

It was "Silent Night." They silently conferred with each other, and then nodded.

"Can you come by the school tomorrow around four o'clock for practice?"

"We got to have dinner before church," Carlos said. "Otherwise, the Salvation Army closes the kitchen before we get done with Mass."

I tried not to think about how pathetic that sounded. I nodded, as if I heard this type of information from young kids every day.

"I'll feed you. Will your parents mind?" I asked, but didn't give them a chance to answer. "I'll make you a permission slip tomorrow. Don't let me forget."

I had a feeling I was going to be spending every last dime of my paycheck feeding the Sacred Heart choir, but I didn't really care at the moment. I had a cappella singers! I remembered my original mission and my voice quieted significantly.

"Hey, Carlos, have you seen Emanuel around here?"

He shook his head. "No, ma'am. I heard Emanuel got in trouble for hustling."

"By the cops?" I asked, horrified.

"No, worse," he said. "His grandma."

I thanked them again and got back in my car. It seemed that for every one thing that went right, something else went wrong. It was a constant struggle.

I drove toward the railroad tracks in the direction of Emanuel's neighborhood. The street was a conglomeration of vehicles wedged into tall snowbanks, some of the cars working, others looking as though they hadn't been operational for a very long time.

I parked and carefully navigated the dirty snow toward the ice encrusted sidewalk that led to Emanuel's grandmother's house. I knocked several times before anyone answered. A woman probably only in her fifties, haggard to the point of looking closer to seventy, opened the door, but only a crack.

"Whatever you're selling, you got the wrong address." She started to close the door in my face.

I reached out and put my hand on the door to stop her. I leaned toward her and discovered that she reeked of alcohol. Taking a better look at her, she might not have been trying to close the door at all, but instead using it for her own balance. I smiled and started over.

"I'm from the school." I figured I'd already long overstepped my boundaries coming here, and now I was impersonating school administration. The school could fire me, if they'd ever formally hired me in the first place. The woman looked at me like I was the cause of her indigestion.

"You sure you ain't the State? I already had my visit last week. We'll pass the next one, I told you! You're s'posed to call before you come showing up anyway." She started to close the door again. Again, I stopped her.

"No, ma'am. I promise you. I'm Mina Borsalino from Emanuel's school. I just want to see how he is doing." I thought quickly. "I heard he's sick."

"He is sick," she slurred. An expression of recognition suddenly came over her face. She waved her index finger at me. "The papers—that's where I know you from. The newspapers."

I was going to correct her about those "papers" being actual news, but she didn't give me the chance.

"I know you," she groggily repeated. She stepped onto the front stoop and shut the door behind her. "You're a pervert. What do you want with this God-fearing house and my kid?"

I digested her insanity, and focused on my mission of discovery, not her ignorance. "I want to see if he's feeling better."

She seemed to consider it. "He would be better if he had him some new clothes and other things. You care so much about him, prove it."

"I would like to see him. It will just take a minute."

Other sets of eyes—none of them belonging to Emanuel—peered out from behind the curtains of the only other front window. I wondered about the caliber of our audience. I swallowed hard, feeling nervous despite the fact that she was a granny. Who knew how big her friends were or what they could be packing? I felt as scared as if I were in the worst part of East LA.

"I'll tell you what," she said, lowering the volume of her slurred words to a confidential sounding level. "I'll sell him to you."

My eyes went wide. "Pardon?"

She nodded. "Ten thousand dollars and I sign him over, right here, right now." She leaned right into my face, spittle flying from her drunken lips. "Between you and me, I got no use for a kid anyhow. I raised my own and that never got me nothing."

"I can't buy Emanuel," I whispered, aghast.

"Why not? You got the money!" Her voice rose several notches. She took in my horrified expression and started back inside, screaming at me all the way. "Forget it. Just you get out of here! You don't know a thing about us kind of people. Get out of here, Hollywood pervert!" She toddled inside, nearly missed the step up, and slammed the door in my surprised face, once and for all.

I took a step backward, watching the windows and the multiple shadows moving behind the thin curtains. Every light in the tiny house was on, and it looked like a full-fledged party was unfolding inside. *Buy her grandson?*

I felt like there was something I should do, but I had no idea what. I jogged down the walkway, practically hurdled the snowbank, and got in the car. I drove out of the neighborhood as fast as possible, checking the rearview mirror to be sure I wasn't followed.

I ended up at the hotel bar where I drank quietly among strangers for a few hours. I thought about what Emanuel's grandmother had said, and to a degree, she was right. I didn't know about her kind of people—nutty, or poor, or what have you. My sudden hiccup told me I might be getting to know the drunken part.

I hated like hell to leave that kid there. I hadn't even found out if he was hurt or not. In my sufficiently drunken brain, I figured there was only one thing to do.

I paid my tab and went outside. I trudged twelve blocks uphill toward the Park Hill neighborhood. Numb from the cold and the booze, I depressed the doorbell of the Borsalino residence.

In seconds, Fee's mother's face appeared in the window. She seemed shocked to find me there, shivering on the doorstep, and she hurriedly unlocked the door and ushered me inside. After a kiss on my cheek, and probably a whiff of my breath, she went upstairs to alert Fee of my arrival. I waited in the sitting room until my almost ex came downstairs in her robe and pajamas.

"You got her up there?" I suddenly asked, pointing upstairs. I'd been referring to the woman who'd answered our telephone in Malibu, but my reference was completely lost on Fee. Plus, my slurring reminded me of Emanuel's crazy grandmother. I knew it looked bad and I confessed it upfront. "I'm drunk."

"You surely didn't..." Her voice trailed off when she looked out the window and scanned the street. "Did you walk?"

I nodded, causing both my head and the house to spin a little. The place was silent. I wondered if her parents were upstairs trying to listen to our conversation. I remembered my mission and got the show on the road.

"I changed my mind about the check. I need ten thousand dollars right now."

"Right now?" Fee's eyebrows hiked up. She took a seat on the antique loveseat and patted the space next to her. "Come, sit down."

"I don't have time to sit," I told her, still trembling from the cold and embarrassed by my sloppy sound. For some reason, I sat down anyway. "Can I have ten thousand dollars or not? It's an emergency."

Previously, I'd considered the smell of Fee's bath powder to be the closest thing to an aphrodisiac in my world. I tried like hell not to smell it now. She seemed oblivious.

"Calm down. Tell me about this emergency," she said in her most levelheaded tone.

I was exasperated. "Jesus Christ, Fee. I give you a dozen good years of my life! That money's half mine and you can't give me a bit of it?"

What do you need it for at—" She glanced at the grandfather clock. "Eleven thirty at night?"

"If I told you, you'd tell me it's a stupid idea and you wouldn't give it to me."

"Try me," she sweetly insisted.

I took a deep breath and rolled my eyes. I quieted my voice as much as possible because I knew what I was about to tell her would sound insane, drunk or sober.

"I want to buy a child."

"I beg your pardon?" she asked, because any normal or sober person would think they'd surely heard me wrong.

"A child."

Fee slowly nodded and looked at her hands, clasped together in her lap. She sounded remorseful. "Is that what's been bothering you? Is that what happened with you? With us?"

"What?" I wasn't following. I shook my head. "I'm asking you for money."

"Mina, we already talked about that and it wasn't your fault. I thought you knew better than to blame yourself."

"No, no, no." I remembered that conversation and I wasn't in the mood to rehash the past. Not now. "This isn't about that. I'm trying to fix something here."

Fee reached over and gently laid her hand on my shoulder. "Hon, you're always trying to fix something. You can't blame yourself because we lost the baby."

I stared at her for a long time. I hated Fee a little for knowing where to reach inside me and hurt me. My voice dropped. I very clearly told her, "I'm not talking about me losing our baby."

"But don't you see that you are?" Her voice was soft, her eyes showed sympathy. I felt my own tears welling up. She continued, "Don't you see that when you make a statement like that—about you losing our baby—you're taking it personally. It wasn't you, that wasn't your fault. You have to accept that to be okay."

So it appeared we were now definitely talking about the baby. I whispered, "Well, I can't be okay with it. I'm glad you're bigger than me."

"We'd both have given each other anything we wanted. I'd have done anything for you, but I can't fix the baby problem any more than you can. I wanted her, too. But I sure didn't want that to destroy us."

Try as I might, I could never make sense of the fact that we'd lost our baby at the five month mark. I'd done everything right; I'd followed the instructions to the letter. I'm a fixer, that's my job. But there was no fixing this. First there was a D and C, then a bunch of fibroids, and eventually they took all my parts, so me and my twin had more in common than our appearance.

No babies for me, not ever. I swallowed hard and regretted having come to this house at all. I was sobering at an alarming rate. I clenched my eyes shut and shook my head. And with Tina out of the baby-making business, there was no chance of handing down my father's asshole genes. Goody.

I whispered, "I told you I'm not here to talk about that, so please stop."

Fee looked confused. "Then tell me why you are here."

"Oh, my God." I slapped my already aching head. "I came here for ten thousand dollars!"

"For a child?"

"For Emanuel, a boy in my class." I attempted to explain. "His grandmother will sign him over to me for ten thousand dollars. I can take her the check and have him tonight."

She stared at me for a long time, just blinking. "There are so many things wrong with this picture."

"I know, I know, Ms. Legal Proper Soapbox."

"Then allow me my say," she said, shooting me that do-not-cross-this-line look. Her voice stiffened considerably. "Kids are not like puppies, all right? You don't just buy one. It's entirely illegal to, and it's ridiculous that you'd think you could. Also, crazy granny might just roll you for the money and you'd never even see the kid. Maybe she'd kill you, all right? Ask yourself what kind of person tries to sell her own grandchild."

"My point exactly," I said, nodding. "I have got to save him."

"No, not like this." She shook her head. "Let's get you into the guest room. You're in no shape to go anywhere tonight. Tomorrow, we'll talk about an alternate solution, I promise."

"You promise a lot of stuff," I said, standing up and almost losing my balance in the process. "You promised you'd love me forever. Bullshit. You've changed, Fiona Borsalino. But here's my promise and I mean it from the bottom of my heart: I will not leave that kid there. Not for a second longer than necessary."

"Promises? I've changed?" She started up one avenue, but before my eyes, diverted to one she apparently found more pressing at the moment. She stood. "Look, first things first—you can't go back there. You'll end up in jail or worse. You're not being practical, and per your usual, you're a bullhead."

"Practical like you? Let me ask you something, how much money did you shell out for all those years of fertility treatments for me, huh? And that Harvard sperm—what'd that set you back?" I started for the door, but stopped before leaving. "I'm asking for ten thousand dollars to save the life of a good kid I already know, not the possibility of what might be, and you're telling me I'm stupid." I lowered my voice, realizing I was probably entertaining the entire neighborhood. "Then again, I guess I already knew how stupid you think I am since we went with brilliant sperm and your eggs, not mine."

I turned the doorknob. In seconds, I was running down Park Hill. I heard Fee calling to me the entire way. I didn't stop until I neared the hotel, whereupon I found it necessary to puke out my guts in the parking lot.

Breathing raggedly, I went into the lobby where I raised a few eyebrows, I'm sure. I washed up in the bathroom and stared at myself in the mirror. I was a well-rounded disaster. I borrowed the front desk phone to call a taxi to take me home.

# CHAPTER FIFTEEN

In keeping with my apparent one to one ratio of right and wrong, I arrived at school with a splitting headache. However, Emanuel was there. In fact, quite a few kids were there—more than usual. Word on the street was that kids were pretty much running things in their own Christmas program and it seemed like everyone wanted in, much to the delight of the hallway reading monitor who got to go to an early lunch as all of her readers were cramming up my airspace in what was normally a quiet room. They were drawing plans and revamping songs, which would have made for nice background noise had it not been for the aforementioned pounding headache.

Emanuel and I diligently and quietly put together the rest of the instruments.

"I heard you came to my house last night," he finally brought up.

"Yeah, sorry about that," I mumbled. "I hope I didn't get you into trouble with your grandmother."

"Nah. She didn't tell me about it. I overheard her talking to my uncles about it."

"I see," I said, focusing on the same washer I'd had in my hand for the last five minutes. I just wanted somewhere to look besides into his deep brown eyes. "Wanna stay around and have lunch with me?"

"You don't eat lunch," he reminded me.

"Maybe I should start," I said, setting the last stand upright. "I brought enough for two in case today seemed like the right day to do it."

"No sense putting it off," he said. He set the drum head on top of the stand and gave it a spin. When it stopped, he tightened it into place. "Done. We're a pretty good team."

I smiled at him. "Yes, we are."

***

After school came two rehearsals, one with and one without the high school kids. Shivan did a pretty good job instructing the girls with their guitars. When Chip added the sax and Roddy kept time on the drums, well, it wasn't perfect, but it was something.

I was familiar with the jazz version of "Silver Bells" they were trying to achieve, and it sorely missed a trumpet. Sadly, the trumpet we did have would never realize its full potential.

Less than two weeks until showtime, I kept telling myself. I was alternately nervous as hell and more than ready for it to be over. I wondered if this was how Fee felt each week before a live show. Of course, generally, the musicians we hired had played more than a handful of days in their lives.

Shortly after rehearsal and before Mass, I fed my new four-part boy's group as I promised I would. They were fantastic, I'll add, and starving when they finished. Thank God Domino's delivers. The boys and a few high schoolers overseeing their practice devoured four pies in about ten minutes. Emanuel hung around, but didn't touch a slice. I asked him to join me at the diner down the street after Mass wrapped up.

We sat in the warm place with its steamy little windows and neon lit signs, both of us hunched over grilled cheese sandwiches and bowls of tomato soup.

"So tell me, since you seem to be the guy in the know," I started as I dipped the corner of my sandwich into my soup. "What's Roddy's story? He seems like a nice enough guy."

"He's okay," Emanuel agreed very quietly. "But his mother is a member of the Melendez family."

I shot him a puzzled look. "What's the Melendez family?"

He put a finger to his lips. "Shh, you want to get us killed?"

"No, I really don't." I figured if living with his grandmother didn't scare Emanuel and the Melendez name did, I should be rightfully terrified. I whispered, "Who are they?"

"Their whole family came here years ago. They pretty much own all the little corner grocery stores, only they don't sell your typical groceries, do you get what I'm saying?"

*Drugs?* I nodded. "I do, I think." Good Lord, it was a wonder that many of these kids bothered to show up to school at all, as rich and colorful as their home lives were, and not in a good way.

"So that sucks, right? Because he's kind of smart and he could probably do something. I don't know what, but probably something."

"He's so quiet."

"Everyone thinks he's gay," Emanuel confirmed, uncorking the story I had actually been trying to get at. He rolled his eyes. "He's love dumb, but he's not gay."

"Why do you say that?" I fished a crouton out of my soup and set it aside. "Why is he love dumb?"

"Falling in love itself ain't dumb," he said, growing significantly quieter. "Falling in love with Brenda Da La Salle is really, really dumb. It can't work. It's like Romeo and Juliet."

I was impressed by his comparison. "She from another gang?"

"Don't use the G-word. Around these parts, we call them 'families.'" He hooked air quotes with his fingers. "Anyway, Roddy's got it bad for Brenda. She is pretty, but it can never, ever work."

"That sucks," I said, borrowing his favorite line. He nodded.

In the background, I heard the bell over the door ding, and I saw Emanuel's eyes widen a bit.

"Your woman's here," he coolly announced. I whipped my head around, and then turned back to face him. Fee stood at the counter talking to the guy at the register.

I arched an eyebrow at Emanuel. "How did you know that was her?"

"Please, it's all over the tabloids." His gaze flitted toward the ceiling as he whispered quite obviously, "I hope you're in the mood to see her."

I slightly sunk down in the vinyl booth. "I haven't decided about that yet."

"You better make up your mind quick, because she's headed this way."

A million uncivilized scenarios wound through my brain and I wanted to disappear. I sat up straight when Fee said my name. She was right behind me. When I saw her, she was wearing the same knit hat that made her hair flyaway with static.

I returned her greeting without overdoing the eye contact. Nor did I scoot over on my side of the booth to make room for her. In fact, I didn't really know what to do, so I hastily introduced her to Emanuel. To my surprise, he shook her hand like a little gentleman, and then the ball was back in my court.

She seemed as nervous as I felt. "I was just stopping by for—"

"Soup?"

"Yeah, Mom is craving it," she said, smiling. "They have her favorite—"

"Broccoli and cheese, I remember," I finished for her. I was still embarrassed about my strange, drunken visit last night. I cleared my throat and drummed my fingertips on the Formica tabletop.

"Well, I'd better get going," she said, looking at the counter. "Nice to meet you, Emanuel."

"It was nice to meet you, too," he chirped, as polite as could be.

She took a few steps, and then doubled back. Clearly, she felt as discombobulated as I did. "You want to get some—"

"Coffee?" I finished. Now this was getting awkward. I vowed to shut my mouth for good.

"How about eight o'clock at..." She trailed off again. I figured she was waiting for me to fill in the answer, but I was determined not to. I bit my lip to refrain from doing what had always come naturally to us. It was like a little word dance we performed. This time, she finished her own thought. "The hotel restaurant?"

I nodded, still gnawing my lip. When she was gone, I expelled the breath I'd been holding.

"Brother," Emanuel said, having witnessed our shenanigans. I nodded and rolled my eyes. "You still love her?"

"Not so loud," I warned him, much as he'd warned me about using the "gang" word. I looked around, but Fee was gone. I considered his question and sighed. "Yeah, I guess I do. But it's complicated."

"Adults are complicated," he said, sounding disgusted.

I looked at my watch. I had an hour before my coffee appointment. I looked at my present date. "So tomorrow's Saturday. You want to do something?"

Emanuel looked at me funny. "You seriously need to get a life, you know that, right?"

"Probably," I agreed. "But until then, you want to hang out? Grab a bite or something?"

I worried about the very real possibility that Emanuel wouldn't eat all weekend. He nodded and I smiled at him, relieved that he'd accepted my invitation.

***

A half hour later, I was washing my face in the same hotel bathroom I'd used to clean the puke off the night before. I felt a little paranoid that someone might recognize me—not as Mina Borsalino, half of Fi-Mi Productions, but as Mina Borsalino, Drunken Music Teacher.

I slipped quietly into the restaurant side of the operation and ordered coffee. Fee showed up a few minutes later, but ordered nothing.

Without bothering to sit down or go through any of the niceties one performs when greeting another, she politely but firmly grabbed my arm, and led me out of the restaurant and into the elevator. When the door was safely shut, she pressed her body into mine and her tongue hungrily explored my surprised mouth. I quickly caught on and melted at her touch, even through my coat.

Emotionally, I had every reason to be hesitant, but my body seemed to have no problem slipping into old habits, and let me say that there was never anything frumpy about our sex life. We'd practically undressed each other before we left the elevator car. My bra was gone. I figured she had to be Houdini to pull it off without removing my shirt. My hand was actually inside her bra as she jammed the key into the door lock of room three-ninety.

Inside, I caught my breath and whispered, "Nice to see you too."

"Yeah," she answered breathlessly.

I didn't know whether to run or stay. "I take it you planned this?"

"I took a chance you'd go along with it," she sweetly answered. Her coy tone transformed into something more lustful when she said, "I missed this body."

We kissed deeply. She broke away long enough to shrug the rest of the way out of her blouse. She slipped off her trousers and gave them a fling, and then unfastened her bra, unleashing firm breasts I remembered and loved so well.

I fumbled with my shirt buttons, but gave up and pressed my fully clothed body against her panties-only one. We crashed into every piece of furniture as we blindly navigated in the dark toward the bed.

When the backs of my knees bumped against the bed, Fee shoved me hard, almost causing me whiplash when I hit the mattress. She proceeded to unfasten my borrowed teacher pants and yank them down to my ankles. She paused only to remove my shoes, freeing my pants before giving them a similar toss in the same direction she'd flung her own clothing. We were creating quite a winter garment pile.

I was helpless to resist when she slipped her hands inside my panties and cupped me with her fingers. Her strategically placed knee wouldn't permit me to budge, and she remained only teasingly inside me. I writhed madly, trying to get as close to her as humanly possible. I'd missed her so much.

We'd reached this point at breakneck speed, and as she was prone to do, she slowed to make love to me. She took her time running her hands all over my body, inside and out. After so many months without her touch, I knew I wouldn't last much longer.

"More. Please," I whispered to her. I felt myself growing emotional. I was needy, utterly desperate feeling, and though I needed to come quickly, I wanted it to last forever.

"I'm here, Mina," Fee said, her words sweet and powerful.

She increased her penetration but not speed. I moved every way possible to plunge her deeper and deeper into me. She kissed her way down to my breasts and suckled each nipple, taut and straining for her hot breath right through my thin cotton shirt.

Her lips returned to my ear. She whispered two words I had neither heard nor felt in four months, "You're safe."

I cried out and exploded, and then collapsed against her after several long moments. My body continued to quiver from her touch long after I came. My tears freely fell, and she laid her cheek against my wet one.

When I'd quieted some and recovered a little calcium in my bones, I stood up and unbuttoned my damp shirt. I tossed it on the pile and looked down at her with heartfelt intent. A neon sign outside was shielded by thick curtains, but provided enough flickering, muted blue light for me to look into Fee's eyes.

I kept her gaze locked on mine as I pulled the bedsheet toward me, effectively bringing her with it. I watched her until the last second before I fell on my knees, peeled off her panties, and wasted no time diving in and pleasuring her with my tongue.

She tasted delicious. I held her bottom in both hands to get as deep as possible, until the tip of my tongue touched her spongy center, the spot I knew so well. I've always loved the happy, needy sounds Fee makes when we make love. My intensity increased in time with her moans until she nearly screamed and her body stiffened.

We made love to each other several times that night. No talking, no making of promises often made in the throes of passion. We had sex—grunting and groping each other like animals guided by our base instincts. Alternately, we made love, cuddling, kissing and stroking each other sweetly. If only for the night, harsh words and hot tempers were put aside. Only our bodies communicated and they did so splendidly, sometimes with vigor, sometimes with great tenderness.

Only when it was morning did I realize that I'd stayed out all night long. I sprang out of bed, grabbing random pieces of clothing and the wrong shoes.

"My sister is going to think I got mugged and killed!" I exclaimed. I found the right socks and sat on the edge to roll them on. I looked at Fee, still lying there calmly, watching me with an amused look on her face. I finished dressing and brushed her shaggy, auburn, pixie cut hair away from her eyes.

I kissed her and whispered, "By the way, that was the best coffee I've ever had in my life."

"Call me your barista," she teased. Her look turned somewhat troubled as she dragged herself out of bed. I wondered if she felt regret concerning our all-night marathon. I watched her slowly dress and soon discovered the reason for her turn of mood.

"I leave town today," she said.

"I see," I quietly replied. We sat next to each other on the edge of the bed. I wasn't sure where we stood. For a night, I'd pretended my heart had never broken. Now, I didn't even know my role for the day, let alone my lifetime. I stammered, "Would you...would you like me to take you to the airport?"

"Dad will." Fee looked down at her lap for a long time, and when her eyes met mine again, they were blurry with tears. "I missed this body," she repeated the same thing she'd said several hours earlier. She laid her cheek on my chest. "And this heart."

We stayed that way for what felt like forever. I finally asked, "What should we do, Fee?"

"I don't want to break up," she said with hesitation in her voice. "But I don't want a relationship that only works when things are simple like they are in Landon."

I figured she needed to be a teacher or without cash for a few weeks to see how really un-simple things in Landon could be. My pennilessness was temporary, not like some Landoners who had to contend with racism and unimaginable long-term poverty.

"Fee, every place comes with its problems," I told her.

"I'm sure. But California is a monster…" her voice trailed off. She looked at me again. "And you've changed so much. I'm not sure we can make it."

"I haven't changed. I'm the same girl who loves you." But the feeling in the pit of my stomach knew she was right. I felt that I had changed. As for Southern California and its famous, sometimes evil, and often shocking trappings, it did make being in Landon look rather much like a picnic. Almost.

In our past, we'd had arguments that had dragged us perilously close to the edge of our marriage. Also in the past, given the slightest hint, like tears or a soft look from her, I would have promised anything simply to stay, simply to feel better for a while. Also, I admit, because I didn't have anything else.

As I suppose many people do when faced with a breakup, I saw that I'd thrown myself so totally into our relationship, I'd utterly lost myself. Despite my feelings of loss and sadness about our divorce, I could see that for once, I actually did have something, if only a ratty school and a handful of kids. I also had my sister.

"What do we do?" I whispered.

She shrugged and wiped her tears on the back of her hand. "I don't know. You could always come back to California."

Yes, things were definitely different.

"Can we agree that we need some time to decide what we want instead of moving forward with the divorce?" I asked. "See what happens?"

She smiled and nodded again. We moved together until my forehead rested against hers. After a short while, we finished dressing and added a layer of coats, and then took the elevator downstairs to the parking garage. She walked me to my sister's old car. We held each other a while. I felt sad, but for once, not utterly needy.

"Tina's sick," I blurted after a few minutes in her embrace. That certainly caught Fee off guard. I felt ashamed of myself for having kept the news from her.

"Sick?" Fee took a step back to see me. "What's wrong?"

"It seems like she's got more cancer than she doesn't, or so that's what I'm learning." I shook my head. "That's why I took over her classes. It's a miserable little parochial school on the verge of total failure. Nothing about this trip is making me like Landon any more than I ever did."

"Hon…" Her voice trailed off. After all, what do you say to any of those things? She pulled me close and hugged me hard. "What can I do? I'll do anything."

"I know you would. But she seems happy with her treatment here."

We were quiet for a while, standing there in the cold garage holding hands. Fee leaned over and kissed my cheek. "Keep me updated, please? And give her my love."

"I will."

I unlocked the car and felt her still watching me.

"Mina?" I turned to see her glistening eyes and the little puffs of warm breath coming from her lips. She shivered. "Maybe I could come back for Christmas."

I smiled at her. "That would be really, really nice."

Fee walked toward her rental car and it was my turn to watch her go. She fumbled with her keys, casually addressing me as she found them in her bag and flicked the door switch. "She was just an assistant."

"Pardon?" I said, momentarily confused.

"The woman who answered our phone was an assistant. It takes three people to do your job. I guess I never really realized everything you do for me."

I chuckled and looked at my feet. "Yeah, well. We both take pretty good care of each other." I opened the car door and started to get in. "Call me. Oh, but you'll have to call the old landline at the house or the school."

"Why?" she asked, concerned. "Is your phone okay?"

I laughed hard, effectively relieving the pressure that had built in my chest. "It is very much not okay." I grinned at her and added, "But I think I am."

I said goodbye to her and drove off in Tina's car before its idling blue smog killed us all. At home, I was greeted by Tina's highly uncharacteristic screeching.

"Where have you been? I waited up for you all night long!"

# CHAPTER SIXTEEN

"Oh, my God," I said, and launched into a series of endless apologies. I felt awful that I'd caused my sick sister even a minute of worry. Tina needed her sleep now more than ever.

"I walked the floors," she went on, not even close to letting it go, I could tell. I deserved it. "I called the police—everyone I knew! I talked to Principal Reeves and all the janitors. Then I talked to the priest and told him my only sister hadn't come home last night, the little harlot."

It was only then that I realized she was doing her best to stifle a grin. My chin dropped to my chest. "All right, very funny. You got me."

"I really did call the police, though. Well, an off duty-cop, a friend. Chuck. He checked it out." She leaned against the center island butcher block and gave me an inquisitive look. "So tell me, is it still considered an affair if the tryst is with your wife?"

I rolled my eyes at her, my cheeks warming. "Who is this Chuck, anyway? And how did he find me?"

"Hotel registration to Fiona, two women entering an elevator, one red bra outside room three-ninety. My sister always had a penchant for red lingerie. It all adds up." She leaned back, folded her arms, and looked smug. "Elementary, really."

"You might consider turning that teaching certificate in for a badge, nosy girl."

She ladled oatmeal into my bowl and I hungrily dove in. We talked and laughed until I set my spoon aside and looked at her. I considered how happy I felt around her. How free we were in a house so long repressed by religion and bad tempers.

"We'd never have been able to go on like this when we were kids," I said.

"I know, right?" Tina grinned.

"I just want you to know, you've given this house a real nice vibe, Tina," I said, nodding. "It's really, really nice and welcoming."

"Well, the company isn't too terrible, either."

I glanced at my watch, blotted my lips on the cloth napkin, and stood up. "I've got to get into the shower. I told Emanuel I'd pick him up today."

"Really?" She looked slightly caught off guard and mightily pleased. "He's a good kid, isn't he?"

"Yeah, he sure is." I headed for the door. "I've got him down to a minimum on his swears, and he's helping me with the program."

"Excellent," she congratulated me, following me into the hallway. "That's right. Go shower. Go and wash away your sins!"

I heard the wonderful sound of her joyous laughter as I headed for the bathroom.

***

I picked Emanuel up at noon and took him to The Men's Shop, a privately owned clothing store that had survived since I was a kid. He thought the name was ridiculous.

"We're getting you some new uniforms," I told him. "You'd like that, wouldn't you?"

I didn't want to make too much of it for fear of embarrassing him, but his pants were coming through in the knees and the butt, and the hems were about two inches too short. Don't get me started on the dingy shirts that, at some point, I'm sure used to be white. I figured I'd pick him up a few things.

He looked at me funny when we got out of the car, but he followed me down the sidewalk toward the shop. "You like to spend money or something?"

"When it's necessary," I told him. "I think we should. It's an investment."

"You're goofy. Everyone around here buys their uniform stuff at Walmart."

I didn't want to tell him that Walmart wouldn't supply me the line of credit that this boutique shop would. I still had no big tangible funds, no matter what terms Fee and I were presently on.

I smiled at him and rubbed my hand through his hair. "You talk too much, you know that?"

The shop owner quickly identified me and established an account on my word. He rushed to ply Emanuel with every possible wardrobe option for a school uniform. We ended up with four pairs of pants, some play jeans, four long-sleeve and two short-sleeve crisp white shirts, a warm peacoat, and a necktie and gloves for good measure. The tailor promised they'd work around the clock sizing things down to Emanuel's thin frame for a Sunday afternoon pickup, even though they weren't normally open on Sundays.

The economy in this town was so bad, the shop owners would do just about anything for an order like the one I'd just placed. I thanked him nicely and we left.

We did end up at Walmart for a couple of dozen pairs of socks. I turned my back when Emanuel picked out some underpants to his liking.

While we were there, I selected some granola for kicks, along with packages of cheese crackers, juice boxes and a bunch of licorice, and threw it all into our shopping basket—things I figured he could take home with him that wouldn't need refrigeration. The thought of this kid going without food killed me.

In the checkout line, I couldn't help noticing how funny people regarded us. At first, I thought it was because I was the whitest, blondest Caucasian woman on the planet accompanying a mixed-raced boy, and I was appalled at the small-mindedness.

I soon discovered my assessment of the villagers was wrong when we reached the checkout stand containing a half dozen tabloids starring my picture. Must be a slow news day in Hollywood. I sighed and figured I'd finally cracked the mystery of exactly who reads this crap, not that I'd know them by sight, but I'm pretty sure they shop at Walmart.

I paid with cash and we left, and then I took him straight to the barbershop where—according to the window sign—they offered haircuts for ten bucks. It cost forty by the time they finished taming Emanuel's exotic mane. He loved it. The kid ran his hand over his closely cropped hair for the rest of the afternoon.

Early that evening, I took Emanuel to a fast-food Italian restaurant where, interestingly enough, everyone spoke Spanish. Emanuel ordered us garlic bread knots and two spaghettis without meat sauce at the walkup counter. I got us glasses of water, and we took a seat at a booth with a checkered tablecloth.

"You want to go with me to pick up your clothes tomorrow? We can leave right after Mass," I said.

"I better stay around the house. My grandma gets funny acting if I'm out too much. She starts thinking I'm up to no good." He appeared to think it over. "But you could bring them to school on Monday and I'll come in early to change."

"That sounds good. Mind if I ask you something personal?" I was building courage right and left. He hesitated, and then nodded, as if he knew exactly what my question would be. "Did your grandma put those marks on your back?"

He looked surprised that I'd noticed. I filled in the blanks. "I saw them when you changed shirts earlier today."

"Those were just accidents," he quietly said. "If they weren't accidents, I'd have to go to foster care, and then what would become of me?" He said it as if he'd heard that explanation many, many times before.

"I see." We were quiet for a moment. "You know people shouldn't hit each other, especially not their kids or grandkids, right?"

"I'm not hitting anyone," he said. "My grandma's too old to be raising kids." It sounded to me like he'd heard that several times in the past too.

"I'm sorry to hear that."

A server delivered two dishes of pasta to our table. Emanuel started to tie his napkin around his neck. I stopped him.

"You're a big guy now, you can lay it out on your lap. Like this."

I demonstrated by putting my napkin on my lap and he did the same, not at all offended by my correction. He dove hungrily into the plate of food.

"So that extra food stuff I bought at Walmart, I thought you could stash that away in your bedroom for a snack when you want one. How's that?"

He gave me an odd look. "I don't have a bedroom."

I knew I'd hate myself for asking, but I did anyway. "Where do you sleep?"

"On the living room floor. My uncles and grandma have the couch and beds." He didn't seem to see this as a tragedy. "Where do you sleep?"

"I'm staying at my sister's house for a while. I'm actually sleeping in my old bed from when I was a little girl." I swallowed hard and smiled at him. "The house belongs to my sister now because my parents are both dead."

"My dad's dead and I don't know where my mom is. Maybe she is too. I'm not that sad because I never knew them." He watched me spiral pasta around the tines of my fork using my spoon as a guide, and he roughly imitated my action. "My grandma's about to lose me."

I stopped swirling pasta and looked at him. "What do you mean by that?"

"State rules. You get a bunch of chances to pass your inspections and stuff, and my grandma finally failed 'em all." He raised his eyes to mine, speaking matter-of-factly. "I could be out of there in the next few weeks even."

"How do you feel about that?" I asked as calmly as possible. I was trying to tamp down my obvious horror that this kid would probably be indefinitely shuffled through the State system.

"Oh, you know. I'll turn eighteen at some point, and then I'm on my own." He shrugged. "Or at least that's what my grandma says. Mind if I ask you something personal?"

I nodded as he had when I'd asked him the same question.

"You love her?"

"You mean Fee?" I asked. He nodded, and then I did too. "Yeah, I do."

"Then why don't you fix whatever they said you did wrong in those tabloids?"

It sure seemed simple enough when he said it. I smiled at him. "Some things are trickier to fix than others. You have to reevaluate what you're doing, or you keep making the same mistakes and you only go in circles. Going in circles makes you crazy. Make sense?"

He set his fork aside. "Not really. She don't seem too bad to me. And she'd be stupid not to want you, that's what I'm thinking."

"I appreciate that." And I did.

I drove him home and tried to get him to take the snacks I'd selected at the store, but he refused. "I'd get into trouble for sneaking. It ain't worth it."

I stuffed the licorice in his torn coat pocket anyway, thinking about how happy I'd be when he was wearing his new peacoat come Monday. I watched him leave the car and walk up the path toward that awful house. I drove away very slowly.

I pulled the car into the barn around nine o'clock and locked up the house on my way in. The lights were off. I assumed my sister was asleep. She called out to me when I started for the stairs.

An hour later, we were bundled under blankets in her big bed downstairs, laughing and whispering like we were schoolgirls. It no longer felt like my parents' bed. Everything about this place had become quintessentially Tina.

The late night chat gave me a chance to catch her up on the program and other things. I told her about Ricky Martinez, the wardrobe diva, Sofia's interesting version of a parent-teacher conference, about our lack of trumpeter despite our new trumpet, and Gabriella with a dozen last name's amazing voice. Tina was thoroughly entertained by my colorful storytelling. When we calmed our gut-splitting laughter and settled down again, she got serious with me.

"So where'd you leave it with Fiona, anyway?"

"I'm not sure," I answered, because I wasn't sure about much these days. "We have our problems, enough of them that we filed for a divorce, and those things don't just go away."

"Did she treat you right?"

I thought about it. "Sometimes she did, sometimes she didn't. But I didn't treat her very well at times, either."

"What was an argument like for you?" She rushed to quantify her question. "I'm curious if they were like Mom and Dad's."

"Yikes. Not like those." Our parents had some doozies, that's for sure. Mostly over religion. Sometimes over me. "You see, Fiona is friends with everyone. As you know, she's very outgoing and personable. She's so generous, at times she's developed a habit of putting others before our relationship."

"What about you?"

"I deal with the business end of things, and all I see anymore are the takers. They want money for this or that, or a reference, or a TV part, or an audition for their niece or neighbor's best friend. It seems like they view us not in terms of friendship, but as speakers, or donors, or a leg up for whatever their cause or favor. Jesus, I see so many takers, I can hardly see the good in people anymore. It's ruined me a little bit." I felt a lump in my throat. "I used to see people more the way Fee does. I used to be more optimistic."

"Is it possible that they're not really the takers you make them out to be, but you feel threatened by them? You know, one more thing standing between the two of you? That would certainly make everyone appear to be a taker."

"I suppose," I confessed. "Either way, it doesn't feel very good."

"I hate the thought of you viewing the entire world through cynical eyes." Tina looked thoughtful. "Did you try to talk to her about it?"

"S-sort of," I stammered. "But every time I did, I felt like I just looked insecure and jealous. Maybe I am a little insecure."

"Little bit?" she asked in a half-teasing way. "Welcome to the club. We all are."

"When it comes to Fee, it feels like everyone gets a chance to look better than I do."

"Do you really think that's the way it is?" Tina didn't sound so sure.

"I don't know." I laid it on the line. "I lost a baby. After that, it felt like I couldn't do anything right again." I hesitated. "Maybe that made me a little nutty."

Tina leaned up on her elbows to look at me. Even in the dark, I saw her sad expression. "I didn't know."

"I didn't tell."

"You should tell me everything." She put her arm around me and pulled me close. "I'm so, so sorry."

"I'm better than I was," I said. "I guess for all my bitching and nagging, I probably deserved it."

"No, no you didn't. You're not better if you don't understand that." She stroked my back. I hoped she couldn't see that I was crying. "You have a right to be sad. You have a right to a lot of things, but blaming yourself isn't one of them."

"That's what Fee said." We were quiet for a very long time. I wiped my eyes on the sleeve of my sweatshirt. "I don't know what's going to happen. We're in such a strange phase right now."

"The phase where you just fuck around?" She whispered the bad word. Still, I was horrified that she could deliver such uncharacteristic language in such a saccharine tone. It definitely lightened the mood in a quick-hurry.

"Tina!" I laughed, despite my tears. "Some good Catholic girl you turned out to be."

"Some good sister you turned out to be," she quietly said after we settled down once more. "And I mean that. A really, really good sister."

I curled into her, my body happily exhausted from the previous night's shenanigans. But I felt something else that felt like relief. I closed my eyes. Lulled by the sound of Tina's quiet breathing, I fell asleep.

# CHAPTER SEVENTEEN

I arrived at school early with Emanuel's clothes still in the store packages. He arrived shortly after me and savored his new clothes from the untying of the packing bows and removal of tissue paper to endless self-admiration in the full-length bathroom mirror. I stood in the hallway listening to him as he loudly narrated events.

"I look like a new man! What a way to greet Monday, huh?"

I continually checked my watch.

"Yeah, well, you better get a move on. First bell rings in a few seconds." I barely had time to finish my sentence when he stepped into the hallway wearing a fine set of clothes and a grin like I'd never seen on him. I cupped my hands over my mouth. "Emanuel, you look incredible."

"I don't know, you think so?" But I could tell he knew better. The bell rang and the swarm began. He ran off to be seen by as many kids as possible, I'm guessing. He called over his shoulder, "See you in a minute!"

When Emanuel finally arrived in music class, he made quite an entrance, greeted by whistles and claps from his peers. Except for Steven Weitrich.

"If he has a benefactor, the school should be made aware," he said in his typically sly sounding monotone. "A fact like that might influence the level of his handout."

"Scholarship," I corrected him, smiling brightly. "A scholarship which is achieved on the basis of grades and good citizenship."

"And financial need," Steven said.

"And grades and good citizenship," I repeated, deaf to his insults on this day.

The over-privileged student smirked. "What would he possibly know about being a good citizen?"

Emanuel turned in his seat to face his opponent, wearing the same wonderful smile he had all morning. "It's what's keeping me from coming up there and kicking your ass right now."

I didn't correct his swear this time, just calmly folded my arms across my chest. "That really is good citizenship."

Many of the kids nodded and voiced their quiet agreement.

"That's harassment, is what it is. Him," Steven first glared at Emanuel, and then turned to me to add, "and you."

The class rumbled a little louder. I clapped my hands, signifying a change of subject. "Let's get started. Is Ricky here yet?"

"Here!" The trilling voice came from the hallway. Ricky made his own spectacular entrance wearing yet another flamboyant outfit. Each one had been gaudier than the last. I wondered what poor Mrs. Duffy next door thought of our guests and the frequently loud volume level.

"Cheers, kiddles!" he said.

Everyone muttered hello. Emanuel's new duds didn't go unnoticed by Ricky.

"Fine threads, little man!" He walked over to him and made a fist. "Bump it."

They bumped fists and Ricky returned to my side. "We need to talk wardrobe," he said out of the side of his mouth. "You know, choir robes, that kind of thing."

I was confused. "We don't have choir robes."

"Exactly." He made a face.

Two weeks to go and we had twice again the number of students we'd previously had in the show, a few strong singers, a boy's group, a semi-functional band, and dreams where wardrobe was concerned, if it only amounted to good intentions. It wasn't a bad way to start the week.

Ricky stayed throughout the day to help. While he was helpful and especially good with the younger kids, I worried that he was seriously cutting into his own classroom time. I asked him about it.

"Don't worry," he said, attempting to dismiss my concerns with a flip of his hand. "I have study hall all afternoon."

Kid had a lot of study hall. He changed the subject back to the same one we'd been talking about on and off throughout the day: those godforsaken choir robes we didn't have.

"It's not in the budget," I told him. I glanced upward, pretending an idea had just dawned on me. "Wait a minute—that's right, we don't have a budget at all."

"I just don't understand how we can have a choir program without choir robes, that's all I'm saying." He folded his arms across his chest as we stood in the sanctuary foyer, which is where our debate had followed us.

I sighed and rolled my neck. The pounding in my head had gotten so loud, I could actually hear it. I furrowed my brow and pushed open the sanctuary doors to discover that the pounding wasn't in my head at all. It was on the stage. A small barn-like shape was being constructed one plank at a time by people I didn't recognize at all. Correction, by women I didn't recognize at all. Hot women.

"Lord have mercy! The Almighty!" Ricky squealed.

It's exactly what I was thinking. Five women in a variety of dress ranging from workout attire and heels to short-shorts and heels were wielding hammers and hacksaws. I walked toward the stage in a daze.

I heard Ricky's voice behind me. "Go get 'em, girl. Grrr!"

A woman in a particularly short sweater dress turned around. I would have recognized her sooner had I ever seen her in actual clothing before.

"Sofia?" I asked. She promptly dropped her hammer, which clattered behind her when she came to greet me like an old friend with a kiss on both cheeks. I grinned. "What on earth?"

"My Mercedes told me how big your classes got—they just blew up—and I was worried that you might be short armed."

It took me a second. "You mean shorthanded?"

"Whatever," she said with a shrug, her eyes sparkling. "So I told the girls at the club and they thought it would be fun to give back to the community. So here we are!"

"Yes! Here you are." I forced a smile and tried not to notice a blond woman behind her with heavers so huge, they'd make excellent airbags. "And you're building a…?"

"A manger for the Baby Jesus! With the scraps from the old Kit-Kat stage!" Again, Sofia's rolling Rs and missing Js absolutely mesmerized me. She stopped suddenly and moved closer to me, her voice dropping to a whisper. "I had to show the girls four storybooks to explain that the manger was where the Baby Jesus was born." She thumped her index finger against her temple. "They are very sweet, but some of them have the boulders in the heads."

I would have corrected that to rocks in their heads, but maybe Sofia knew something about them I did not. I noticed a row of wide-eyed and wide-mouthed boys watching the proceedings with real preadolescent interest. Raul, the high school boy who'd been designated scenery manager, was awestruck. He turned and gave me a thumbs-up. I grinned at Sofia. Along with some miscellaneous physical parts, I was growing to love this woman's enthusiasm most of all.

"Sofia, what you're doing is great. I'd like to invite some other parents in to help with the project if you don't mind."

"No! I don't mind at all! The more the merrier."

"Good," I said, nodding toward the row of boys. "Perhaps you could make the announcement?"

"Absolutely." She winked at me and her eyes sparkled.

Nobody could say she wasn't a brilliant businesswoman. "Listen up, children! We need the big strong muscles to help us with the scenery. So go home and tell your parents that me and the girls will be here tomorrow night and every night until the program!"

The boys did everything but cheer as they scampered out of the sanctuary. I wondered if we'd done something unholy in the church, but I figured God knew it was for a good cause.

I watched Ricky help Sofia with her fur coat and escort her up the aisle of St. Mary's. He would probably have designed an entirely new wardrobe for the dancers by the night's end. Judging by the scant clothing they wore, he could have them sewn by midnight. I looked at the empty pulpit and signed the cross, looked up at the ceiling, and mouthed thank you.

My a cappella group wrapped up their practice session. I fed them as usual—sub sandwiches this time—and released them to go to Mass. I was also about to leave when the janitor informed me that I had a telephone call. I followed him to a small outer office. It was Tina.

"Are you okay?" I asked.

"Yes, well, no," she stammered. "Well…"

"Yes or no, Tina?" I felt panic rising. "What is it?"

"I'm on the City Arts Board and I'm obligated to attend a function tonight that I forget all about."

I was confused, not for the first time today. "You sure you feel like going out?"

"No! You have to go in my place," she exclaimed. "I have two reserved seats. There will be food and it starts at seven." When I didn't answer right away, she carried on some more. "Oh, please, Mina! I don't want to leave a bad impression on the board. They're my only networking connection to possibly find a new job." She sounded desperate. "Pretty, pretty please?"

"Fine." I glanced down at my borrowed black slacks and sweater and dusted some chalk off them. "I don't know that I'm dressed for it."

"There's a pretty scarf in the bottom drawer of my desk." She sounded rushed. "It's at the Fine Arts Center, otherwise known as the Grassley Baptist Church."

"Got it," I said and hung up. I started for the other building to retrieve the scarf when I caught a glimpse of Emanuel. I waved him over. "C'mon. We're going to try out your new coat and tie."

We showed up at the Baptist church where we were presented with a series of food courses. They included a poor imitation of Hungarian dumplings—still slightly frozen inside, imitation crab—I don't even like the real stuff, and veal—it's a fucking baby cow. Following my lead, Emanuel ate only the dumpling-cicles.

We sat at banquet tables along with a bunch of Landon's version of stuffed shirts while they talked art and music, and then we took our assigned seats to wait for the program to start. The theme for the night was *A Jazzy Little Christmas*, which I figured would just about put me to sleep. My days were getting to be as long as they'd been in California working for a television network.

I was staring into the distance when I caught sight of a familiar face across the room, which was unusual, since most everyone I'd gone to school with had apparently long since bailed out of this shabby little town. A boyish face framed with thick, dark hair, looking every bit the part of a Kennedy, studied me in return.

I quickly realized it was Thomas Weitrich, still dressed to the nines, and now with gleaming veneers. Still the biggest fish in the smallest pond. No matter what accomplishments I'd made in this big old world, here in Landon we seemed to have fallen into our old roles: he as the hotshot, and me, the riff-raff.

He looked away after a bit. I considered everything that his son could have possibly told him, and sighed when the stage curtain parted and the sweet sound of a trumpet filled the auditorium with a wonderfully controlled, gentle version of "Silent Night" that was truly moving. My eyes opened wide when I recognized the pint-sized trumpeter. Suddenly, I knew exactly why Thomas Weitrich had graced the audience with his kingly presence.

I could hardly sit through the remaining forty minutes of the show. When the final applause died down, I grabbed Emanuel's hand and moved against the exiting crowd, employing as much courtesy as possible. I reached the stage just as the young and talented Steven Weitrich was snapping his instrument case shut.

"Steven!" I called to him. He froze at first, and then looked around. I knew he'd recognized us, so I could only assume he hoped no one else saw us engaging him, as if we'd somehow damage his reputation. He made a bored face and sauntered to the edge of the stage. I focused on the music and my goal, not on the child. I smiled at him.

"That was sincerely an outstanding performance!"

Despite their earlier near-tussle, even Emanuel was quietly respectful. He stood by my side. I guessed he'd figured out my mission.

"Thank you," Steven was obligated to say. He started to go. "I have to meet my father."

"Wait!" I grabbed his pants leg and stopped him from leaving, happy that I hadn't succeeded in tripping the kid right off the stage. I turned him loose. "Can you come down here for a minute and talk to me?"

Steven rolled his eyes. "You're going to beg me to play in your stupid program and I'm going to say no. Conversation expedited."

"Why would you say no?" I asked. "The school might close in the spring and this is your last music program. Don't you want this to be a show worth remembering?"

He looked thoughtful before he took a seat on the edge of the stage. He leaned toward me and spoke quietly. "I'd sooner forget this whole school ever happened. When it finally closes, I'll get to go to a nice boarding school, and it will make me *very* happy to be gone from this town."

His tone bordered on vindictive, but I can't say I didn't understand him to some degree. It also sounded as though there was more than simply "this town" he wanted to escape. I leveled with him. "I'm anxious to get back out of here myself."

"Then you understand why I don't want to further involve myself in this venture." It was the most personal we'd gotten since our rough beginning.

"C'mon," Emanuel mumbled, starting to leave. "Who needs him anyway?"

At some point, Thomas Weitrich had come up behind us. When he spoke, I nearly jumped out of my skin. "Son, we've got a dinner reservation."

I turned around and forced a smile. From his haughty tone, I figured he was taking Steven somewhere for something better than the partially frozen fare we commoners had dined on only an hour ago. The man dressed and carried himself like he was fresh out of East Hampton, not the north side of Landon. It crossed my mind to be intimidated, and then I laughed at old ghosts.

"Good to see you, Thomas," I said. "I was just complimenting Steven on his performance. You must be very proud."

"Musical genius runs in our family," he said, as if I should have already known.

I glanced at Steven. Even he rolled his eyes at his father's arrogance. I'd bet theirs is a hell of a competitive household. Suddenly, I felt as enterprising as Sofia.

"I was just asking Steven if he'd be a part of our Christmas program at the school. We don't have a trumpet for our band and we thought maybe he'd like to step in."

Thomas chuckled and did everything but scoff at the idea. "Steven has got a lot on his plate these days. Thank you for thinking of him, but I don't think there's any room on his schedule to play with your little ragtag band."

I squeezed Emanuel's hand tight so he would refrain from correcting the senior Weitrich despite how fond he was of correcting the junior one.

"Our loss," I said, smiling. "I mean, performing at Sacred Heart wouldn't exactly be a jewel in the family crown, right?"

"Come along, Steven."

"No scholarship possibilities there," I smartly told him, still smiling a smile so phony, my lips were quivering. "It was nice to see you. I can't get over the family resemblance here. Amazing."

"Naturally." Thomas also made a small smile. "Like father, like son."

From the corner of my eye, I saw Steven's look of disdain for his father. Something told me that no matter how much he enjoyed his privileged lifestyle, he didn't want to be any more like his father than I did.

"Well, let's hope not," I said. It was out there before I could stop myself. I kept the same phony grin on my face, trying to remain strong in my sneaky pursuit of a trumpeter.

"I beg your pardon?"

"I said—"

"I heard what you said." He stepped toward me, his eyes burning with hatred, just like in the good old days. He quieted his voice. "You'd be wise to not disrespect me in public as I am the author of a large percentage of your paycheck."

I felt some growing confidence that in reality, I had money. I certainly wasn't dependent upon the school for an income, and now, neither was my sister. "It's not like when we were kids. You can't hurt me, not at all."

By now, Thomas' face was red with the fury that I'd caused. Yay. I kept cool and smiling. He leaned in close enough so only the boys could hear our exchange. "In fact, Steven will no longer be participating in your show."

"Only if he wants a grade. I doubt your fancy-pants private school will take him with an F on his report card." I shrugged again. "Just saying."

"I'll do it." The voice belonged to Steven.

I turned to look at him, feigning surprise.

"Steven, don't be ridiculous," his father said, attempting to laugh it off.

"You'd better do what your father tells you," I told him. "Everyone else does."

"I already said I'd do it," Steven said, more to his father than to me.

"In that case, I'm forced to repossess the instruments my family donated." Thomas had a smug answer for everything. "Not only do you not have a trumpeter, you now no longer have a band."

"Those old things? We threw them out," I told him. "Some of my friends sent us new ones. I gave them to the kids to do with whatever they want."

"I want a band for the Christmas program," Emanuel quickly put in, also grinning.

"Done," I told him.

Thomas turned toward his son. "You're not playing your trumpet in that program, period."

I lit up. "Steven, I happen to have an amazing new student trumpet—"

"I'll take it," Steven said, practically growling and still glaring at the elder Weitrich. "It's my life and I'd like to make a decision for myself once in a while."

Father and son stared at each other for a while.

"We'll talk about this later," Thomas told him. He turned to glare at me, but I just smiled and gave him a little goodbye wave.

Steven followed his angry father. I looked at Emanuel.

"You knew that was going to happen, didn't you?" he asked.

"I hated to pit him against his father to get my way."

"Nah," Emanuel said as we watched them go. "I don't think he wants to be like that douchebag anyway." He didn't even bother to look my way when he added, "Sorry."

***

I drove Emanuel home, but he hesitated before getting out of the car. "That true what you said back there?"

"Which part?"

"You really anxious to leave here?"

I studied my little friend for a few seconds. "I'd be a liar if I said I wasn't anxious to leave Landon."

He got out of the car and slammed the door. I called to him, but he disappeared inside the house.

I slowly drove away, wondering why I would say such a thing to a child. For all the things I was anxious to leave behind in this crappy town, there were two very good reasons to want to stay. Tina was one. I swore I'd tell Emanuel first thing in the morning that he was most definitely the other.

# CHAPTER EIGHTEEN

Emanuel was a no-show at school on Tuesday. I oversaw the ever-expanding class as if I wasn't worried sick about him. I wondered if Tina's cop friend was as good at checking on kids as he was with grown women engaging in a much needed romp.

After school, I conducted our strange, loosely assembled band. To my surprise, Steven showed up at about the halfway point. Who was I to complain?

Looking about as repulsed as if I'd forced him to stand in a soup line, he accepted the student trumpet and warmed up. I nodded hello so as to not make a big deal out of his presence. Trying not to smile, I started things from the top once again. It wasn't perfect by any stretch, but it wasn't horrible.

Feeding the now massive crew was getting to be a challenge, but I even had help with that these days. It seemed more and more parents—especially the men, thank you Sofia's crew—

showed up at night to help build or paint. With that bunch came the owner of a butcher's shop who provided hot dogs and chips, the manager of a trattoria who donated beans, rice, and something that—given my limited Spanish—sounded like cow's stomach, and good old Bernie from the hotel with his noodle-potato pie.

Not to be outdone by the locals, the chain store, Hy-Vee, catered to us in fine style one night with chicken and dressing.

Each owner or manager gave us a speech about their store's offerings and plied the kids with business cards to take to their parents. The kids got a nice lesson in American economics to go with their dinner. I figured it would be hard for some of them to return to the soup kitchen after several days of fairly adventurous cuisine.

Late that afternoon, I left practice in the very capable hands of Ricky to keep an appointment I'd made with my family's old lawyer. Once at Attorney Gerald Dueling's office, I explained Emanuel's situation and asked him outright about the laws surrounding gay adoption. He seemed appalled that I'd even consider it.

"First off, the kid already belongs to someone—a blood relative, no less," he said, practically dismissing me on the spot. He closed the notebook he'd opened without even making a mark in it. My heart sank. "You can't take a child away from his biological family. Period."

"I have reason to believe that the child is already involved with Social Services, and that in his present home, he is being abused."

He shook his head. "That's hearsay."

"The child told me himself."

"Then call Social Services." He stood up, an indication that I should be on my way. "I'm sorry, but I can't help you."

"You can't help me or you won't? What's your real issue with me?" I felt my saucy attitude slowly rising. "I could sue this law firm for refusing to represent me on the basis of sexual orientation."

A sly smile came to his cracked lips. "Well, I simply don't practice family law."

But I felt I knew better. I stood up and stormed out of his office, happy as hell that it had been a free consultation. I could see why this old fart and my father had once gotten along so famously. I was near tears by the time I reached downstairs. Before I could exit through the revolving door, I heard a voice behind me.

"Miss! Excuse me, miss?"

I blotted my eyes and turned around. A guy who looked like a shorter Greg Kinnear was chasing me. I waited for him to catch up, and then waited some more for him to catch his breath. He wore tiny glasses and a three-piece suit. Though he dressed the part, his smile made him seem out of place in this firm.

"I'm sorry, I couldn't help overhearing what you were talking about." Still breathless, he thrust his hand out for a handshake, but I just stared at him. He went on, "I'm Larry Bennett."

"Who are you?" I asked.

"My mother is Gerry Dueling's sister. I'm his nephew," he explained. I considered that they couldn't look less alike if only comparing his smiling face to his uncle's grimacing one. Larry suddenly appeared embarrassed. "Oh, you mean who am I to this law firm? Of course. I'm an attorney. A new one, and I'm trying to specialize in family law and human rights, that sort of thing."

"I think your uncle made it pretty clear he was unwilling to help me."

"I take my own cases," he said, and lowered his voice. "We can arrange to meet elsewhere if you're not comfortable in this building."

"No, I'm fine," I said, hope slowly creeping back.

"I've only been here a short while. I just graduated, but I'd like to take a crack at your case. Would you care to follow me to my office?"

I did. It was about the size of a broom closet, and in fact, could very well have been one at some point.

He eyed the low-hanging ductwork above us, grinned and shrugged. "Pardon the décor." He had some gray hair at his temples and sun creases around his smiling eyes.

I began, "No offense, Mr. Bennett—"

"Call me Larry."

"No offense, Larry, but you don't exactly look like a lawyer who just sprang from college."

"Oh, I'm forty-five," he said quite openly. "I spent twenty years teaching high school before the Great Recession." He made a slicing motion across his neck. "Got the ax like hundreds of other folks did. I decided to take my unemployment and go to law school. Took me two and a half years."

"That's fast."

"I don't like to waste time." He smiled. "I've always wanted to help people."

"I like ambitious people." I made a face. "How did you end up in Landon?"

"Economics. My uncle was hiring when no one else was, not that he planned on employing a new lawyer, but my mother's his baby sister, so that didn't hurt." He sat down. So did I. "Let's start with basic information, shall we?"

I told him everything about my struggles to have a child, my sister's cancer, my sudden teaching job, and my estranged, almost ex-wife.

"That's all very good, but I was hoping to learn more about the boy," he sweetly said.

I rubbed my forehead. "I'm sorry. You're not a shrink."

"That's okay. If I was, I would say you're reacting quite normally to your environment, given what you've been through." He poised his pen above his notebook. "Shall we start again?"

When we finished, he had a few pages worth of notes, which was more than his uncle was willing to give me. He stood up when I did.

"I won't lie to you, this is tricky." He frowned and looked through his notes. "My uncle was right about the difficulty in removing a child from his own family. Biology has first priority. Second, there's a matter of establishing whether or not the child is a citizen. Do you know if he is?"

I shook my head no. There were a lot of gray areas surrounding Emanuel Diaz.

"And are you planning on returning to California?" He looked at me.

"Yes. Well, I...I'd like to." I stammered. "What is the right answer for that?"

He grinned. "That you'd be willing to stay if given the opportunity to parent would certainly look good in your favor, if it comes down to it." He reached out his hand and I shook it. "I've got your contact information. I'll first check with the State and see where Emanuel stands in the system. But Ms. Borsalino, I warn you not to get too optimistic. I've seen more of these things fail than I've seen them succeed."

"I thought you said you were new at this lawyer thing." I said.

He quieted significantly. "I saw too much of it as a teacher. Too much injustice for kids. That's why I'm here."

I thanked him for at least trying, but left feeling less than excited about my prospects of saving this child from his present horrid lifestyle. I drove to Emanuel's house before going home. Of course, his drunken grandmother answered my knock.

"He's not here," she announced, prepared to slam the door in my face.

I was familiar with this scenario by now, and wedged my foot in the doorway to prevent that from happening. "I just want to know if he's okay, that's all."

"You reconsidered my offer, didn't you?" she asked, smiling. Her expression turned to one of sheer hatred. "Well, it's too late! The price has gone way up!"

And then she did succeed in slamming the door in my face, or more pointedly, on my foot. I limped back to the car and drove away.

*\*\**

On Friday morning, my favorite missing pupil showed up in class wearing one of his new uniforms. To my surprise, it was crisply ironed, but he looked tired. I called him to my desk before the bell rang.

"I was worried about you," I told him. He shrugged and looked away. I figured he'd heard his grandmother yelling at me nights earlier and was probably embarrassed. "About what we talked about the other night, about my leaving Landon."

His gaze flicked back to focus on mine, but he didn't say a word.

"You are the best thing about Landon as far as I'm concerned," I said, staring him straight in the eyes. As other kids were filing in, I lowered my voice to a whisper. "If I had to leave here, it would hurt me to leave you most of all."

It didn't seem to help. He nodded and slowly walked toward his chair. It felt odd.

Odd seemed to be the theme of the morning when the announcements had not come over the intercom a whole five minutes after the second bell rang. I stood beside the podium tapping my toe, impatiently waiting. There was supposed to be a prayer, then the pledge followed by a rundown of school activities, all of which Principal Reeves delivered in her slow, flowery tone. We'd waste half the class if she didn't get a move on.

Ricky entered the room and glanced at the intercom. I shrugged and motioned him toward me. "Keep an eye on these guys. I'm going to check on our beloved nutty Principal Reeves."

When I reached her door, it was closed. I knocked and pushed the door open when there was no answer. Principal Reeves had cleared the paperwork off her chair and sat with her face down on her desk. Fearing the worst, I ran over to her.

"Hey!" I said, shaking her shoulder. She slowly came around. "Should I call an ambulance? Can you hear me?"

"I can hear you," she groggily whispered. It was then that I realized she'd been crying. I let go of her shoulder, unsure of my role. I started to gingerly clear a corner of her desk when she swept her arm along an entire side and made a clean sweep of things.

"You're messing up your filing system," I said, trying for a laugh I didn't get. I sat down on the spot she'd cleared. "What's going on, Principal Reeves?"

"There's been a change of plans," she said bleakly. "They're closing the school. Sacred Heart will cease to exist after today."

"They? Who are they?"

"The leaseholders."

"Today?" I asked to be sure I'd heard her right.

She nodded. "Yes. I'm sorry you wasted your time on the music program."

"Wait a minute, they can't just tell you today without any real notice."

"They didn't." She opened the top drawer of her desk, withdrew a stack of typewritten letters, and handed them to me. I briefly scanned the top few, and then skipped to the back.

I felt frustration creeping up on me. "These go clear back to August."

"Yes, they do." She sighed. "Ten years ago, the church sold the school to the public school board."

"Wait...why would the church sell the school?"

"Not the school, just the building." She sadly shrugged. "Too many liens on the building. It was cheaper to let someone else settle them. In turn, the agreement said we could stay here for as long as we paid the buyer rent, which worked great until we couldn't."

"What about church funding?"

"Practically nonexistent."

"And tuitions?" But I already knew the answer to that one.

"Even more nonexistent than the church funding. And now, out of the blue, our primary funding family, the Weitrichs, have discontinued scholarship assistance."

"Oh, God," I absently said. Thomas Weitrich had once again flexed his asshole muscle. This time, I was to blame. I honestly had not seen that coming, and I certainly hadn't meant to jeopardize the school in any way. My guilt was rapidly mounting. Still, it seemed nowhere near the level held by the frazzled principal.

"First the plant left, then the recession, and practically all our students are on scholarship. We were overextended as it was. And now...this is all my fault." She looked stunned as she summarized the school's gloomy history. "I pulled every last trick out of my hat to make rent."

I handed her the letters and looked at her. "How far behind are we?"

"Three months," she admitted. "It was either rent or payroll. They're also saying we violated the terms of our contract. Apparently, renting space to the city for storage is considered subletting, which is forbidden according to today's letter, which I received registered mail, the…the bastards."

I'd never heard her use any such language. I couldn't help but hear Ricky's voice in the back of my mind, insisting that the public school system wanted Sacred Heart permanently closed.

"Why didn't you say something?" I demanded.

She made a soft laugh. "I didn't think they'd throw us out. I didn't think they were serious."

"Been there, done that." I couldn't help but be sympathetic. "What could the public school board want with this building anyway?"

"Storage, ironically. Seems that's all Sacred Heart is good for." She looked as if she might start crying all over again. Her voice cracked when she said, "How ungodly."

"Did your board know you were in this kind of trouble?"

"We don't really have a board anymore. As I said, we have very little funding from the church. They know we're in dire straits, but you can't raise money when nobody's got it. I handle bookkeeping on this end and it's clean as a whistle, I guarantee it. The little bit of money we get from tuition is reported on the up and up, it's just not enough." She sighed so deeply, I thought her round little body might deflate on the spot. "I've blown through most of my retirement to make ends meet around this place."

I looked at her, the multiple official notices, and the office heaped high with paperwork that would mean nothing by the end of the week. I tried to put myself in her strange, wounded place. I wondered if, under similar circumstances, I'd behave so selflessly to forgo my pay and retirement to feed and educate a bunch of starving actors. It wasn't a good comparison, I admit.

I shook it off, felt a surge of internal electricity, and swung into the mode I operate in best: fixer.

"Let me take a look at things. I'll need your ledgers from the last six months, a copy of your rent agreement, all bills, and all your city documents. Everything, I mean it—don't hold back." I stood up. "But first, you'll make the school announcements because the students and staff are wigging out. Everyone's wondering what's wrong."

"I couldn't possibly speak to them." Her voice cracked again. "Could you?"

"Fine," I reluctantly agreed, much as I'd reluctantly agreed to do everything that had me in this school to this point. "Go get cleaned up. You don't want anyone to see you like this. Then we'll go over all your options." She left the office, and I added under my breath, "If there are any options left."

I went toward the intercom system and looked at the few announcements laid out for that morning. I recalled the order of things as I'd gotten used to it: Prayer, Pledge of Allegiance, announcements, lunch menu. I could do this. I pushed the button, instantly sending feedback squealing throughout the school. I heard complaints from all the way down the hallway.

"Oops, sorry," I said, moving my lips away from the microphone. "Good morning, Sacred Heart. Principal Reeves has an appointment this morning." I rolled through the steps in a performance that was rocky at best. On the tail end of the prayer, I added that the school was always facing struggles, sort of a foreshadowing for the teachers in the event that I wasn't the fixer I gave myself credit for being. "Please pray for Sacred Heart's strong future. Meanwhile, be calm and carry on."

Hey, it worked for the Royals.

For the rest of the morning, I left Ricky and Mrs. Duffy at the helm of the choir while I pored over the books with Principal Reeves. While I studied bills and invoices, payroll and contracts, she paced and prayed with her rosary. It was clear to see the school had been in trouble long before Asshole Weitrich pulled his funds.

At nearly eleven o'clock, I asked the pacing principal to get us some coffee from the diner downtown, which was my polite way of getting her out of my hair so I could think, and then I made my last resort phone call.

"How much?" Fee asked when I'd finished explaining the dire straits Sacred Heart was in.

"Six thousand in rent, utilities, salaries, termination of old agreements…" I listed the items off before announcing my rough tally. "Looks like twenty thousand would catch them up and keep them in business through January, pending resolution of small and funky rent contract clauses."

There was real concern in her voice. "Twenty grand is just a bandage on a pretty serious wound."

"I know that, I know, " I said, thinking as fast as I could. "We need an ongoing solution."

"Will you listen to yourself?" I heard her chuckle softly. "You're saying 'we.' You're so used to fixing things, you've taken ownership of Landon's problems."

"Not Landon, just the school."

"I'm not saying it's a bad idea," she started, which usually meant she was saying exactly that. "Any money we leave in Landon needs to go to your sister. She's a victim of that institution too. She's family. She's the one we need to worry about."

I was quickly growing exasperated. "Fee, do you know how much dough we give to every conceivable charitable cause? We give to animals, the disabled, to disabled animals, for God's sake." I was too frazzled to think. "We should do this."

"Give me a minute to wrap my brain around it." She was quiet for a while. "Hold up…what if I could arrange a crew to fly there and beam the big holiday show back via satellite? It's our Friday night, after all. We were only planning a rerun. We could donate commercial proceeds to the school. Better yet, we could talk to the students, let them tell their sob stories, which will certainly catch the interest of a channel in our network. My God, we'd be talking about ongoing money for the school if it takes off, and in this day of reality TV, it really just might work."

A bad feeling crept over me. "I don't know…"

"It would be one of those rise-up-against-the-odds-type stories. Get personal with the kids, see what their lives are like."

She was fully engaged in creating a business plan. It was like we'd switched hats. As her idea ramped up, so did my fears. I remembered the god-awful stuff on the music channel on my first day of class as a babysitter only.

Most starlets I'd seen in the magazines and tabloids of late were not really starlets at all, but reality TV stars. Young single mothers, kids binge drinking on the shore with Bumpits in their upsweeps, moms with too many kids, fighting housewives…our children's heroes weren't heroes at all. They were melodramatic freaks, the new norm that society measured their own personal lives against. My concerns wound through my brain, conspiring to give me the headache of the century.

Fee was still going on. "It'd be a heartwarming sob story, a ratings win for sure! In the meantime, you'd get to do your Christmas show for a bigger audience than Sacred Heart could ever hope to have, and the world will see how you spearheaded the whole…"

She went on. My head spun. Her idea, albeit a strong business plan, was reminiscent of the same one Ed Sullivan offered to Bing Crosby on another one of my sister's god-awful favorite movies, *White Christmas*, but the consequences here would extend much farther than simply embarrassing the old General.

Putting poverty-stricken Landon into a veritable life-ruining spotlight would only stoke the fires of a hungry reality furnace we were all already roasting in. It was the worst possible idea for Sacred Heart—the *absolute* worst.

"No," I blurted. "We are not conducting a show development meeting here, okay? The money, even the Christmas concert, it's only for the school. Nothing more. You have to promise me you won't do anything with it."

She stopped talking and sighed. "Okay. I just want to help because I love you."

Jesus, that was certainly good to hear. I closed my eyes and smiled with relief. "I love you, too."

"So we can agree upon that," she said.

"Yes, we sure can." I chuckled and swung back around to the pressing matter at hand. "Twenty thousand. Can you make it fly by noon your time? At least it will save this month."

"What about January?"

"The school might not be open in January. At least we can give these kids a Christmas program to remember." I balanced the phone on my shoulder and rubbed my fingers on my temples. "I got to hand it to you, that was an outstanding plan you laid out. You have a better head for business than you give yourself credit for."

"You've got a more creative mind than any of us gave you credit for." She lowered her voice. "I'm sorry I didn't tell you before. Hon, it's going to be a great program, one they'll always remember. I'm proud of you for what you're doing."

I felt warm through and through. Much as I would have liked to advance the conversation, I had a school to fix.

I hung up and called Principal Reeves back into the office. She'd returned long ago and had been straining to hear my phone conversation from the hallway. I knew because I could see her outline through the milk glass window. She practically fell through the door and pulled a chair up next to me.

I accepted one of the coffees from her, took a sip, and stifled my grimace. I'm sure it was terrible long before it was cold.

"First of all, it's my understanding that the city contract is month to month," I said.

"Correct," she said, nodding.

"Cancel it immediately. Refund them a prorated month."

She looked as if I'd just slapped her. I explained what I felt should be common sense. "You can't offset the rent by five hundred dollars if there's no rent to offset."

"Okay," she said, looking through a business card file and selecting one. "I'll arrange to have the stuff out by tomorrow morning."

"Good," I went on. "My wife is wiring us the money now. Then we'll talk to the public school board and throw ourselves at their mercy, using the whole don't-throw-us-out-at-Christmas angle. Whatever it takes."

"Yes, Jesus!" she said, clapping her hands together in prayer.

"Whoa, before you go praising Jesus, keep in mind that this is only a temporary fix to bring the school square through this month. Come February, you're back to the possibility of missing rent. That or not making payroll. We need a plan."

"We should pray for a miracle," she said, her eyes wide. She took my hands in hers, but I wriggled mine free.

"We should pray for money," I amended her proclamation. "And in case we need a backup plan. We need to figure out where to cut corners."

Her expression went blank. "Most of the students are on scholarship. There's not a lot of money coming in these days."

I nodded. "Which means you will have to make some tough decisions. You may have to cut some of those scholarship recipients and combine classes, which includes cutting staff. I can put some numbers together for you so you can see how that would impact the budget."

"I've already cut some staff, you know that much," she said, referring to my sister's joblessness come January.

"I know it sounds brutal, but I don't see how else you can survive." I drew a line through my own name on her payroll roster. "We'll start with my position, naturally. I'll stay, but I won't take a salary. I'm not sure anyone else will be willing to do that given the economic conditions of this town."

"No teacher will teach without a salary!" She shook her head. "And no student shall be turned away! Every child deserves the same opportunities."

I sighed. "Sadly, that's not the way it works in the real world."

She straightened her posture, her decision obviously made. "Well, that's how it works at Sacred Heart."

I started to tell her that she was nowhere near having the luxury of making those bold declarations. Irritated, I blew a stray blond lock of hair away from my eyes. "So what's your plan?"

"Prayer." She stood, crossed the floor, and dumped both awful coffees in the garbage can. "The Lord will deliver. I absolutely expect a miracle."

She marched out of the office.

I slumped in my chair and whispered to no one, "And it will definitely take a miracle."

# CHAPTER NINETEEN

Friday had proven to be about the longest day of my life. By evening, we'd secured a day's extension and a Monday meeting where we'd find out if the public school board would accept our late payments and allow Sacred Heart to stay in the building at least until January. One worry was momentarily shuffled to the back burner.

Saturday night after Mass, I slipped into the sanctuary to the sound of hammers hammering and quiet, polite laughter. Only a few late-stayers from the service were kneeling or lighting candles. Even Fee's mom greeted me at the door with a hug before trotting off to build and paint with the other volunteers.

I saw Principal Reeves on her kneeler. I slipped into the pew and went to my knees right next to her. From the corner of my eye, I saw Roddy waving a little wand with a long streamer on it, skipping down the aisle as he made a demonstration to the smallest children in the program rehearsal. His flittering and fluttering certainly wasn't helping his case for being straight much.

On stage, I saw Sofia leading the building crew with the rest of her lady friends. She gave me a nice wave. I returned it. I heard Principal Reeves next to me continuing her one-woman prayer campaign to save the school. She paused only long enough to ask me a question in her sweetest, most patient voice.

"My Mina, have we professional dancers in our presence?"

Ah, the strippers. I gulped and whispered, "Yes, ma'am."

"And Lord," she said, loud enough so that I could hear. "Thank You for the abundance of help You've directed our way, in all its voluptuous forms. In Your Son Jesus' name, amen."

We both crossed ourselves and slid onto the pew. I felt my cheeks growing warm. Shortly behind the small children, I saw a few wild acrobatics happening. I hurriedly stood, excused myself, and hoped to shield that image from our fragile principal. I practically ran to Abby, the high school cheerleader in charge of those circus tricks.

"Hon?" I held up a halting hand. "I thought you were teaching the kids to dance."

"I'm not much about ballet. Roddy's got that covered." She grinned. "But I'm all about making a spectacular entrance. Look what I taught Juan."

I stopped Juan from taking backflip flight, nearly putting my own back out in the process. I looked at the blond cheerleader girl with desperation. "Abbs, do we need to have some parental permission slips signed to do this sort of stuff?"

"Well, I'm pretty sure every daddy associated with the school is up on that stage." Abby said, referencing the stage crew led by Sofia. She sweetly grinned. "If you approach them right now, chances are they'll sign anything you'd like."

"I see," I said, trying not to smile. So far, I had a waiver "list" that included everything from simply working with high school helpers to singing a variety of religious Christmas songs in a few languages. Now I was about to add hair-raising acrobatics to that list?

I turned around to see one of the older boys lift Mercedes up in a pretty and delicate ballet move that probably had tons of liability attached to it. I slapped my hands over my mouth and called to Ricky. He ran over to me. I gave Abby the one-minute sign.

"We need to create a liability waiver right now and get every parent on the premises to sign off. Can you help me?" He nodded and followed me to a side office.

"What do you think about the streamer-sticks I put together for the little kids?" He excitedly asked me. "I got the material and dowel rods donated by Sanchez Hardware."

"I think they'll be beautiful," I told him honestly. "At the same time, I'm afraid someone will poke an eye out. But this should help, right?"

I handed him a handwritten letter requesting permission for everything but actual breathing. He nodded, added something at the bottom of the list, and handed it back to me. I read it.

"Permission to measure for wardrobe?" I asked him, shaking my head. "Ricky, we don't have a wardrobe budget. We've already been over this."

"I'm creative to the nth degree. Don't you believe in me?" he asked, refusing to glance away from my glare.

I nodded, rolled my eyes, and smiled. "Yes, I really do."

"Good." He laid the sheet inside the copier. "We'll need ninety-eight copies."

"Ninety-eight?" I gasped. "We started with twenty-nine choir students, then that doubled! Wait…are there even ninety-eight kids in the school?"

"Ninety-seven," he said, pressing buttons like he knew what he was doing. The machine roared to life. Obviously, at some point the church had been able to afford better equipment than the school. "Remember that boy you recruited? The tough-looking one from the Red Bucket Singers? He's a high school dropout. Still, permission is required."

"Good thinking," I said, patting him on the back. The Red Bucket Singers had become the name for our four-part boy group. I nodded. "You're something, Ricky. You've got an eye for detail and you're tremendously organized. You've got mad skills."

"I know," he quietly said, beaming at me.

Moments later, we marched back into the sanctuary armed with pens and a stack of permission slips. They were signed within minutes. Shortly thereafter, we were snacking on pastries from a local bread shop. It was heartwarming to feel some sense of community in this small, though barely existing school. And to think much of it had been spearheaded by a kindhearted stripper!

***

The days—weeks, even—ran out quickly. We were down to the line and still had only a shaky musical performance. That wouldn't be all bad if the supplemental show didn't include a rag-tag band, as Thomas Weitrich called it, shepherds who forgot their lines, and angels who continually ran into each other, killing any dreams of allowing them to carry lighted candles.

On Monday morning, Ricky really showed me his ingenuity. He came in shortly after I arrived in the morning, lugging a heap of blue velvet garments. Panting from the effort, he dropped them onto the floor and practically collapsed beside them.

"What is this?" I said, slowly circling the blue velvet mess. I wrinkled my nose. "Ooh, smells a little ripe too."

"Smells musty," he corrected, shaking out a length of fabric and smoothing it on the classroom floor. It was an ancient choir robe. "It's just the collars. They're yellowed too. I can pop them off and sew on new ones."

"Wait a minute." I sat down next to him and his pile. "Where did you get these?"

"First Church of God, now defunct." He grinned. "They were throwing them out, I was doing a little Dumpster diving. It was meant to be." He threw his head back and laughed. "Oh, you should have seen me with these on the city bus!"

I smiled at the image. Still, I wasn't sure about the robes. They smelled like they'd been pulled out of a Dumpster. "Are you sure you can get them clean?"

"They are clean. They were wrapped up. But these collars," he said disapprovingly. He ran his finger along the underside of the one he was holding and popped the threads securing the yellowed collar. Like that, the collar and its First Church of God Singers patch was gone, leaving a velvety crew neck. And did I mention that these robes were about two feet longer than our average singer's height?

He didn't seem put off. "I'll shorten each one up, use the cut-off hems as sashes for the angels, then use the leftover angel gown material to make little collars."

"Rob from the robes for the gowns, gowns for the robes..." It sounded good until the next thought occurred to me. "And where did we get material for the angel gowns?"

"Robbed the school," he said without missing a beat. He nodded over my shoulder. I turned around and squinted as sunshine bounced off the snow and through the windows. There was a good reason for that.

He nodded. "Forgive me for loving *The Sound of Music*. Maria inspired me!"

The curtains were gone.

I turned back toward him. "You don't need to share everything with me." He started to speak, but I stopped him. "Seriously, some things are better left a mystery."

He pursed his lips into a thin smile and tipped his head oh-so sweetly.

The first bell rang.

"Don't worry about clearing this out of the way," I told him, rising off the floor. "I'm taking the kids to the sanctuary all week for practice. You can make this classroom your sweatshop."

He looked suddenly troubled. "Wait, Mina. I have to tell you something."

"Yes?" I said, doubling back to face him.

"I dropped out of school," Ricky blurted.

I stared at him for a moment, not as horrified as one might think. This kid's talents didn't lie in academics. Sometimes, they just don't.

"I know," I finally told him. I walked to the doorway to greet the incoming students and redirect them to the sanctuary. I felt Ricky's gaze on my back. I think he'd expected a lecture from me, but I didn't feel it was necessary to make him feel as if he'd disappointed one more person in his life.

I caught Emanuel, walked beside him on our way to the sanctuary, and asked him if he'd been sick.

He looked thoughtful, and then shook his head. "No."

"Okay, well, you've been gone and it's...it's close to the program," I stammered, which I'd been doing a lot of lately. "I was worried about you, actually."

"I'm fine," he said. I felt him casting me little sideways glances all the way to the church. I was doing the same thing to him.

"You want to meet me for lunch today? My room?"

He shook his head again. "My foster mom packed me a lunch."

I watched him walk ahead of me and catch up with the other kids. He didn't engage with them, just walked along behind them.

My footsteps slowed. Foster mom? It felt like my heart was wedged in my throat. I suppose if I was a better person, I'd have been happy that he'd gotten out of that horrible house. Now he had a foster mom who packed his lunch and even managed to iron his clothes. He looked good, but sad. I felt awful.

I blinked hard and vowed not to lose it. I'd contact Larry the Lawyer as soon as I could, let the guy exhaust his bag of tricks, and see where that got me. I hadn't even talked to Fee about the possibility of fostering a child. Maybe she wouldn't want someone who wasn't of her own biology. Hell, our very relationship was iffy. These thoughts went through my head until it throbbed.

I finally tried to comfort myself with the notion that if things with Emanuel didn't work out, I'd be back in California this time next month anyway. To hell with Landon and its failing Sacred Heart, my sister's devotion to it, and her years of tireless work...

\*\*\*

Two hours into rehearsal, I left Ricky and Roddy in charge so I could attend the school board meeting with Principal Reeves. Apparently, I'd been elected keynote speaker because as soon as we entered the room and shook hands, our sweet principal clasped her hands together and nodded for me to begin.

For the next two hours, I basically talked the school board down from the ledge. When they didn't appear to have softened, I politely added that our big-city attorney Larry Bennett was curious as to why the building was so dramatically underinsured in the first place after the science "wing" burnt down. I dropped some other liability-centered words into my bluff—asbestos, lead paint, basically anything that came to mind—as I imagine the only thing the school board disliked more than their Sacred Heart contract was the thought of involving legal folks to explore it.

This seemed to shift the tone of the meeting. We ended up shaking hands to uphold the contract from here forward. I walked out of there praying that Principal Reeves would be able to do just that. After the day I'd had, the week—hell, the month I'd had—I was ready to go back to the West Coast.

I saw the parked cars as soon as I turned onto Tina's road and became paralyzed by fear. Cars were parked and idling all along my sister's driveway. I practically ramped the snowbank, jumped out of the car, and ran inside to see what had happened.

As I was making my entrance, many laughing, smiling familiar faces began filing past me on their way out. About eight girls from my music class were pulling on stocking caps and mittens, and a few carried guitars on their way toward the door. They greeted me cheerfully, but my return greeting held only a fraction of their enthusiasm.

I hurried past the center island kitchen block which was covered in leftover cookies, fudge and empty mugs of what smelled like hot chocolate. My sister sat next to the fireplace in her lounge clothes, smiling radiantly.

"Tina, is everything okay?" I asked her, confused. "What's going on?"

"The girls just wanted to say hello and sing a few carols," she said, almost giddy about it. "It was really very nice. Wasn't it nice?"

Only then did I turn my head to see Attorney Larry Bennett sitting next to her on the fireplace hearth. I swallowed the lump that had formed in my throat, nodded at him, and then looked back at her.

"But you're okay?"

"Mina, I'm okay," she said, suddenly worried looking. "Oh, the cars! You must have been so worried!"

She patted the bench seat next to her but I only stood there, surely looking dumbfounded. Adrenaline spike over, I wanted to collapse. I finally eased myself into a rocking chair facing the pair. They looked nice sitting there together.

"I'm sorry to have intruded," Larry said, looking rather embarrassed. "I actually came out here to talk with you, but then you were gone, and, well, the girls showed up—"

"Yeah." I rubbed my winter hat off and dropped it into my lap. "It's been a crazy, crazy day."

"Yes, so I've heard." He nodded in the direction the girls had just exited. "They sound wonderful. You must be terribly proud and excited."

"Actually, my sister's to thank. She taught them everything. I just helped out."

"Don't be so modest," Tina shushed me.

"Well, to both your credit, they seem like fantastic girls." Larry grinned. He was an okay guy. "Before I begin, are you in the mood to discuss business, or should we meet later? After the show, perhaps?" He chuckled. "I'm not charging for this house call, don't worry."

I smiled at that and shook my head. "Not worried, and yes, this is a fine time."

He cleared his throat, turned serious, and in seconds, Larry Bennett was once again in polite business mode. "First of all, you'd have to become a licensed foster care provider which involves some classroom time and various home studies to get approval."

"Okay," I said. My sister seemed unfazed by our conversation, nor did she need to ask about the subject who'd prompted such an inquiry. She knew without me telling her that I wanted Emanuel. "I can handle that."

"I'm sure you can," he said, smiling. "Then we'd have to look into getting an ICPC—an Interstate Compact for the Placement of Children, an agreement that would allow you to take Emanuel with you to California, if that's what you chose to do." He dipped his chin. "But it won't come quickly or easily, and it will be expensive."

"I don't care about expense." As the business side of our company and as a woman who'd recently practically panhandled to get to Landon, it sure sounded weird hearing those words come out of my mouth. I nodded at him. "What else? Tell me everything."

"It could take up to twelve months to secure the ICPC. You have to ask yourself a bunch of tough questions." He ticked them off on his fingers. "One, would you be willing to remain in Landon for twelve months if it comes down to it? Two, is your partner in agreement on every one of these issues, or are you doing this independent of her? That will determine the nature of the home study."

"Sure," I said, unsure as hell about every bit of it.

"And three, if the whole thing falls through and Emanuel can't be moved out of state, would you be willing to live in Landon to remain with the child until he is eighteen years old?"

Nobody said a word, maybe nobody breathed. My head nodded without me specifically giving it permission to do so. I guess it was bypassing my brain and communicating solely with my heart at this point.

"Good," he said, expelling a relieved breath. I got the feeling that he understood my desire to get out of Landon on a very personal level. "Then we can start the home study process and see about getting you licensed. We'll see how long this will take and whether or not you need to established yourself here, short or long term."

"She'll stay with me, naturally," Tina put in.

I shot her a grateful look, and returned my attention to Larry when he started talking again. "I communicated with Social Services. Emanuel has recently been placed with a foster family."

"Yes, I learned that today." The tone of my voice markedly changed.

"From what the caseworker told me, this is a good family."

I gulped hard, nodding for him to continue anyway.

"It might not be easy trying for an interstate agreement if the family takes a shine to him and wishes to adopt him right here. The state of Iowa loves to keep kids around their school and friends. You can understand that."

"I do." I lowered my eyes and pretended to study something on the floor to avoid looking at my sister or my lawyer. Suddenly, I felt as vacant as I had after losing our baby. I forced what I hoped was a semi-convincing strong façade. "So you're thinking it doesn't look good?"

"But it doesn't look terrible, okay?" He was obviously trying to cheer me up. "Emanuel is an American citizen. His mother is MIA and his father is deceased. That's all the information I have on the little guy right now."

I stood up, an indication that I was going to take a shower so that I could cry alone. Larry took it to mean that he should go and he also stood.

"I'm sorry. I wish I had better news," he said. "Can you try to stay optimistic? I'll do what I can."

"I know you will." I shook his hand.

He turned to Tina. "Don't get up. It was lovely to meet you and your very talented students."

"So nice to meet you as well," she returned.

"Thank you for the delicious hot chocolate and the fudge."

Tina shrugged as if dismissing his thanks "I've always got plenty of both. Come by anytime."

I would have been happier about this sweet interaction had I not been so absorbed in my own misery. When Larry left, I took his newly vacated seat next to my sister.

"I don't want to live in Landon," I quietly confessed.

"I know you don't."

"I don't know where I belong."

She smiled, put her arm around me, and pulled me close to her. "You belong with Fee and me. And if I'm not mistaken, you just might belong with Emanuel."

I looked at her. "If I can make this happen, can I take you with me? Can we get you somewhere else? Get you better?"

"Don't tell me you want me to go with you to California." She chuckled.

"Nah," I said. "California tried to kill me. I feel like I'm running away from problems all the time. Landon, California... I don't want to run away anymore."

"You never ran away from me," she said, laying a hand over her heart. "Oh, you tried. But I always kept you right here, and that's the truth."

I asked what I had to. "Tell me why the girls were here."

"They didn't know if I'd be at the program or not. They wanted to say goodbye." Her eyes sparkled with happiness.

I'm sure it seemed weird that I burst into tears and buried my face in her shoulder. "Should they say goodbye, Tina?" I tearfully asked. "Are you going to get better?"

"Mina," she said, stroking my back while I trembled. "Don't talk like that. Please."

"I can't help it!" I sobbed. "Are you going to die on me, Tina? Please, please, don't do it."

She held me and shushed me until my sobbing finally subsided. I caught my breath.

"Mina, I can't promise you I won't die. Eventually we all do, right?" she whispered sweetly. "But I'm certainly in no rush, I promise you that much."

# CHAPTER TWENTY

On Wednesday, two days before showtime, I walked to the classroom carrying a tray containing two coffees—one for myself and one for Ricky, who'd be in any minute, or so I presumed.

Arms full, I kicked the door open, and then almost let it slam back in my face. I set my bag down and slowly re-entered. The lights were on, the sewing machine was already whirring, and a clothesline was strung from one end of the room to the other. Sturdy as it looked, it bent in the middle under the weight of the robes hanging across it.

Mesmerized, I followed the sound around to the other side of the clothing room divider and found Ricky hunched over his sewing machine.

"Ricky?" I softly called to him. His head snapped up. His eyes were wide, he seemed tired, he wore a hanky on his head, and looked as if he hadn't slept. He glanced at the wall clock.

I nodded. "Yeah, it's morning. Have you been at this all night long?"

He flipped the switch on the machine, effectively killing the noise. Without breaking eye contact, I handed him the tray with both coffees since I no longer felt worthy of mine.

He peeled off the lid of one of the cups, took a long swig, and closed his eyes for a minute before he stood up and motioned for me to follow him.

"I tore the old collars off the robes, strung 'em up, and let 'em air out all night long. About three o'clock this morning, I found some Febreze in your desk and just Febrezed the hell right out of 'em." He plugged his nose and made a tired, comical face. "Next, I opened the windows and froze 'em out. In all, they're smell free."

I sniffed the air, which smelled like fabric softener, and nodded in agreement. He took another long swig of the coffee.

"Then I attached the new collars and jazzed 'em up a bit." He grabbed a robe off the line and held it up to his body. "What do you think?"

The robe had been pressed, redressed, and now bore tiny initials on the collar that read SHCS. I gasped and clutched the smooth, velvety fabric.

"It's amazing," I muttered. My grin burst out in full and my voice reflected it. "They're all absolutely amazing!"

"Yeah, well." He pretended to take it in stride, but his pride was evident. "I cheated on the initials—they're iron-ons. But they look like the real deal, right?"

"Amazing," I kept repeating. It was really all I could say.

"Now I just have to finish the angels, and get the little rug-rats in for a fitting, and—"

"No," I firmly told him. "No, you don't. You go to the back of the room and lie down on that cot for a while. I'll find you a blanket somewhere."

He didn't argue, just headed toward a canvas cot that had served as an emergency sick bay since until recently, the music room was empty most often. I doubted it would be terribly comfortable, but I figured even poor sleep was better than none at this point. I ran around the freezing classroom shutting windows, and then retrieved a blanket from the supply closet. Ricky was asleep before I could spread it over him. I wondered if I'd ever known anyone who worked harder than this kid. I smiled and gently covered him up before going over to the sanctuary to greet the "rugrats."

The rest of the teachers were kind enough to loan me their kids for a two-hour, all-school rehearsal. I'm sure they didn't mind the extensive coffee break, though many of them brought their coffee right into the sanctuary to watch the practice. A few parents joined us as well. By now it seemed like everyone was in on the program. It was really no longer my show at all. The kids fumbled and bumbled their lines and footing, and if the show hadn't been the following night, I would have laughed more than I worried. As it was, I was a little worried.

Though he now brought his own lunch to school, Emanuel surprised me by showing up in my classroom at noon. Ricky, Emanuel and I scooted three desks into a circle. Two of us spread out our lunches while Ricky sipped herbal tea.

"Come on, join us," I said, offering him half a peanut butter sandwich.

"You don't get a figure like this—" He ran his hands over his hips. "By eating garbage like that."

"You're really a little queen, you know that?" I chuckled.

"You say that like it's a bad thing," he fired back.

Emanuel rolled his eyes and shook his head, but he clearly enjoyed being with the grown-ups. I asked him about his foster home, only because it was the right thing to do.

"I have a lot of sisters now. They're constantly primping and doing their makeup." Emanuel made a face and looked at Ricky. "Kind of like living with four of him."

"Oh, burn," I softly said, smiling, and we bumped fists. If anything, Ricky was flattered by the comment. He clearly did put a lot of time into his appearance and wide-ranging fashion styles. But I worried about him. "Ricky, what are you going to do now?"

Everyone was quiet for a moment. Finally, he shrugged. "Put on this show."

"And after that?"

"Given the times, does anyone in Landon know what they're doing after next week?" He shrugged, all traces of attitude gone. "It may be the one thing I have in common with these pathetic people."

I nodded because I understood what it was like to be the odd man out. Emanuel nodded because the kid was growing deeper and more mature by the second. I appreciated his respectful behavior. In fact, he hardly even swore anymore...

The bell rang, interrupting the daze of admiration I'd fallen into. Emanuel started to go.

"Emanuel?" I stopped him from leaving. "Can I ask...are you happy?"

"I don't get hit now," he finally said after mulling over the question. "I get lunch *and* dinner."

"But are you happy?" I prompted.

He stared at me for a while. "If I tell you I'm not, what would you do about it?"

I shook my head and quietly admitted, "I don't know."

"I'm okay," he said. "The Petersons are fair people."

I nodded, unable to talk about it anymore. "I'll see you right after school, then?"

He nodded, collected his backpack, and headed out.

All afternoon, I tried not to think about what I could not control, but instead focused on the fact that Emanuel was safe, fed and apparently fairly well cared for. That made it possible for me to help Ricky suit up every last kid in a choir robe. I made a rough tally and was about to announce that we were short four outfits when he pulled out four long red stocking caps and matching scarves.

"For the Red Bucket Singers," he explained before I could ask. He calmly shrugged. "I told the Salvation Army we were short. They made this donation for their own little group."

"Is there anything you haven't thought of?" I asked him.

"Let me see...uh...no." He giggled like a girl and held the items out for my inspection. "They'll wear them over black turtlenecks, also donated by the Salvation Army, and wear their uniform pants."

"I've got to come up with an extra pair," I said, remembering that one of the boys didn't belong to Sacred Heart at all.

"Salvation Army," he said, pulling a pair of matching pants out of the bag. "They're all used, but you'd never know it."

I grinned while I watched him lint roll the hats and scarves. "Ricky, why don't you ever ask me about my personal life?"

"Why don't you ever ask me about mine?"

I looked at my shoes and chuckled as I admitted, "I'm afraid it would make me sad."

"I'm afraid talking about yours would make you sad, too." He sweetly grinned and added, "It's really all about you."

"As it should be," I teased him back. "So why don't you come to my sister's house for Christmas? We won't talk about anything that will make either one of us sad."

"And leave behind my love-filled life and glamorous apartment for even one second?" He gasped. "Who will look after the rose garden?"

"Join us, okay? Promise me you will. I won't take no for an answer."

"I wasn't planning on saying no." His brown eyes danced under the shadow of the oversized hanky on his head. A few curls sprouted from beneath it. The bell rang, and he gathered the last of the angel costumes into his arms.

"Let's get to the sanctuary and turn the rest of those little devils into angels. If anyone ever questions whether miracles really happen in church, they never will again."

\*\*\*

The show had become one giant case of product placement. A little netting for the skirts of the girl angels was donated by Saffron's Fabrics, therefore a tiny patch bearing the store logo dangled from their satin belts. Same with the ribbons they twirled—that was Walmart. I guess even the big guys like to get in on local action. In addition to the ribbons, they'd sent each of the children's families five dollar gift cards, all in exchange for a mention in our cheaply photocopied program.

The lights strung around the place were dotted with occasional placards reading, "Sanchez Hardware," the same store that donated Baby Jesus, which was actually a Baby Bella doll, the most sought after toy of the season, in exchange for a program mention and a raffle afterward for Baby Bella, courtesy of "The Wonderful Folks at Sanchez Hardware," of course.

The program also contained mentions of the restaurants and markets that had provided food for our hungry singers over the last few weeks as well as the local soda distributorship who'd brought juice and water. The Men's Shop—where I'd bought Emanuel's clothes—supplied nearly a hundred pairs of new, bright white socks. Even the Kit-Kat Club got a mention under its "corporate" name to avoid raising any Catholic eyebrows. It seemed Landon had really taken a bite out of our program.

Thankfully, I hadn't experienced any troubles with the rival families that Emanuel had previously mentioned to me. Everyone who'd been involved in helping bring the program together had only been absolutely cordial. There were the strippers, the daddies who came to help them, and the mommies who came to keep an eye on the daddies helping the strippers, but there was no real tension. I'd witnessed busty Havana Anna swapping a gnocchi recipe with Principal Reeves, and a crew of Amish-looking farmwives raising a manger alongside sturdy women in hot-shorts who could barely speak a word of English. I thought of Ricky's joke about miracle making in the church. But in strange, small ways, it was really happening.

Our final dress rehearsal wasn't without its problems, but the effort made by everyone was obvious, so I wasn't filing any complaints. I gathered the kids around me before the bakery representative served them their cookies and business cards, God bless free enterprise.

"It's wonderful. It's better than I ever imagined it would be." I paused a second, contemplating whether I should mention that Gabriella had been slightly pitchy, or if I should remind the Red Bucket Singers to coordinate their first breath, or if I should tell Roddy not to step on the wise men when he entered the manger.

"Just perfect. I can't wait to see it tomorrow. You've really made your town proud of you, and you've made me proud of you, too. Get over here, all of you. I want to give each and every one of you a hug before you go get Mr. Alejandro's cookies."

I was almost knocked down by the little ones' ambush hug attack. That was followed by dozens of embraces from the older kids, ranging in style from endless clinging to hit and runs. After I pried Mercedes off me, I went to Emanuel. I knelt in front of him and pulled him close. His thin body was rigid, out of the practice of hugging, if he'd ever been in any kind of practice to start with.

I patted his back, and as the kids had largely dispersed on their mission of cookie seeking, I whispered in his ear, "You made coming to Landon worth it. I want you to know that."

When I pulled back, we both looked a little embarrassed and emotional. I laughed to break the tension I'd caused. He leaned very close to my ear and whispered something before scurrying off to join the others. I slowly stood and watched him go, stunned beyond all measure. I didn't have even a moment to process it because of the tall, slender human barrier suddenly standing in front of me.

"Music teacher?" the woman demanded. Surprised, I nodded. "I need you. Now."

The smile I'd worn for the children quivered slightly. They were otherwise occupied and didn't seem to notice I'd been intercepted. I followed her obediently, snagging my coat off the last pew as we exited the grand sanctuary doors.

Nervous about her forceful tone, I wordlessly followed her until we reached the sidewalk beyond the church, well out of view of the others. Once there, she performed an about-face and pressed her mouth against mine for several long seconds. When at last she pulled away, our breathlessness was evident by the little misty clouds between us.

"I mean it," Fee said, her desperation clear. She sexily gazed at me with her big brown eyes. "I need you right now."

We went to the same hotel, employing an almost business-like approach to getting thoroughly laid by behaving coolly on the way to, and while inside of, the elevator. We dared not give prying eyes a show. However, inside the room that Fee had rented especially for the occasion, we attacked each other. We threw our clothing everywhere.

"Wait," I said, breathless from our haste. I hurriedly pushed the door open a few inches and hung my red bra on the outside door handle. Fee gave me a funny look. "I'm just leaving my sister a message."

She didn't ask about it, just covered my mouth with hers and edged me toward the bed. I have always thought Fee is absolutely beautiful. Her dark, deep-set eyes and olive complexion conspire to make her a very desirable woman, while her fun, pixie cut hair gives the distinct impression that she could be every bit an ornery tomboy.

Despite a diet containing mostly horrid on-set craft services and too much caffeine, she's somehow maintained this firm, exquisite body that knows and loves me all too well. We used to joke that we were like those magnetic Scottie dog toys you played with as kids. Our bodies simply and helplessly connected, our curves melded softly together, our hands gently and efficiently explored each other. There were no words or wrong moves. Our lovemaking was instinctive and entirely loving. I'd realized how very precious that was more than ever during our time apart. Simply enough, I would never love another body, or the soul inside it, the way I love Fiona Borsalino.

Her hand edged downward and tenderly found me, and I also reached for her. I slipped my fingertips inside her wetness and we slowly moved together. Having emerged from the threshold of losing Fee for real, forever, I was overcome by the sensation of her sweet body and the emotion that came with having her again.

"I love you," I whispered.

Her movement slowed, further stoking the want building inside me. She nibbled my ear and said, "I love you more."

I writhed against her, unable to hold myself back for another second. She strained against me, and for several noisy moments we were absolutely one, as close as our bodies and hearts could get.

"Don't move," she said afterward. "Don't go anywhere."

"I won't," I quietly assured her. "Fiona, I'll never go anywhere again."

# CHAPTER TWENTY-ONE

I first noticed something strange was afoot while peering out the side door of St. Mary's. The line for the Christmas program was astonishingly long. It wound around the building and down the block. I wondered what the church's maximum capacity was to remain in accordance with the fire code.

At *Viva Friday!*, when we hit max capacity in the studio, we simply ushered a few hundred of the overflow fans into an outer lounge where they could watch the show on floor-to-ceiling screens in the comfort of leather theater recliners. This, of course, gives them a chance to shell out for twelve dollar cocktails and even more on a variety of officially licensed *Viva Friday!* fan merchandise, like boxers and camisoles—even VF-stamped fuzzy handcuffs in an array of colors.

On *The Ellen Show*, the overflow area has been coined The Riff-Raff Room, and deals in sweet things like baby onesies,

T-shirts and fancy bottled water, her image stamped on all the merchandise. I guess that's the difference between clean, daytime humor TV fare and the racier nighttime fare VF offered. I felt more disconnected from that life every day.

Judging by the line, I wished more than anything that we'd had fan merchandise for sale at the school program. But the cost of entry to our little show was by donation only, and who in Landon had any dough anyway? Given a wealthier audience, Sacred Heart would surely benefit from the proceeds of twelve dollar cocktails and forty dollar T-shirts this year. I guess I'd joined Principal Reeves in praying for that year-end miracle.

Back to the something-strange-is-afoot part. It occurred to me that our audience might be stretching beyond Landon, despite my firm insistence that it remain private to the townspeople. The certainty came when I caught a glimpse of Marlaine Du Pont of the famed California Du Pont Wine family, a socialite who loved nothing more than to attend Hollywood functions and in fact, fit in quite well in Hollywood. Not Landon. I assumed she wasn't in Iowa scouting snow grapes for a pinot noir.

When I saw Don Rubenstein also standing in the line in the bitter cold, I began to pace the floor. It wasn't good old Don's Jewishness that had me wondering why he was at a Christmas program. That he was president of Rubenstein Broadcast Network had me on the phone with Fee. Or with Fee's voice mail, anyway.

I took the phone as far away from the children as the tightly stretched cord would allow, and proceeded to yell at her as much as my whispering could convey.

"You promised me faithfully that you would not make this show into a three-ring circus! I just saw the wine socialite and the network president outside this church. Don't you care about these kids at all?" I noticed some of the students looking my way and figured I'd best keep my cool. I bitterly added, "Call me! No. Get here, *now!*"

I returned the phone to its cradle and shot them a little grin. I looked at the lot of them, half in angel costumes, half in choir robes. I saw Steven Weitrich sniffing the air first and his choir robe next.

"Does anyone else smell fish?" he asked.

"I think it's drifting over from the downtown restaurant," I quickly lied.

He seemed to buy it and didn't make further inquiry. I sighed with relief and wondered how many more lies I'd tell before the night's end. These kids had seen their share of troubles—hell, even the Weitrich kid apparently had his problems. I silently vowed to keep them as far away from media scrutiny as possible. I resumed my post at the door, much to the background grumbling about letting in a bitter draft.

As the line progressed toward the main entrance, I counted seven more affluent Hollywood types, including A-list movie star Shoshana Davies, and Clive Bartel, head of Bartel Records. Each time I'd spot a familiar face, I'd slam the door and march to the phone to place another pissy message on Fee's voice mail. She was incredibly smart to avoid my calls. By the time I saw Johanna Louise Rutger join the line of shivering program patrons, I was furious. Now what business did a world-class opera singer, a record producer, a label maker, a network president and a handful of A-list actors have in Landon?

"Fame whores," I muttered, assuming there would indeed be a live broadcast of Sacred Heart's Christmas program beamed to the country in place of *Viva Friday!* "Yeah, follow the spotlight, letches."

"Who's a letch?"

I jumped at the sound of Emanuel's voice. I slammed the door again and turned toward him. He stood there with a crisp collar and the tie I'd bought him peeking just over the top of his choir robe. His shoes had been polished to a high shine. He looked well cared for. I wondered if he was being loved just as much.

"Nobody," I said, interrupting the odd, longing, motherly daze I seemed to drift into every time I was around this kid. I pretended to straighten his perfectly straight tie. "You look great. Are you nervous?"

"No," he said. Giving it a second thought, he amended his first confident statement. "Not really, anyway."

"You'll be great," I assured him, squeezing his rail thin shoulder. "There's nothing to worry about. Nothing bad can happen. Everything will be just fine, I promise."

He looked perplexed. "You trying to convince me or you?"

Just then, Fee came into the holding room. I promptly left Emanuel, marched over to her, and grabbed her coat sleeve without so much as a hello or good-to-see-you. I pulled her into the coatroom. "I need you," I demanded of her.

"Sexy," she muttered, peeling out of her coat and dropping it on the floor. "Isn't it a little sacrilegious to do this in a church, hon?"

I ignored her funny opener and went straight to the point. "Did I or did I not ask you to *not* broadcast the kids' program on the network?"

"You did." She nodded, collected her coat, and made an exaggerated shudder. "Brrr, it's suddenly very chilly in here."

I went on. "And did you or did you not promise me that you *wouldn't* do that?"

"I did." Again, she slowly nodded.

"And did you or did you not—"

Fee raised her hands in a halting way. She couldn't tolerate speeches, and she was growing obviously impatient with mine. "What's your point?"

"What are all those people doing out there?" I whispered loudly, as if anyone could hear us in the coatroom.

She shrugged, looking bewildered. "Coming to see a show?"

I stared at her. "You honestly don't know what I'm talking about?"

She blinked. "I absolutely don't know what you're talking about."

I believed her. What can I say? "I'm going with innocent until proven guilty, but I find it very hard to believe, considering who all is here tonight."

She tipped her head like some kind of innocent puppy dog. "Who's here?"

I heard Ricky calling my name from the main holding area. "Okay, never mind. Forget about it." I started to go, but doubled back to wag my finger in her face. "If I find out that you had anything to do with this—"

"I had nothing to do with anything," she said, crossing her heart. Her eyes were impossibly wide with innocence. "I just thought we were going to have a little preshow closet hanky-panky, that's all. I'm the good one here, okay? According to all the tabloids, I am most definitely the good, innocent one."

I'd started out of the coatroom again, but doubled back one last time and kissed her hard just to shut her up. "My ass," I muttered when we pulled apart. "There is *nothing* innocent about you. I'll tell the tabloids myself."

"I'll alert the media," she said, chuckling softly.

"That's what I'm afraid of," I called to her as I marched out of there. I found Ricky as soon as I entered the holding room. "What's up?"

"Your sister is here," he said, pointing toward a crowd in the opposite corner. There she was, thin and pale, in a sweater dress and tights, no doubt looking like a rock star to her flock. I made my way over to her and extracted her from her posse for a hug.

"How do you feel?" I asked her.

"I feel amazing!"

And Tina looked amazing surrounded by her flock, I thought. "Quick question for you," I said, pulling her aside. "Did you just come in the front?"

"Yes," she said, smiling sweetly. "They let me cut the line. Nice, right?"

"Yeah," I smiled and nodded. "And when you were out there, did you see anything…ah…unusual?"

"Unusual?" Tina furrowed her brow.

"As in, oh, I don't know, trucks or a camera crew?" Like there's a subtle way to slip that into a conversation.

She looked horrified. "Oh, no, Mina—you didn't!"

"No!" I shushed her and moved her further yet away from the children. "Jesus, why does everyone always think I'm the bad one? I'm a good person! I didn't do anything. I was just asking, that's all."

"The paparazzi, then?" Tina seemed thoughtful, and her eyes grew wider in her thin face. "Would they come all the way to Iowa?"

I figured I'd just go with that for safety's sake. "I doubt it. But you can never be sure with some of those blood-sucking scoundrels."

"Good," Tina said, leveling her gaze at me. "Because I'd hate for them to dig up any dirt on all the hotshot audience members we have in our presence tonight, right?"

I gulped.

"Don't they know some things are private?" Her tone said that I'd better not be up to anything tricky, but it wasn't me we needed to worry about.

"How well I know it," I said, patting her shoulder. "Okay, no worries. It's almost showtime, and then this whole damned thing will be over, hallelujah and thank God."

Tina smiled at me. "Hon, relax. You've done a great job. It's over. Just enjoy yourself."

What a novel idea. An impossible, novel idea. I nodded agreement for her sake, and walked with her to the sanctuary.

Three seats up front had been reserved for Fee, Tina and myself. I cast little sideways glances at the packed church audience, picking out several more famous faces amongst the Landoners, and then I saw something that presented yet a new problem.

A bunch of young men and women entered the church in the same puffy purple and black coats with an insignia patch on their chests that I recognized because it was painted all over town. Tina clutched my hand in a death grip that made me question my belief that she was merely a weakling.

"Oh, no," she whispered. "It's the Melendez familly. They never come to these things."

I instantly recalled Emanuel's story about the rival families. Tina nodded toward a different section of the church where about a dozen folks with handkerchief bands around the arms of their coats were seated. They got to their feet and observed the newest audience members while they strode to a different section.

I swallowed hard. "I take it those are the Da La Salles?"

"You guessed it," she whispered.

We watched in silence as the rival families stared each other down, and then slowly took their seats in a standoff to see whose butt could hit the pew last. I swear it took forever. I hoped like hell that the national headlines on Christmas Day wouldn't star something about a bunch of Hollywood bigwigs getting bumped off, accidental victims of the ongoing Da La Salle-Melendez "family" war in Landon, Iowa.

I got on my knees and started praying for reasons that had nothing to do with being nervous about the children's performance.

In seconds, I heard a stirring at the back of the church and the sound of people turning around in their pews. I crossed myself and turned around. The children were in the sanctuary doorway, grinning in my direction.

I excused myself down the aisle and went to them with all the last-minute things I had in my mind—no shepherds whacking the wise men with rubber canes, be mindful of sharps and flats in our jazz band selections, watch those pitchy highs, be still, be patient, be good. I reached them and started to speak, but nothing came out. I was suddenly overwhelmed. Everything we'd worked hard for was happening tonight, and I was willing to bet that some of these kids had never worked so hard on anything in their entire lives. I was overcome with pride.

"You'll be fine," finally emerged from my lips. They looked at me a little puzzled and suddenly, as if just noticing that the church was far more packed than during Mass or their usual programs, they looked collectively nervous.

"Will you walk us out?" Suzette, looking particularly worried, asked the question. I had walked them out during each and every rehearsal to ensure they had adequate spacing between them. This time, I shook my head.

"Not this time," I whispered loudly enough for them to hear. Their eyes were big as saucers, but I calmed them as much as I could. "It's not my program. This is all yours." My admiring gaze landed on each face, from the littlest angel to the tallest choirboy. "And yours, and yours, and yours, too."

I saw Steven Weitrich looking as nervous as the rest. Almost reluctantly, he held up his fist and I bumped mine against it. "And yours. It's all yours."

Luis swallowed so hard, his Adam's apple visibly bobbed. He nodded.

"You know what to do." I laid out my last-minute instructions. "This is your night. Have fun."

I walked back down the aisle alone and took my place again between my sister and Fee. Tina shot me a worried look and almost started to rise, but I shook my head.

"It's okay. They've got this," I said.

The sanctuary lights went down except for a single spotlight trained on the Red Bucket Singers. I heard a small, perfect, collective intake of breath, and then Carlos's heavenly a cappella voice filled the church with the first line of "Silent Night." By line three, delivered in Rafael's deep baritone, I was choked up and thankful that there were otherwise no houselights. When the four of them finally harmonized, I heard surprised gasps throughout the church. It was clear how invested these boys were in their heartfelt performance that lasted only a single, powerful minute.

There would have been thunderous applause to top it off had the spotlight not gone immediately to Gabriella on the opposite side of the stage. She overlapped their finish, starting up a sweet rendition of "Joy to the World", accompanied by Roddy's quiet piano, a few well-played bells and a single guitar.

When she hit the first high note with her grand vibrato, everyone knew we were in the presence of some kind of real, raw talent. She wrapped up her intro, and the lights came up to reveal the jazz band swinging everyone into high spirits. Down the aisles streamed the rest of the students, directed by Ricky, lit only by the flashlights they carried with Sanchez Hardware tags dangling from them. The kids were loud, and clear and beautiful. I smiled big.

Angels spun their ribbons in rhythmic designs, the Red Bucket Singers took their turn harmonizing a chorus, and Mercedes only wiggled her ass once in the ballet dance. I shot her a thumbs-up.

Encouraged by the audience's obvious glee, Gabriella's voice grew stronger and she took more improvisational liberties in her solo. Not to be outdone, the backup grew louder and clearer, more heavenly with every moment.

With slight apprehension, I glanced down the row at Principal Reeves, relieved to see her doing everything but jumping out of her seat and getting down with them. Her orthopedic shoes slapped the wooden floor in time with the jazzy rhythm.

I next looked at Abby, the cheerleader who'd led the smaller kids to a row of pews stage left where they normally sat to sing their part. For some reason, she'd felt it appropriate to permit them to stand on top of the pews instead, and they danced as they sang. That was fine by me. Their parents had signed waivers.

All manner of clapping and dancing was happening on stage regardless of family differences or where anyone had come from. Whitney Houston would have been proud. Our old Catholic church was in full, multicultural rock-out mode.

The combination first number was at least ten minutes long. It brought the house down. And that was only the beginning.

Thanks in part to our Sacred Heart alumni, the audience enjoyed a blended jazz band rendition of "Silver Bells" with Chip alternating lead with Steven, who played his borrowed trumpet. The boys were obviously way ahead of the other musicians, but even they seemed encouraged by the overwhelming audience approval they were getting. Though I'd only heard him play a handful of times, I'd bet this was the finest performance of Steven's "genius" musical career so far.

Confidence made all the difference in the world—in the universe—to these kids. Once they knew they could do it, they did it better than anyone could have shown them. Give a kid an instrument or a voice and tell them they can, and believe me, they will.

Six songs into an eight-song program, the lights dimmed, which was not part of the plan. Next, a spotlight illuminated a group of girls, including Shivan and her two young guitar students, sitting on the corner steps of the stage. They strummed a gentle introduction four times before my brain fully engaged.

It was "Song for a Winter's Night", my mother's favorite. My heart clenched when I felt Tina squeeze my hand.

"It's your song. Go to them," she said, her eyes sparkling.

I started to refuse, but that was before I saw Shivan holding up my old guitar. I looked at my sister, and suddenly knew exactly why the girls had been at her house that night. I'm sure my reaction was anyone's guess.

Tina nodded toward the stage. "They're waiting. Don't disappoint them."

It was the longest walk ever to reach the seven girls perched there with welcoming expressions. My shuffled footsteps seemed to echo off the high-pitched church ceiling. Shivan handed me my old guitar. The fifth time they began, I lightly strummed along, so out of practice I was afraid I'd embarrass them.

Apparently, Tina knew quite a bit more than I did about teaching kids to harmonize. After all, I'd only found the Red Bucket Singers already doing their thing. These girls' voices blended blissfully, and just barely into the beautiful song, I began lip-synching the words for fear I'd otherwise burst into tears, ruining their planned moment. I was happy to be in their music and in their world if only for the duration of an old song.

I felt something else, too. I felt my mother's presence. I wondered what my father would think of me now. I quickly concluded that I would never stop wondering about him, or if I could have done anything to make that situation better. I guessed I'd start by not punishing the good people around me. I knew from my own experience just how much that hurt.

I rested my head against my guitar when they'd finished. The applause was so loud, my ears rang. The students—*my* students—cheered me on. I finally stood, my rubbery knees barely supporting me as I quietly thanked them.

I thought about *Viva Friday!* winning an Emmy and four Golden Globes, and how Fee and I had stood in front of the cameras with our cast and crew around us. Standing before Sacred Heart's music students and their families, nothing—bar none—had ever felt so wonderful. Somehow, my numb feet returned me to my seat where Fee clasped one of my hands and Tina took the other.

I was relieved to hear the opening notes of "O Come All Ye Faithful." I swallowed hard and concentrated on angels circling back around and filtering down every aisle, making way for the wise men and acrobatic shepherds who backflipped their way to the stage. I breathed a sigh of relief when they safely landed, and felt Tina do the same.

Flocks of five-year-olds wearing animal masks joined them. Luis lifted angel Mercedes to "light" the holy star. At her touch, the Sanchez Hardware and Kit-Kat constructed manger lit up brightly to the zing of bells.

In the manger were Joseph and Mary, my newest, sudden concern—in other words, Roddy Melendez and Brenda Da La Salle.

"Oh, no," I whispered. I turned around and craned to see both families. Nobody flinched. I took a deep breath, re-upped my prayer, and clenched hard onto the hands I held. In the end and much to my relief, no gunfire rang out, only proud, loud applause. So when the kids launched into the finale, "The Hallelujah Chorus", an audience sing-a-long, I sang along at the top of my lungs and for what I felt was a good reason.

Roddy and Brenda further pressed the issue by emerging from the manger with the Baby Bella doll in tow. I was pretty sure that the rival families would once again be at war the next day, and I had no clue how these two kids would survive such an impossible young love paradox. But for one night, they looked on each other with sweet eyes as they held hands before the choir, their complicated families, God and everyone.

When the song ended, around four hundred people sprang to their feet with thunderous applause and cheers. The kids stood there, frozen. I'd forgotten to tell them to bow. I stepped in front of the row of pews and demonstrated what they should do. They followed suit several times, proudly bowing, and even clapping and cheering themselves.

I caught sight of Steven Weitrich, bowing, applauding and wearing the most genuine smile I'd ever seen grace his face. I wondered if he was at long last enjoying a bit of camaraderie with his peers, or if perhaps he was inspired by what he'd been a part of, and full of wonderment about what life might hold for him. Maybe he was just glad it was all over, but I choose not to think so.

My sister's status had escalated to legendary. Everyone came to congratulate her on the performance, and she constantly deferred credit, insisting that it was me. I shook my head. After all, I hadn't taught them to sing. I just put a little zip into it.

I left her to contend with their praise and went to Fee at the doorway. She was graciously thanking the Hollywood folks who'd come to witness a performance at a school in the middle of the United States on Christmas Eve for no apparent reason.

# CHAPTER TWENY-TWO

I reached Fee just as Don Rubenstein was heartily congratulating her on a job well done.

"I had nothing to do with it," she said, turning toward me. "It was all Mina."

"Well, it certainly was lovely and heartfelt," he said, shaking my hand so hard, my teeth rattled. I smiled at him.

"Do you mind if I ask how you knew about our music program?" I was at the height of my curiosity.

"A little birdie told me," he said with a wink. He leaned in close and whispered, "A little *loudmouthed* birdie named Mrs. Bernard Fontaine. I've been contributing to that musical refurbishment program of hers for years and never saw the result of any of it. Then I heard you were connected with this bunch. How could I resist? How terribly impressive! I wondered what would cause you to drop out of sight for so long! You really gave the newspapers a lot of time to spin their lies."

Sadly, much of what I'd seen in the tabloids about me was true. I was about to correct him when Fee gently elbowed me.

"Oh, Don, you surely knew better," Fee quietly responded.

"If I didn't then, I do now," he agreed.

It was undeserved praise, but I appreciated it. Miracles everywhere. I thanked him again for coming to the show.

"My absolute pleasure. I had no idea you were so good with children." Maybe it was just the holiday talking, but old Don was exuberant. "I hate to talk business, but the network's starting a new channel of all family-friendly programming. I never would have guessed it was your cup of tea." He was referring to the often gross *Viva Friday!* He looked ashamed. "Could we possibly get a meeting?"

"We'd have to talk it over first," Fee sweetly told him.

"Of course!" He wholeheartedly agreed. "But I'd love a call when you come back to California."

"That would be nice," she said, looping her arm through mine. She leaned in close. "Don't expect it until well after the holiday. We're adopting a child."

My eyebrows nearly hit my hairline.

"Congratulations!" he said, pulling us into a threesome embrace. "Another superpowered collaboration, I am sure."

Fee thanked Don again and politely sent him on his way. Before I could inquire about her statement, Larry the Lawyer came over, carefully escorting my fragile sister.

"That was wonderful!" he said, breaking free of Tina to give us both a hug. "I was missing my city, but wow! If this is how a small town celebrates the holiday, count me in."

"Unfortunately, this might be the last concert old Sacred Heart will see," I told him. "The school's in bad shape."

"Oh, I don't know about that." The voice came from behind us.

I turned to see the president of the public school board. I couldn't even remember his name, only that he looked like Santa Claus and had behaved like the polar opposite during our meeting earlier in the week.

"We've recently acquired the old Ballingall Depot which will be suitable for climate-control storage. That pretty much eliminates our need for your drafty old building." He tossed a glance in the general direction of the school, as if pleased to be rid of it. "You may as well hold onto your lease for as long as you like. I believe the terms will hold up."

My sister hugged the old guy so tightly, she almost knocked him over, even with her tiny frame. He looked surprised, and pleased, I'll add.

I heard my lawyer whistle under his breath. He smiled and said to Tina, "Remind me to get in your good graces."

"Talk to me about how we can keep music in the school and you certainly will be." Tina winked at him.

"Well, then, I promise to exhaust every avenue," he said, grinning.

We laughed.

The school board president nodded at me. "Thank you for an enjoyable evening."

"You're very welcome." I looked at Tina, who practically had sunbeams shooting out of every pore.

"What about the adoption?" I asked Larry, hungry for answers.

"Yes! Attorney Bennett, the paperwork we talked about?" Fee switched into business mode. Apparently with me at the creative helm of this place, we'd completely switched roles. "I have our home study in order. Are we ready to proceed?"

My eyes went wide.

"We are," he said, patting his coat pocket. "I couldn't see any reason to put it off until tomorrow, being that it's the holiday and all."

"Excellent," Fee said. She did an about-face and left us.

Larry whipped out a sizeable envelope of paperwork and started flipping pages. He talked as he did so. "You know, it is amazing how fast things come together when a parent voluntarily terminates rights and designates a permanent custodian."

"A parent?" I was thoroughly confused.

"Yes. Emanuel's mother is alive and living in Coralville," he calmly announced. My stomach plummeted as I was unsure what he was going to say next. "Social Services had tracked her down and was about to terminate her rights. The state of Iowa gives preference to a parental designee, and now that's you. Seems Emanuel's biological mother likes his odds with you girls much better than with her own mother or the State's foster care system."

"Oh, my God," I muttered, wondering if I would fall down.

"Of course, I immediately contacted Fiona for her consent. I was sure I wouldn't have any trouble getting yours. And we expedited a home study." He waved a pen at me. "You'll sign this now, and then finalize things before a judge after the holiday."

Fee returned to our huddle with Emanuel in tow.

"Emanuel is ours?" I stammered. "He can go home with us? To California?"

Larry nodded.

My hands covered my gaping mouth. I knelt before him. "Emanuel, would you like to…?" Try as I might, I couldn't get the rest of my question out.

"I already told you," he said, in a tone that hinted at the ridiculousness of my inquiry. Besides, he had told me. Only the previous night, he'd whispered in my ear that he wanted to go with me. It had seemed improbable at the time. Now anything seemed possible. I hugged him tight.

"*Attención! Attención!*"

We turned to the source of the excited shouts. As the last of the audience filed out, Sofia burst through the line and came running toward us. She clutched a brown accordion envelope to her generous bosom, and prattled in Spanish as she pranced and flitted down the aisle.

"What's she saying?" I asked.

"It's a miracle," Emanuel interpreted. "We are saved. The school is saved." He looked at me and rolled his eyes, much as he always did at Mercedes' classroom antics.

Sofia dropped to her knees in the middle our huddle, a dangerous move given her extremely tight and short dress. She dumped all the proceeds from the voluntary collection onto the floor, and we stared at the heaping pile of hundred-dollar bills and checks with lots of zeros on them.

Sofia yammered some more record-fast Spanish, signed the cross, and then proudly announced, "More than six hundred thousand dollars!"

Our whoops filled the church. I thought Principal Reeves was going to hit the floor. My sister reached an arm out to steady her, as if the old woman's rotund figure wouldn't take us all down with her. We gasped and laughed.

I hugged Emanuel. "Isn't that great?"

"What do I care?" he said, smiling. "I'm going to California!"

I laughed louder than I'd ever laughed in my life.

# EPILOGUE

"Quiet on the set!"

It was about the fifteenth time Emanuel had bellowed the same order through a bullhorn and I was long since sorry for having given it to him.

Fee and I covered our ears and shouted our protests until he put it down and came over to us. He took his seat at the table where we waited for him on our newly dressed studio set, Lot Twenty-Nine. Only weeks before it had looked like a storage warehouse, but that was before the set dressers had transformed it into an extravagant clubhouse.

In days, six child actors would converge on the set as members of *Bluefish, Inc.*, a computer savvy, mismatched, musical high school bunch in the habit of saving the day when the adults could not, all with a hopeful message. Based on a new best-selling series of young adult books, it was part of DRN's new lineup of family friendly programming, thank you Don Rubenstein.

"Bring on the wardrobe," I said, tired already.

"Bring on the wardrobe!" Emanuel shouted through the bullhorn, creating screeching feedback.

"Manny, hon, if you're using a bullhorn, you don't need to shout too." Fee made a face and waggled her finger in her ear.

"Okay," he said more quietly, though still through the bullhorn.

"Hard-headed kid," Fee muttered. She shot me a condemning look. "He gets that from you."

"And his flair for drama comes from you," I added, never missing a beat. We shared a playful smile.

I directed my attention toward the stage where our youngest cast member was just emerging. She was a sixteen-year-old Asian-American teen, cute as heck in a fun, funky blouse, striped tights and a skirt that was way too short.

Apparently, our eyes hit the skirt at the same time, and Fee and I instantly voiced our protests. Ricky came onto the set, his hands on his hips, looking rather dismayed. He wore his working hanky on his head and a tape measure dangled around his shoulders. He defended his position all the way.

"Family friendly programming," I said. "Do I need to remind you what that means?"

"Well, I bought the fabric in accordance with our wardrobe budget," Ricky said in his queenly way. "I can't sew what I don't have. When will you people learn that I can't always make something out of nothing?" He looked exasperated as he folded his arms over his chest.

"Find a curtain, for Pete's sake," I told him.

"Funny," he said.

"Scoot over so I can see, please?" The voice came from the laptop computer perched on the table between us. My sister—our new associate producer—was video conferencing with us. She looked unsure upon seeing the wardrobe creation. "Wow, how short are they wearing them these days, Manny?"

"Who cares," he dreamily answered, obviously smitten with the cute girl. In turn, she seemed flattered that he'd noticed. He sighed, his eyes droopy with admiration for her. "It sure looks good to me."

"That's a no," Fee and I said together.

Ricky launched into another of his lengthy girlish tirades, as he was prone to do, and we battled him thoroughly, as we were prone to do. It was becoming a new standard, and none of us really minded. Finally, my sister let out an ear-piercing whistle that jarred us from our bickering and almost blew the computer speakers.

"Hello? Two hour time zone difference? I have a date," she announced. She held up her watch to the camera to confirm the time.

"With Larry?" came our chorus of teasing, drawn-out, childish voices.

"Indeed," Tina said, grinning from ear to ear. "So if you don't mind?"

"I like Larry," Emanuel said matter-of-factly.

I nodded my agreement before advancing the meeting. "Okay, Ricky, one inch above the knee, nothing more, get it?" I commanded.

He threw his hands up in the air and stormed off-stage. I probably would have felt a little bad about his apparent aggravation if we didn't know how much he loved his job.

"Next up? The final pilot script. Everybody good with it?"

"As of last rewrite, I like it," Fee said.

I agreed and so did Emanuel.

"A yes on this end as well, though I'm not sure how much I know about it," Tina said. "Keep in mind that, as the school's biggest benefactor, and now that we're without any Weitrich money, if you go down, we all do."

"Really? You have every right to be worried," I said in a sarcastic tone. "We have absolutely no idea what we're doing here. We've never created sensational television before. We could all be eating government cheese next month."

"All right. Very funny," she conceded.

I tsked at her anyway. "A little faith in the West Coast branch of this operation, please?"

"Speaking of which," Fee changed the subject. "Jane Silvia needs our company's new legal name by this time tomorrow morning to file the rest of the paperwork."

"Good old Attorney Silvia," I muttered. "How about Fi-Mi-Em-Ti Productions?"

"The last part sounds like empty," Emanuel said.

"Yeah," I agreed. "Doesn't really roll off the tongue, either."

Emanuel looked thoughtful, which usually signified trouble. "How about Manny's Hot Mama Productions."

"No," my wife and I said at once. I told him, "Family programming, remember?"

"I know," Fee said, brightening. "Since we're now officially the Smith-Borsalinos, let's pick something to reflect that."

"You took your Smith back?" Tina sounded gleeful.

"We all did," I said. "If Gabriella with a dozen hyphenated last names can swing it, we surely can too."

"Such a sweet family!" Tina clapped her hands together. "You do Sacred Heart proud."

Her corniness inspired me. "How about Good Heart Productions. No names—everyone counts."

"Love it," Fee said, without hesitation.

"Me, too," seconded Tina.

"I liked the Hot Mamas," Emanuel said. We threw paperclips at him and he pretended to fight us off. "Okay, fine!"

Fee looked at me and smiled. "Love, do the honors?"

I put on my most official sounding voice. "I'd like to formally call to order the first official meeting of Good Heart Productions."

Emanuel scooted off his stool and made his own announcement using that godforsaken bullhorn: "Good Heart Productions, family programming that doesn't suck."

Bella Books, Inc.

*Women. Books. Even Better Together.*

P.O. Box 10543
Tallahassee, FL 32302

Phone: 800-729-4992
**www.bellabooks.com**